GOLDEN BOY

Kate Moore

A CANYON CLUB Novel

www.BOROUGHSPUBLISHINGGROUP.com

GOLDEN BOY

ISBN 978-1-522843-49-8

For the Mill Valley Library
Wednesday Afternoon Drop-In Writers Group
With thanks for your fellowship, encouragement, and laughter.

ACKNOWLEDGMENTS

The Loner and *Golden Boy* are works of fiction. Both the Canyon School for Boys and the Elizabeth Hutton Cobb School for Girls, or the Glen, are as fictional as Hogwarts. Grindstone, too, is a fictional heavy metal rock band. Researching Grindstone's history and its music took me to fascinating places on the Internet and in our local library. There is no dearth of writing about the lives and music of rock stars. *Louder than Hell* by J. Wiederhorn and K. Turman and *Rock Stars Do the Dumbest Things* by Margaret Moser and Bill Crawford were invaluable resources. I had further help inventing this fictional world from Jeff Symonds, rock musician, teacher extraordinaire, and bass guitarist with the Megan Slankard Band. A shout-out must also go to Martin Karlsson of Stockholm, Sweden, who offered invaluable tips about Swedish rock bands. Special thanks to the Mill Valley Drop In Writers Group for listening to many scenes and offering support and insight. And final thanks to my husband for his unflagging support, good humor, and willingness to live on an unvaried menu of take-out delights. The mistakes are my own.

GOLDEN BOY

Two roads diverged in a wood, and I—
I took the one less traveled by,
And that has made all the difference.

—from "The Road Not Taken" by Robert Frost

Chapter One

Seven years earlier, with money from his now vanished trust, Josh Huntington had purchased a brown-stucco duplex four blocks from the beach in a little town south of the L.A. airport. When he bought the place, he never expected to live there—or to be landlord to the particular tenant whose urgent knock had roused him at noon from a dreamless sleep.

He opened the door. Emma Gray looked like a landlord's worst nightmare, with her leather-gloved fist stopped midway in its path to his door. Dark rouged lips, nose piercings, and smoky, kohl-lined eyes intensified the glare she gave him. Purple streaks in her hair hung long and straight over her ears. Her black skull-and-crossbones tank top bared trails of lurid floral tattoos running across her collarbone and down her upper arms. A wide, metal-studded black leather belt cinched her waist above an incongruous schoolgirl-plaid pleated skirt. Her slim legs, encased in fishnet hose, disappeared into unlaced industrial-strength black boots. And she looked seriously aggrieved that he'd opened his door wearing only a pair of black silk boxers.

"Don't you ever wear clothes?"

"Not in bed."

Her gaze dropped. He might have made her blush. Hard to tell under that Swedish death metal band look. At least she lowered her fist.

"What's the problem?" he asked. "Sink? Refrigerator? Shower?" It was a mistake to think *shower.* The very word triggered images his brain ought not to entertain about his tenant, this prickly, independent, don't-touch-me-ever, single-mom tenant whose rent he needed. He might be at low tide, but not that low.

They stood looking at each other in the common second-floor entry under the breast of Venus overhead lamp fixture while he waited for whatever she intended to say. He had time to imagine several intriguing possibilities before she finally got the words out.

"I need your help."

He did not move. He did not betray by so much as a flicker of a glance the satisfaction it gave him to hear those four words from this girl who did practically everything herself. Her constant stubborn independence irked him, though he was less amused the few times she called him out on his landlord duties.

"Do you?"

She glanced back over her shoulder at her unit. That meant she was thinking of her son Max, a tow-headed six year old. "Yes."

"What can I do for you?"

"My babysitter didn't show and hasn't called, and I'm due at work in fifteen."

He noted what she could and could not say. "You want me to watch Max?"

"He can take care of himself, really. He has toys and snacks. He can play while you...whatever. You just have to check on him once in awhile and call me if there's blood, vomiting, unconsciousness, or visible bones."

He should not have her on, but the temptation was too strong. "Define 'once in awhile.' Like, every five minutes, or every half hour?"

She blew out a short, sharp breath. "If it gets too quiet, you know, you should check."

"So you want me to keep my music down and my door open."

"Can you do that?"

It was clearly instinctive for her to doubt his capabilities. To ask for his help, Ms. Self-Reliance had to be desperate.

He straightened and stopped his teasing. "Listen, let Max know the plan. I'll put on some clothes and take him to the park or something. How long will you be gone?"

"Six." She turned away. "Thank you."

He left the door open and drifted back into his bedroom to find some shorts and flip-flops. Her accepting his help was a slight admission of his usefulness, and he contemplated how to take advantage of his minor victory.

* * *

Hours later, Emma glanced at her watch. Five-thirty. Half an hour of her shift to go. No word from her landlord.

She should have been more specific with him about what he should not do with Max. Maybe the park had been a bad idea. How could she be sure that Huntington would watch her son carefully? What if they went to the beach?

Emma stopped herself. Huntington would never do anything that required such a high level of energy. But there was another problem. She hadn't heard from her sitter, and that did not bode well for the week ahead. She would have to find another option she could trust. One not her landlord.

At least Daddy Rock was having a good day. Just a block up from the Strand, tucked between the local surf shop and an outdoor taco stand, the vinyl store was a fixture on the Avenue, the long retail street that connected the beach towns south of the L.A. airport. Daddy Rock's overflowing bins of LPs from all eras and genres of rock music drew fans from around the South Bay, especially metalheads. Today, Leo the floor manager was not complaining about them. Business was too good, and they were a main reason. She was trying to stay on Leo's sweet side. He wanted her to work extra shifts for the next two weeks. She didn't know how she would manage the time with her end-of-term school workload, but a private Grindstone benefit concert was coming up and she wanted a backstage pass. Leo, who in another life had spent five years as the band's road manager, was her best shot.

Grindstone. For the first time in seven years the band was going to reunite, and British rocker Steve Saxon, the band's lead guitarist, would return from Sweden. To certain fans of heavy metal, Saxon was "the shredder of shredders" for his lightning-fast leads played against a blast of industrial whines and shrieks, as if he were pitting his axe against some giant machine. That guitar-playing had won him male fans, and his shoulder-length black hair, ripped abs, and rough-edged voice had drawn hundreds of female groupies to each of the band's legendary after-parties.

Whatever he was to those legions of fans, to Emma Saxon was one half of her DNA—the living half. She had never met him, but his absence shaped her life. She'd learned his identity in her seventeenth year and tried unsuccessfully to meet him. This upcoming concert was the first chance she'd had in years to try again.

The track playing through the store speakers was a California psychedelic arrangement of "Right Now," by Sammy Hagar out of his Van Halen days, telling his baby not to wait, that tomorrow was far away and yesterday was gone. Leo believed the song sent a subliminal message to buy, and Emma had to admit customers mouthed the refrain as they flipped through the bins. Emma counted nearly thirty. Tonight Daddy Rock would stay open till nine, and the customer level would not dip down until people drifted out to look for food. Usually she worked in the back at her computer, answering email requests from hardcore fans of obscure bands. Her main job was finding albums for them. Online the store proclaimed: *Send us your want list, and we'll find anything for you.* That was one way to survive in the digital age, and it created the perfect job for Emma. She preferred working in the background to working on the sales floor. She had been the Daddy Rock want-list girl for almost a year, entirely behind the scenes until recently.

Not that anyone who once knew her was likely to wander into Daddy Rock, but it was possible that her grandparents, who raised her, still had people looking. She sent them a careful letter once a year to let them know she was alive and not in need of their help, but she could never be sure. Nor could she be sure that her trail was completely cold. The plan remained for her to keep moving, pay cash, and look unrecognizable in case she might be spotted.

Only, now that Max was in school, her old habit of often changing apartments no longer worked. She had stayed in one place for his kindergarten year then picked another place for his first-grade year. It was a good place, too—except for her landlord.

The recollection of those black boxers had stayed with her all afternoon. It was not the first time she'd encountered him in his underwear, and the effect was building like repeated bee stings. Josh Huntington was long and lean and golden, from the tawny fall of hair over his brow to the gleam of darker golden hair on his chest and body. Today, without meaning to, she had looked straight at his crotch where his Wee Willie Winkie—as she and Max called Max's boy-part—would be. Even with her limited experience she knew Huntington's adult male penis would be nothing like Max's little pink nubbin.

She knew exactly where she stood about sex, too. It was overrated, and it was bad for her. Max was the only good thing to come out of her brief experience, and until she accomplished her goals and got her life back on track there would be no sex for her, not even if women were supposed to be empowered to act just like men. But she was close now, just weeks to go. Much like earning her degree, it had taken patience and luck to find a way to reach her impossibly distant, reclusive father. As long as he remained in Sweden he had been beyond her reach, but now, with his return to the States, the opportunity she'd been seeking so desperately had finally landed in her lap.

The persistent mental image of her landlord's distracting black boxers was doubly annoying because she had a pretty good idea of the amoeba-drowning depths of the man's shallow character. In the fall, within a few days of settling into her unit, she had discovered that he was a Canyon boy of the worst sort: the careless, charming variety. He dressed like Canyon and drove like Canyon, and he had expensive Canyon tastes. She had no idea why he was living in a run-down box of an apartment in the only low-rent beach neighborhood in the South Bay.

He was twenty-eight, and last week he had gone to a Canyon reunion, confirming what she had guessed about his background. In a limo, no less. His class at the exclusive high school, the class of '05, was four years ahead of Emma's at Canyon's sister school, which meant that their paths had never crossed at games or dances where girls schools and boys schools mixed, but she was sure that his cousins had been her classmates.

She knew the Huntington name. She had put it all together. His family's branch of the Huntingtons lived on an estate that sprawled over several acres of prime west-side property not far from her grandparents' home, part of the landscape of her childhood. It was a brick Georgian affair with columns, suitable for the president of a small college, right in the heart of what realtors liked to call "the platinum triangle." No question about it, Josh Huntington knew her old world.

He would have been away at college when the story broke about her disappearance. Still, at this critical moment, when her plan to reach her father was coming together, she couldn't afford to let slip anything of her connection to that other life. So she had done her best to avoid him over the past few months, except to pay her rent or to get him to do his job as her landlord and fix something in her apartment.

In the beginning it had been easy. Though they shared an entryway, and though Max was curious about their neighbor,

Huntington's existence seemed to be non-stop partying and traveling. He returned home after midnight most nights and surfaced late in the day. In the fall he'd left his key with Emma to go off for a week, leaving her to collect his mail and admit his cleaning person. In January, he'd loaded his green Range Rover with snowboarding equipment and disappeared for another week. She'd seen him once a month to give him the rent and twice as often to tell him to turn down his music.

Then, abruptly, he'd stopped working or doing whatever it was he did most weekdays. Midday on a Friday, he had come home from wherever, and since then he'd hardly left his apartment. He appeared to be on a perpetual vacation.

He'd never installed curtains in his place. Wednesdays, when she had neither work nor classes, were the worst. Occasionally he managed to put a shirt on over his usual cargo shorts. Emma tried to get her studying done in the morning before he woke and wandered to stand at his window in those boxers of his, drinking coffee and looking toward the ocean.

Laughing at herself for letting her sexy landlord distract her, she put his image out of her mind and straightened the LPs in a Megadeth bin. Recently on weekends Leo had assigned her to the store's death metal section and insisted that she dress the part. From her online work she'd learned the bands and their output, and she had to admit that dressing the part worked with a certain group of customers, two of whom now approached flashing the sign of the horns, the hand signal of true fans.

Brandon and Todd were thin twenty-somethings who made their musical affiliations clear in both dress and hair statements. Brandon, garbed in all black, went for the big-hair look of the early Megadeth lineup, while Todd, in a green fatigue jacket, favored the close-shaved appearance of Tool. The friends were regulars in the metal section and had a perpetual debate going over the origins of the grindcore sound, with its aggressive percussion and heavily detuned guitars. Brandon, who ended up in Emma's aisle whenever she worked it, argued that the distorted sound originated with the band Siege playing at maximum velocity. Todd claimed Napalm Death was the source of the really great innovation.

This time, Emma pulled a D-beat album from its bin for them to hear, for the sake of turning the argument in a new direction.

"Hey," Todd said, nodding to the sound of the first track. "You really know your stuff."

Brandon nodded. "Told ya she was good. Listen, Emma, you've got to get us passes to the Grindstone reunion gig."

"Those guys are still alive?" Todd said.

"They have new livers," Brandon said with a laugh. Then he turned. "How about it, Emma, what have you heard?"

Emma shrugged. "It's a closed event, for high rollers only."

"Yeah." Brandon's taco breath was one of his distinctive features. He was a regular at Tacos Jalisco next door. "But everybody knows that Daddy brokered the deal. It's a charity thing, right? So the store's bound to have passes, right?"

"Not at five hundred dollars a ticket," Emma said. If tight-fisted Leo Grant gave out passes, it would not be to the likes of Brandon and Todd.

She threw a glance toward the store offices. Like Leo, Daddy Rock himself, the owner of the store, had been close to the band members back when he was producing albums. In a way he and Leo were both still profiting from their association with the disbanded Grindstone. The store had the kind of band memorabilia—guitar straps, picks, handwritten lyrics, and the famous rider from the 1990 tour—that drove fanatics mad. It had taken Emma a year to prove to Leo that she knew her stuff, but when he hired her, the job paid off in the first week. She'd managed to snag a hat her father wore on tour with just the bit of DNA needed to prove her connection to him. At least her grandparents had not lied when they finally revealed his identity. Leo had not missed the hat, and she'd returned it to its place of honor in the glass case.

Upstairs in his office, behind the chaos of his desk, Leo hung a large framed black-and-white picture of the band and its crew from their last tour. The band members had signed the picture, or Leo had added a note naming each person and his role in the band's entourage. From the first time she saw the picture, Emma studied it every chance she got, but the questions about her history remained unanswered. She did not think any picture could explain how her debutante mother and her rocker father had met, loved, and parted, leaving a child behind. In her seventeenth year, her grandparents had finally told her one version of the story, but she wanted to hear her father's side.

"But you know where the concert's going to be?" Todd insisted. "Bran has been to every serious metal concert since 2010. He never misses. He's a genius at getting into places you think are closed—parties, clubs, whatever. We could take you with us."

Emma shook her head. It was inevitable, she supposed, that guys into Swedish death metal would have heard the rumors of a Grindstone reunion, and Brandon had been going on about the concert for weeks. He had the kind of serious music addiction that created her job, the constant quest to find something no one else has heard, some never-publicly released track that would blow his friends away. Neither he nor Todd had ever seen the band live.

"It's only a couple weeks away, Emma. Come on, give us a clue. They can't keep the venue secret for—"

"Mom!"

The voice made Emma spin around. Max charged toward her from the end of the aisle, clipping a life-size cardboard Paul Stanley and sending it toppling. Behind him, Josh Huntington caught and righted the tumbling KISS vocalist as Max slammed into her.

"What's wrong?" She detached Max's grip on her hips so she could look at him. She saw no blood, bruises, or scrapes.

"Nothing." Her landlord stood with his hands in his khaki pockets, a dark blue V-neck silk sweater stretched across his shoulders and chest, the exposed parts of him covered with that golden hair. He looked so relaxed, so unruffled, so sure of himself.

"Nothing?" He had no clue that the word *Mom* spoken with a certain inflection could send a woman from calm to high anxiety faster than a Tesla could hit sixty.

"We came to ask about your dinner plans. Burgers? Pizza? Tacos?"

She was conscious of Brandon and Todd staring at Huntington as if he came from another planet—which he did. Planet Privilege. For her, that planet had exploded years ago like Superman's home. Now she lived on Planet Ordinary, where people paid their own way in life. They worked and cleaned and cooked and saved and made it to the end of each month on their own efforts. On Planet Ordinary, she was in charge of her own life and Max's. She'd been in charge since seventeen.

"I serve healthy food. At home."

She indicated that Huntington should turn and move down the aisle. She didn't like that he'd come into the store, especially not when she was on death metal duty. And she didn't know what he'd heard.

He merely raised his brows. He did not seem to notice the two metal geeks. "Max is hungry."

"Did you give him his snacks?"

"And then some."

"Hey, are you the kid's dad?" Brandon interrupted.

"I don't have a dad," Max announced.

Huntington's hand came to rest on Max's shoulder. His lazy gaze shifted to Brandon. "If you're interested in Grindstone reunions, you might look for their 2008 release for Voltage. *Toxic One*." He glanced at Emma. "That was their last reunion tour, right? Do you have the album?"

Emma nodded. "Aisle 12, bin 25." The answer came automatically, but another part of her brain registered Huntington's disturbingly accurate knowledge of Grindstone.

She took his arm to turn him and lead him away from the conversation, but she must have been distracted because Huntington made a little move and his hand found the small of her back, as if it belonged there, and he was suddenly leading her. Max skipped and turned in front of them, running his hand along the tops of the bins.

Huntington leaned in and whispered, "You have admirers."

He meant Brandon and Todd, but how he figured that, Emma had no idea. She shook her head to deny it. "I'm almost done here. Can you take Max home?"

He stopped. "*Thank you* would be nice."

"Of course. Thank you."

"Hey, let me get some food. Healthy, if you insist. I've got to take off at six, so I'll bring Max back here. Salad?"

"Okay."

She didn't like the expression in his gaze. He was just the sort of manipulator who would use an act of kindness to get what he wanted. Of course, she had also seen the kind of tall, beautiful women he liked—a limo full of them. His hand on her back didn't mean that he wanted anything from Emma except rent.

Which was good.

Chapter Two

The Sunday night drive from the beach to his parents' house took half an hour, a record for L.A. As the gates of his family home opened to the click of his remote, it struck Josh that taxpayers in most states might reasonably object to a governor's residence of the size and style of this Georgian brick mansion in which he and his older sister grew up. That the place now seemed super-sized to him must mean his time in his tiny box of a South Bay apartment had affected his judgment.

He left the Rover in the drive and headed through the gardens to the terrace. There he found his mother entertaining guests. The good news was that he had not had sex with any of the three golden-haired women sipping jewel-bright cocktails. The bad news was that his mother had thrown them each in his path in the way a fishing boat throws out chum.

He knew them all. The women were as familiar with his mother's pool and tennis courts as Josh. While he was at Canyon, they had attended his mother's alma mater, the Elizabeth Hutton Cobb Academy. His mother remained a big booster of the school, better known as "The Glen" for its location in a green hollow between the flats along Wilshire Boulevard and the heights of Mulholland Drive. The academy was the girl version of Canyon, a school for L.A.'s female elite.

Paige Crawford had spent her high school and college years competing internationally in freestyle skiing events. Tamila Easley, the only brain in the group, had gained a reputation as a documentary filmmaker. Mackenzie Burke had a history and trust fund like his. No college had suited her for very long, and she had spent more time addressing envelopes for her mother's philanthropic functions and traveling a regular circuit of fashion weeks and polo tournaments than she had taking courses or exams. She knew English dukes personally, but he doubted she had a degree.

Idly, he tried to imagine the women in front of him in death metal attire and failed. If they had tattoos and piercings, those marks of worldliness or rebellion would be discreet and covered by fine lingerie. On the surface only flawless skin and confident sexuality showed. They did not wear metal-studded black belts, even if their handbags sported plenty of bling. They were on track to inherit the social positions of their mothers on the boards of symphony, opera, and museums, heading various charitable efforts, being photographed in designer dresses coming and going from glittering events or in the living rooms of a *Vanity Fair* spread.

"Josh!" His mother acted at surprise better than anyone he knew. "What brings you here tonight?"

"Am I interrupting? I'll take myself elsewhere."

The women smiled and squealed and jumped up to give him air hugs and kisses, asking what he was up to, checking him out, telling him he looked good, and inviting him to join them. His mother's pool boy offered him a cocktail, which Josh declined in favor of a beer.

Mackenzie filled him in. As she talked, Josh noted that the thong under her white designer jeans gave definition to the perfect twin globes of her spectacular ass. "We're planning a mini-reunion for some girls in our class. Your mom has offered her house."

His mother was a marvel. How easily she managed to remind him of the refined taste and effortless glamour of the life he had lost along with his trust: When he'd failed to keep his job at Canyon for a full year, his father cut off his funds indefinitely. His mother had come to the school's centennial gala, patted his cheek, and told him she had a plan. Josh supposed he had been summoned here tonight so that she could unveil that plan.

He settled in and entered the conversation about catering, seating arrangements, and music. The music provoked the most disagreement among the three planners, who argued the merits of different DJs and different sounds. There was no mention of Grindstone.

The women wanted his opinion. They remembered him leading the C-Notes, the men's *a capella* singing group at Canyon. The chief perk of being a member had been frequent invitations to sing at local girls schools. A second benefit had been the way it annoyed his father.

Josh's mind drifted in and out of the conversation. Ordinarily he would be planning to take things further with one of the women, observing the details of sexual interest and looking for signals of availability. Instead he considered whether he could excuse himself and head straight for the pool. Something had put him off his game.

Inevitably, the women asked about the Canyon scandal.

"So what's the scoop?" Tamila said. "You must know what really happened. Weren't you working there or something?" There was the tiniest hint of a sneer in the question.

"Tell us. It must be something big," Mackenzie suggested. "My dad claims that old Headmaster Chambers was the only reason my brother got into college at all."

"What did Chambers do? And how did he get caught?" Paige wanted to know.

Josh gave them the version of the scandal that did the least damage to the school, making it ancient history: Chambers's grade-tampering and his dipping into the till. He didn't tell them about the years of systematic tyranny over scholarship students. He didn't tell them Chambers had fired him as the assistant development director at Canyon, and he didn't tell them about his classmate Will Sloan buying an unpaid bond and saving the school. They would not remember Will Sloan, anyway, the scholarship boy who had been a despised outsider in high school—though they might have heard of him as the newest tech billionaire on the block with the sale of his startup Z-Text.

The women were polite enough not to press him even if they assumed Josh knew more than he was telling. They were wrong, at least about any recent developments. Ever since the school's centennial gala he'd become an outsider in his old crowd. He had heard nothing from anyone connected with Canyon except a few remarks from Will Sloan's fiancée, Annie James, comments about the fate of Ulysses, the scholarship student whose admission to Canyon had unraveled so many of the school's secrets. Indirectly he'd heard there was an interim head of school now in place, Dr. Archer, one of the most revered faculty members, and that the New Directions committees, which Josh himself had invented, were busy meeting to shape the school's future. No one had called him for his opinion on anything. He hadn't even heard from Sloan, though Annie sent him almost daily texts as she and Sloan planned their upcoming wedding. His friends had invited him exactly nowhere. He knew the drill. He'd essentially been blackballed from the Canyon "club" for airing the school's dirty laundry and allying with outsiders.

When he offered no gory details of the scandal, his mother's guests checked their phones and said their goodbyes.

"You have to come to our party, Josh," Mackenzie said.

His mother followed the women out, leaving him to nurse his beer and reflect as he watched the pool shimmer in the evening light. He liked women, and he liked sex. He probably liked sex more than most of his friends. Maybe not more than Sloan, but Sloan only wanted one woman. Josh found there was something he wanted in nearly every woman he met.

He remembered when Dr. Archer required their history class to watch the movie about Oscar Schindler saving people from the Nazis. They were supposed to write papers about an historical figure as a role model. What had fascinated Josh about Schindler in the film was not the hero's growing compassion for the oppressed, but his insatiable attraction to women—secretaries, mistresses, factory workers—and his ability to win their affections. Not one woman in the film seemed to dislike Schindler or resent his attraction to the others. Josh's younger self had found Schindler to be a perfect role model, a man of impeccable taste who wore silk suits and offered every man he met a drink and every woman a place in his bed.

If he hadn't yet slept with any of the young women his mother dangled in front of him tonight, it was only because, when he'd known them earlier, he'd tended to go for women with more experience than most high school girls. His piano teacher, one of his mom's tennis partners, newly divorced, and Headmaster Chambers's secretary, had all taught him a great deal by the time he graduated from Canyon. Josh supposed that if he still had a preference for a type of woman it was for the sexually experienced.

Yet, tonight, his mother's guests had not exactly stirred him.

Maybe he should be thinking about giving Mackenzie a second chance. She could probably match him in experience by now, and she had been the friendliest of the lot. She might consider him for a brief hookup even without his money. He knew better than to expect more than that from any other woman from his old crowd.

It all came back to the trust. Without it, he just wasn't himself.

His mom returned and settled at the table. The pool boy brought her a drink.

"Mom, what was that all about?"

"Just a chance for you to reconnect with your own kind."

He took a judicious swig of his beer.

"You are a charming piece of eye candy, darling, not unintelligent, and entirely presentable. You are at just the age to attract the right sort of woman, the kind who would never be embarrassed to have you on her arm."

Trust his mother to sum up his worth like that. He could be reasonably sure she was not on crack, but she was deluding herself if she thought he had any immediate marriage prospects. Not that he was looking for that kind of commitment. "I think you are confusing me with an escort service. I can find my own dates."

"Not if the gala was any indication. That sweet redhead was entirely wrong for you."

"It's true," Josh agreed. "Annie James is too good for me."

Two weeks earlier he had taken Will Sloan's love, not yet his fiancée, to the Canyon anniversary gala. Taking the newspaper reporter to the event had been one of those good deeds that never go unpunished. That night, seeing Annie with Josh, Sloan had finally proposed to the woman. Supporting the two of them against Chambers had cost Josh his job and his Canyon friends, even if it had been the right thing to do. At least he could take a large share of the credit for Annie and Will's current wedding plans.

His mother sat up in her chair, her version of strong emotion. "Nonsense. Red hair is utterly wasted on a woman like that. You don't know yourself if you think that sort of good girl is for you. You need a very different sort of woman."

"What sort?"

"A woman who will appreciate your gifts and make use of them."

"My gifts?"

"A man who can make himself agreeable to a woman is always useful."

"And you have someone in mind…for me to make myself agreeable to?"

"Actually, my assistant has a curated list she will email you. Twelve suitable women."

There was something more, of course. Josh waited for it.

His mother sipped her drink then said, "For each woman you make an effort to...know, I will provide you with a check for a month of your trust."

So, this was his mother's plan—to put a woman of her choosing in charge of him?

"You're serious," he said.

"Very. And I think you should move home."

He looked so like his mother. He wondered whether as a boy like Max Gray he had ever clung to her, whether she had ever ruffled his hair or worried about blood, vomiting, unconsciousness, or visible bones. He did not remember when she'd last taken any notice of his affairs.

She stood. "Of course, your father has a different idea. I believe he has a list, too."

"What sort of list?"

"A list of five men who would be willing to hire you."

"As many as five?" His father must have pulled some strings to find five friends willing to hire him. At least Josh had found the Canyon job on his own.

"Think about my offer, darling. I'll give you until the girls' Glen reunion. You'll be there, of course."

* * *

His apartment had shrunk by the time he arrived home. It was, after all, less than half the size of his family's garage.

His unit was dark. Emma Gray's unit was marked by a single bright square of light coming from her living room. As he came up the stairs he could see her slumped over a pile of books on the round table that stood under her living room window. Her laptop was open, but she looked dead to the world.

He turned to his own door and found a sticky note posted to the doorjamb. In the dim light of the entry he could not make out all the words. It appeared to be a list.

Opening his unit, still warm from the afternoon sun, he tossed his keys on the console table, flipped on a lamp, and read Emma's note:

Thank you for taking care of Max. I will be happy to return the favor.

Please choose one of the following:

1) one apartment cleaning
2) one healthy meal
3) one car wash.

He didn't think. He'd had enough of other people's lists.

He pivoted and crossed the narrow entry and knocked on Emma's door. His knock reverberated in the small space. Through the window he saw her start and lift her head from the pile of books. She had removed the heavy dark makeup, the earrings, and the dye from her hair. A red crease from the edge of a textbook marked her cheek. She looked confused for a moment, as if she did not realize what had wakened her, until she saw him at her door.

When she opened it, he strode right in and waved her note under her nose.

"What's this?"

"My offer to repay you for helping with Max this afternoon."

"What makes you think I require repayment?"

Oh, but he would. She could be it, with her scrubbed face and bare feet, her lingering vanilla scent, and the red crease on her cheek. He had only had a beer at his mother's, but now he felt the more potent buzz of a mix of anger and sexual frustration.

"That's just the way things work. You do me a favor. I do you a favor. We trade favors."

Josh looked at the list. He did not think she had any idea what she was saying.

"Usually 'trading favors' refers to a very different set of activities from the ones on your list."

Alarm flickered briefly in her gaze, and then her expression turned stubborn. "That's my list."

"So I can pick anything on this list and you'll do it?"

He'd put enough innuendo into his voice to make her peer at the list again, trying to see it in his hand. "Yes."

"How much notice do I have to give?"

She looked utterly exasperated and tired and vulnerable. The red crease on her cheek was livid against her pale skin. She was not a beachgoer.

"Mom?" Max stood at the other entrance to the living room in a pair of fire truck PJs. He looked between the two adults. "Are you sleeping at our house tonight, Josh?"

"Hi, Max. No. Sorry I disturbed you. Just talking with your mom."

"Mom made you a thank-you list."

"I know. We're talking about it."

Emma turned to the boy. "Go back to bed, Max. You have school in the morning."

"So do you, Mom. Mom says she doesn't need sleep," Max confided.

"I have a paper to finish first."

Josh looked at the stubborn expression on Emma's face. "Do you? Then, Max, you'd better head back to bed, buddy."

Her unit, the one of the two he had not fixed up before moving in, had a salt-and-pepper shag carpet that looked like matted dog fur. He scooped Max up under one arm and carried him to his room, the only furnished room in the apartment as far as he could see. The boy's room had a bed, a large wicker trunk, and a folding bookshelf, everything used but neat and orderly. He high-fived Max and promised another outing someday soon.

When he returned to the living room, Emma was back at her computer. A pool of light from her crook-necked desk lamp contained her. She did not look at him.

"Thank you."

He should walk out the door and tear up her silly list of favors. Instead, he crossed the room and stopped to stand at her elbow. "Did your babysitter call?"

"No."

He picked up a pen and scrawled a name and number on a piece of paper with her notes on it. "Call this place. Max can go after school. Lots of working moms send kids there."

"How much does it cost?" Emma asked.

"It's free."

"How can it be?"

"Trust me. The place is well-funded." He didn't know how much Sloan had donated to the Center, but he knew it was a chunk of change. In addition to her newspaper work Annie James ran the Center's communications, and Sloan had been willing to shell out a big bucks donation to get close to her.

"I can't accept any more favors from you."

"Without giving something in return, you mean?"

She swung around to stare at him, defiant.

He arched a brow. "Then make some other babysitting arrangement."

He didn't know why he was angry with her. Maybe he'd had a couple of spectacularly uncomfortable erections because of her, but that was just deprivation. She was not his type physically or in any other way. His mother was right about him and good girls, and he had a feeling that Emma was a very good girl despite her weekend death metal attire.

He felt obliged to warn her anyway. "When we *do* start trading favors, I won't be trading for kale salad."

Chapter Three

Will Sloan expected his very good life to get even better. He wasn't a loner anymore, and in a few weeks he would be married to the woman lying beside him. The thing that worried him at the moment, that had caused him to lie awake in their bed after a noise disturbed him earlier, could not change that. Still, he was wide awake and unlikely to drift off before his alarm <u>sounded</u>.

He shifted onto his right side so that he could watch Annie sleep in the faint light of a foggy beach dawn. They were living in her brown-shingled cottage on the highest dune overlooking the Pacific, the place where he'd first come to understand her. At night she plaited her deep red hair into a loose braid, but now wisps of hair curled around her pale face from the warmth of their shared bed.

Ten years earlier he had asked her to marry him in the Hall of Canyon Men. She'd turned him down. At the time he had blamed her for what seemed a pathetic weakness of character in the face of obstacles that he had known, even then, young and broke as he was, he would overcome. They had parted and remained apart for a decade. He had meant to forget her and thought he'd done so…until he saw her again. That had been at a Canyon alumni party organized by Josh Huntington the previous fall.

Since then Will had come to understand her better. What he had seen as weakness all those years ago was really a stubborn determination to do what she believed was right. And as they planned their fast-approaching wedding together, and as he watched her gentle resistance to every effort of her controlling sisters to manage things, he had come to appreciate her quiet strength even more.

Without opening her eyes, she reached for him, finding his left hand and drawing it up to tuck under her chin. "What are you worrying about?"

He laughed at her knowledge of him. "Jack Joyce."

"The boy who became a mercenary."

Will kissed her forehead. "Arms consultant."

"Oh, right."

In the past month, as they'd worked to save his old school from scandal and its shaky financial position, he had told Annie a lot about Jack. She had known him as a boy when she worked in the

Canyon Prep admissions office, but at school he'd been the class nerd known as "the invisible man" because he'd kept such a low profile. Both Annie and Will had only recently learned that as an angry high school senior Jack torched the school's original sign—an act of vandalism of which Will was accused, and for which he'd nearly lost everything he'd earned the hard way at Canyon: his diploma and his scholarship to college. Annie had defended Will then and given up her job to do it. Jack had never been revealed as the real vandal. And what troubled Will into wakefulness now was that, as far as he could see, Jack had taken no steps to reconcile himself with the past.

The guys who'd known Jack Joyce in high school would never have predicted his future—that he would drop out of college to become an arms consultant to mercenaries. Last year he'd come back to L.A. with a lot of cash and apparently as much anger as ever. He'd reconnected with Canyon only to shut it down. Using an assumed name, Jack had offered unscrupulous Headmaster Chambers a bond to cover some school needs created by the man's unethical manipulation of funds. Chambers had taken the bond, not recognizing Jack as a profound enemy, and Jack had let Chambers get further and further behind in the payments until he was in a position to foreclose and take over the school. When Will and Annie and Will's other classmate Josh Huntington uncovered Chambers's misdeeds, Will had also discovered Jack's role—and was able to buy the bond outright on several conditions.

It was one of those conditions now keeping Will up.

He had agreed to let Jack use the campus to host a benefit rock concert featuring the old heavy metal group Grindstone. According to Jack, the concert would launch a new video game, and most of the proceeds from the event and from sales of the game would go to support brain-injured veterans. There was a story there, and Will was sure of it. Something specific had happened to Jack to bring him back from the Middle East with this specific mission, and it sounded crazy, but something about him still seemed...off.

Annie tugged on Will's hand. Her expressive brown eyes were open and full of concern. "Tell me," she urged.

"I'm worried about giving Jack permission to use Canyon for this benefit concert."

She half laughed. "You think he might burn down another sign because he's still angry over something that happened when you were all in school together?"

"*I* was still angry, remember?"

The thought of Jack Joyce in control of the campus for a long weekend was starting to scare Will. What would Jack do ten years later as an angry ex-arms consultant? With his knowledge of weaponry and explosives, his devoted security people, and his invitation to a couple thousand anarchy-loving metalheads, he could easily do some serious property damage—or cause the school's reputation to take another public relations hit.

"One does have to wonder why you and Josh and Jack have all returned to Canyon," Annie said. She stretched, distracting him momentarily. "I have a theory about that."

"You do?"

She nodded solemnly. "I think you all want to undo a past choice."

"Do we get to undo the past?"

"*You* did." She kissed his knuckles. It was the lightest touch, and it stirred him. As her touch always did. "You should ask Jack to hire Josh."

"Because?"

"Josh is good at event planning."

"Does Huntington actually do work?"

Annie punched him playfully. "Also, Josh is smart, and he loves Canyon, and it's hard to be angry around him."

A few months earlier, Will would have been jealous to hear her speak of Josh Huntington this way, but he had misread her then and underestimated his former classmate. "I'll give him a call."

"You, my husband-to-be, may be even smarter than I thought."

Annie smiled at him, warm and soft, and ready to forgive him all over again for the past, for misjudging her and staying away so long out of bitterness. She was fully awake now, and she opened his hand, flattening his palm against her collarbone in invitation, and with a glance at the bedroom clock he decided that the next billion-dollar tech innovation could wait.

He slid his hand down to take hold of her waist and draw her body up against his, informing her of his intention. He leaned forward, but she pressed her hand to his mouth, stopping him.

"You have to promise me that you will tell Josh what worries you."

He promised.

She moved her hand, and he pressed his mouth to hers. *Let the forgiving begin again.*

* * *

Outside Josh's window, a low damp fog obscured his view of the beach and left only the flattened landscape of a modernist painting, shingled cottages and patches of square stucco in faded shades of olive and rust. He took a deep hit of espresso. The Monday morning neighborhood was dead, as if the population had vanished in the gray mist. His tenant certainly had. A dark oil spot on the driveway below his window marked the place where she parked her pathetic mustard-colored car.

He was listening to Rod Stewart singing, "Ooh la la, I wish that I knew what I know now when I was younger," and trying to understand what had made him so angry with Emma the night before. He didn't do anger. The emotion was a total waste of energy.

His gaze returned to the oil spot like a Rorschach blob on the pavement. He had not been a landlord before, so he might not actually be angry with his tenant, rather just annoyed with her demands. She could ask him to fix this or that, and being her landlord meant he had to deal with the plumbing or the gas or grout or whatever it was that needed fixing. When he'd had his trust, he could fix such things with a phone call to someone else. Since becoming a landlord, he'd been learning just how much he did not know about such ordinary stuff.

He did know his manners however. Emma had been the rude one, not thanking him for his help with her son Max. He'd gone totally above and beyond the call of neighborliness, and she had barely managed a thank-you. And then she'd insisted upon repaying him with a list of services, as if he couldn't just do a kindness. He wondered if she had the slightest clue how plainly that list revealed her estimate of his character.

Of course, he had probably reacted *so* badly to the list because his mother had wound him up with that plan to manage his life. He didn't need a woman to tell him what to do. He had been taking care of himself for years. In fact, his parents could hardly claim to have parented him at all. He and his sister had looked out for themselves with occasional help from a series of cooks, nannies, coaches, and drivers.

So, maybe the anger wasn't really about Emma Gray. He should tear up her stupid list and just let her alone. He had other things to do.

He reminded himself that the main benefit of being fired by former Headmaster Chambers was that he was free again. He had no plans, no obligations. When he'd had his trust, he had relished days of freedom and spontaneous adventure in places like Cabo and Bali. So, he wasn't in Bali or Cabo, but with Emma gone he could play his music, lounge in his favorite chair, and look at his neighbors' walls all day if he chose. He had some serious thinking to do about his cash flow.

He rolled his shoulders and felt the knots in them. He should get a massage. A place down by the pier gave a Shiatsu massage as good as any in Tokyo. He should see if they could take a walk-in. He put down his empty cup, pulled on a sweater, scooped up his keys and phone, and slipped his feet into his old boat shoes. He'd stop for tip money at the ATM on the way. Once he had the knots worked out, he would think of his next move.

As soon as he reached the long sloping main street that led down to the pier, he realized that the population hadn't disappeared after all and his mood lightened. The whole town covered about one square mile between the sand and the Coast Highway, a square mile of cottages and condos, small apartment complexes and duplexes like his, and the really big places that dominated the Strand. From nearly every dwelling, residents could see or hear the surf. Locals liked to say that there was no life east of the Avenue.

This morning people were hanging out in all the usual places, huddled at outdoor tables under heat lamps with coffee and muffins, or finishing up a workout in the sand at the end of the pier, or zipping along the Strand on bikes or inline skates. It wasn't Malibu, but the beach lifestyle was alive and well. Not everyone felt compelled to pour into L.A. to make money. He picked up an Americano at Java Jack's and headed down toward the Strand.

Owned by his Canyon friends Trevor Lynch and Greg Shields, the Power Plant microbrewery was closed at this hour, but its beery smell mixed with the salt air of the beach. Some volleyball players had strung their net anticipating a brighter afternoon, and an old guy in red trunks with a full mat of white chest hair charged up from the beach rotating his arms like windmills, apparently invigorated by a plunge in the surf. A woman jogged by pushing a stroller with a golden retriever trotting at her side.

She was a random woman with a child, but the sight flipped his mind right back to Emma Gray.

His intense attraction to Emma made no sense. Yes, she was female, but she was not his type in any way, and yet the puzzling thing was that around her, without any touch or body contact, he got erections—the kind that came on fast and hard. Last night she had invaded his dreams. Probably because of all that talk about trading favors.

She didn't have a clue, of course. The woman was nervous and awkward around him. He had caught her startled glance at his crotch the other day. Hard to miss how quickly she'd backpedalled from *any* apparent interest in sex. The women he usually connected with would be more frank and open, letting him know where they were willing to go with their curiosity.

He didn't think there was a man in her life despite the two metalheads from the record store who apparently worshipped her musical geekiness. Max had chattered away quite happily in their time together, but he'd made no mention of one. So, Emma was a clash of contradictions, tough and independent but gentle with her son. When she was not in her death metal getup, she looked like a kid herself, but she had a kid, a kid who'd announced that he didn't have a dad.

Josh did the math. At seventeen, someone who was not part of her life anymore had knocked up Emma.

Having Max had likely interrupted some of her plans, because she was going to school now. Josh could think of a number of scenarios that could account for a nice young girl getting unintentionally pregnant—a torrid farewell to her high school boyfriend that went too far, or a frat party in her first semester on some campus where she had too much to drink and hooked up without protection. The real mystery was why she had chosen to have Max alone and keep him. She must have parents somewhere who should be part of the picture. If a boyfriend knocked her up, there must have been some conversation, some joint decision-making about a kid, yet Emma and Max were on their own and clearly had been for some time. She did not seem to have anyone in her life, except maybe the babysitter who disappeared on her and her followers at the record store.

Josh tossed his cold coffee into a trash bin. He should be thinking about how to get his trust back without caving in to his parents' demands. He should not be devoting so much mental energy to his tenant.

Serious sexual deprivation was making him crazed. His favorite waitress, Melissa from the Power Plant, had moved on to his friend Lynch. Annie James had been an idle dream; she had always belonged to Sloan. And he had no prospects on the horizon. So, maybe the truth was that he was angry with Emma because for no reason he could understand she turned him on and they weren't going to have sex. Having her next door was an exercise in frustration he didn't need.

But…it didn't have to be that way, did it? If he could get Emma out of that Swedish death metal costume and do something about her reluctance to admit she wanted him, maybe they could get something going. He could get her to unwind a bit, and she could tide him over until he went back to his real life with his trust and his Canyon crew. He would think about that during his massage.

He turned back up the hill toward the center of town. Outside the bank he stepped up to the ATM, stuck his card in the slot, entered his PIN, and punched the fund level he needed.

The reply came back instantly:
TRANSACTION DENIED. INSUFFICIENT FUNDS.

Chapter Four

After school, at the light on the Coast Highway, Emma took Max's hand firmly in hers. They were walking up to the Center Josh Huntington had recommended as an afternoon-care option. Emma had texted Maria Felix, but she'd had no word back yet from her friend and weekend babysitting mainstay.

Now that Max was six he didn't like to hold Emma's hand crossing the street, but the highway was more than a street. In the late afternoon, the impatient ebb and surge of commuter traffic made its six lanes potentially lethal to pedestrians.

"Josh did not make me hold his hand," Max reported.

Of course he didn't. Her landlord had no sense of responsibility.

"Did you cross the highway with him?"

Max watched the traffic until she gave his hand a little shake. As they walked he had offered details of the afternoon he'd spent with their neighbor and landlord as if he were measuring her ways against the ways of a superior being instead of a do-nothing incompetent.

"We waited for the light. Just like you do."

"Where did he take you?" They got the green and began to cross.

"To a place where kids play and draw and stuff."

"The Center? Where we're going?"

Max nodded, looking at her as if Josh Huntington's taking him to a storefront community center that catered to the ninety-nine percent seemed an ordinary event. Emma didn't think so.

Nothing about her landlord made sense. She was something of an expert in the matter of landlords, and she'd never had a landlord under fifty. In the beach cities, landlords in the big complexes were faceless entities hiding behind their office managers. Landlords of little post-war stucco cottages were retired couples where the husband was handy and the wife careful of their pennies. Landlords were not...sexy.

To be fair, so far he had not pushed to take advantage of the favor he had done her. Not yet, anyway. He'd only hinted that her list of favors was not what he had in mind.

He probably thought she was crazy, what with her thank-you lists and her bipolar fashion sensibility. For weekends at Daddy Rock when Leo wanted her to mingle with customers on the floor she wore her death metal gear, but for school she wore her cloak of invisibility, a generic twenty-something student look designed to be ignored. Huntington was the only person who saw her in both. It was unfortunate that he no longer had a place to go each day. This morning she had caught a glimpse of him sprawled in the oversized leather armchair that dominated his living room reading the paper in his inevitable boxers.

And...he must have bills to pay. Emma had made a rough calculation in her head of just how expensive he was—car, clothes, mortgage, meals out, and taxes. Not to mention his garage full of expensive sports gear.

She and Max reached the Center. She had called the number and been assured by the director, Louisa Ruiz, that Max would be welcome in the afternoons, so they made their way up a stairway decorated with primary-color kid artwork to a second-floor set of rooms. A large central space was partitioned into sections where different age groups gathered. At a long table in the middle a skinny dark-haired youth wearing drug-dealer shades was helping a group of middle school kids with homework. In a corner, a pair of couches, a rug, and a low bookcase made a cozy spot where a woman with deep red hair was reading aloud to a group of children sitting atop cushions on the floor.

Max tugged her sleeve. "That's Annie, Mom."

"Annie?"

The woman glanced at them and waved at Max.

"Josh knows her. Can I go listen to the story?"

"Sure."

Josh knows her. That explained a lot. Emma was not wrong about his character after all. He had taken Max to this place not out of the kindness of his heart but because he was interested in a woman here. Emma watched the beautiful redhead welcome Max to the group, and at her encouragement the other kids made a space for him and a brown-haired girl who had to be close in age to Max handed him a pillow to sit on.

"Ms. Gray?"

Emma turned to find a smiling thirty-something woman at her side, dressed in tangerine from the butterfly clips in her shoulder-length brown curls to the beads on her sandals.

The woman stuck out her hand. "Hi, I'm Louisa, the director here. Let me show you around, and if you'd like to sign Max up for one of our afternoon programs, we can take care of the paperwork."

Emma let herself be led away, doing her best to banish thoughts of her landlord from her mind. She relaxed a little as she looked around. The Center was nothing she'd expect her upscale landlord to recommend. It was warm and organized and about as chic as a school cafeteria or a church basement meeting room.

In her office, Louisa cheerfully shifted an open bin of file folders to clear an orange plastic chair for Emma and handed her a clipboard with some forms to fill out. "Look these over while I check on the group in the computer room. I can answer any questions when I return. Basically, we meet participating children at school at the end of the day and walk or carpool them here to the Center. You provide an afternoon snack, and we provide activities and tutoring or mentoring as needed."

Ballpoint pen in hand, Emma sat in the bright orange molded plastic chair Louisa offered her in a corner of the cluttered office and confronted the first form attached to the clipboard. Its blank spaces invited her to spell out her identity as if it were simple, but one glance reminded her of all the reasons she usually relied on her friends to babysit Max. An organization wanted phone numbers and the sort of information that made a person findable by someone who might be looking. Suddenly Emma felt tired from school and work and keeping it all going. Her brain refused to come up with another dodge, an invention, something to fill the blank line for nearest emergency contact.

She shook off the momentary fatigue. She was used to giving her invented name to people. It was the name she'd picked for herself at seventeen when she'd taken charge of her life. At the time, the one thing she'd been sure of was that her old name, the one given to her by her grandparents, did not fit the truth of who she was—and she had learned how useless that old name was when she went in search of her father.

Until that night, she had believed her old name was like a magic pass that opened doors. She had been wrong. She had also believed she could handle herself and alcohol, and that the world would treat her kindly and gently as always. The man from Grindstone's road crew who sneaked her into the hotel where the concert after-party was in progress had disabused her of those ideas. His name was Ron, and he had expected sex in return for helping her. He'd been unwilling to hear "no," and she'd been in no shape to fight him off. When her flailing arms failed to stop him, she'd just lain there. Their encounter had gone downhill from there, and the last thing Ron said to her that night still burned in her brain:

"You little rich girls are all alike. You can't drink, and you think daddy's bank account makes you hot, but you don't even rate a screw from the guy that carries Saxon's bags."

When she awakened on a sofa in an empty hotel suite with her panties sticky and bloodied, she had not gone home. The girl she had been no longer existed. She wasn't sure then of who she might become, but she had known that she needed to be tough and independent.

It had proved easier than people imagined to disappear, to rely on cash earnings, no-contract phones, and a network of moms like her who were on their own and who looked out for one another, laughed together, and raged and cried together. Once a year, on her mother's birthday, she mailed her grandparents a letter letting them know she was still alive.

Emma straightened in the plastic chair and picked up the pen again. From beyond the little office she could hear the familiar rhythms of mom-talk, sweet endearments and sharp cautions mixing as women like herself collected their kids. She didn't know any of them, of course. The beach was a new neighborhood for her. She had lost touch with most of the people with whom she'd traded babysitting turns when she took the job at Daddy Rock—except Maria, who was like a mother hen to a dozen or more moms like Emma. Maria was the one who found the babysitters or the clinics or the jobs that people needed, and she kept them all going, taking things one day at a time and encouraging baby steps to get where you wanted.

Maria was also the babysitter who'd bailed on Emma yesterday. If Emma hadn't heard from her, it had to be because someone else needed Maria even more desperately. But she'd be back. Emma couldn't imagine her friend disappearing forever, and when she was back everything would be okay. In the meantime, Emma would just have to manage.

Louisa returned, and Emma rose and thanked her, offering the half-filled out form. "I'm sorry for taking your time. I don't think this will work for us. We're so new to the area that I don't have anyone nearby to list for an emergency contact."

"Why don't you put Josh down? He's your neighbor, I take it?"

"Next door."

"Perfect. He's here often enough. He helps the older kids with their high school and college applications. He's sort of a pro at it, actually. I'd hire him if I could."

Hire him? Emma swallowed her disbelief. She couldn't imagine Huntington hanging out in a place like the Center. At random the image of Huntington in his black silk boxers surfaced in her brain. She dismissed it with a little shake of her head.

Louisa's warm smile remained in place.

Emma held out her hand to take back the forms. She listed Josh on the emergency contact line and wrote his cell number in the blank space, but she told herself she would never need him. The form was just a form. She and Max would get where they needed to be every day just as they had before, and she would only need the Center for backup for a few weeks. Then her plan would be complete.

She would have to do something nice for her landlord, though. She did not want to owe him anything, and whatever Huntington's motives, he had done her another favor by giving her the Center's number.

On the way home, she decided what she could do to keep the favor count even. She had never seen him eat anything. No food smells came from his unit, except in the morning, the delicious odor of rich dark coffee beans. She had seen and heard the device in which he ground the beans: a smart grinder he called it, the sort of expensive hardware that people put on wedding registries. He ground beans and fired up his espresso machine whenever he woke up. Ten seemed to be his idea of rising early.

She took Max into the market and led him to the produce section to choose fruit for his lunch while she considered what to make for her landlord. Whatever she made, it would have to be something simple and effortless as she could not imagine Huntington heating or mixing or doing anything more elaborate than selecting the timed-cook option on his microwave.

She was standing in front of a bin of avocadoes when Max tugged at her sleeve. "Are we done yet, Mom?"

"Sorry. I was just thinking of what to make for our landlord."

"Josh? Are we making him something? Oh, because he helped us get to the Center."

"Yes. But I don't know what."

"A sandwich would be good. With lots of stuff on it."

She looked at her son. He was right. A sandwich would be perfect.

"Good idea. Thanks, Max. You can help me make it."

* * *

Josh opened his door.

It was getting to be a thing, this opening the door to his tenant's particular knock. Even over the sounds of the Red Hot Chili Peppers—*"Give it away give it away give it away give it away now, I can't tell if I'm a kingpin or a pauper"*—he could hear her knock. She never messed around with that knock. And lately she seemed to knock whenever he was feeling the pinch of his situation.

It was on the tip of his tongue to say something biting, but she had Max with her. The boy was holding out a square package wrapped in brown paper and string.

"We made you a thank-you sandwich."

Josh shot a glance over the boy's head at his mother. She was using the boy as a shield. Smart move. He couldn't say any of the things that came to mind with an innocent six-year-old looking up at him.

He accepted the sandwich. The thing had to weigh half a pound.

"What are you and your mom thanking me for this time, Max?"

Max glanced up at his mother and shrugged. They obviously hadn't rehearsed this part. "I'm going to go to the Center. After school."

"Good plan." That wasn't it, though. Emma was holding something back.

"We saw Annie. She read to us."

"What's in the sandwich?" Josh asked the boy.

"Avocado, bacon, tomato, onion, cheese, and bread. I picked all the good stuff. Mom grilled the onion."

"Sounds great. Your mom went to a lot of effort." He looked at Emma again, who took hold of Max's shoulders as if she could steer him back to her apartment and end the conversation. Having the boy there was obviously a two-way street, so Josh could force her to make an admission she'd rather not make. "What sandwich-sized favor have I done?"

"I used your name on the emergency form at the Center. Don't worry. They'll never have to call you. I always get home on time to pick Max up. They just needed the form filled out."

"My name on the emergency form?" Obligating him to help if she was unavailable? It said so much about the absence of people in her life, but this made the sandwich a pathetic thank-you. He hefted the thing in his hand. It wasn't any of the things he was used to, not tacos from Guisades or Thai from Jitlada or dinner at Mozza—

The ATM message from earlier flashed into his brain. A conversation with a cute teller inside the bank had revealed just how badly he was dipped. His automatic bill payment system had kicked in just as he'd set it up to do, but no paycheck had been deposited, no trust check arrived. Hence, insufficient funds. He had checked all his accounts and found no hidden stash of cash. So, no, Emma Gray had to do better than an avocado bacon sandwich, even if it was as thick as a brick.

He had a sudden flash of exactly what would suit him. "What about a massage?"

"A massage?" Her voice went up an octave. She looked horrified, but he knew better. She was not as indifferent to him as she pretended. A massage meant touching, and her expression meant that Emma imagined touching him, imagined it instantaneously as he made the suggestion. Her eyes betrayed her. Emma Gray was a woman resisting an attraction, and he felt the tug between them.

"Neck and shoulders. Twenty minutes," he said, trying to be cool about it, to reassure her. Still, she'd have her hands on his body, which parts of him found to be an extremely interesting idea.

"I don't know anything about massages," she said. "Hire a professional."

She was hard on a man's ego.

"I'll give you directions."

"What's a massage?" Max asked.

"It's—" Josh and Emma started to answer as one and stopped.

Emma reached out with a finger and tapped the sandwich she'd brought. "That's a great sandwich. It's the perfect thank-you. Unwrap and eat. No effort required."

Josh looked at her. "If being available for Max in an emergency is worth this monster sandwich, what favor do I have to do to get that massage?"

"No favor. We're done now."

She pivoted Max around and marched him back to her unit.

Josh shut the door. He felt as if he were free-falling. His parents were calling the shots, women were ignoring him, and he was accepting handouts from a tenant. He clearly needed to get his trust back.

Going about it by following his father's plan meant starting over again, accepting a job of his father's choosing and meeting his father's conditions. Once again he would have to keep himself employed for a full year from day one of a new job, and once again he would have to find a project through which he could contribute to something larger than his own pleasure. Those were his dad's conditions. Josh's original project—getting his classmates at Canyon to give the single largest ten-year class gift in the school's history— had succeeded thanks to Sloan. It wasn't breakthrough medical research or world peace, which were out of his league, but it would have satisfied his father…if Chambers hadn't fired him.

Josh shook his head. His father's conditions for regaining the trust made his mother's offer look good. Date her candidates and collect money. A year of hookups and handouts. That was better than finding a job and completely starting over.

He crossed his living room, heading for his apartment's tiny kitchen. He had not eaten for hours. He unwrapped his tenant's sandwich and put it on a plate. Between slabs of beautiful, thick dark bread were layers of artfully arranged ingredients. Emma had definitely made an effort to repay the favor he'd done her.

He took a bite, and his mind swung back to the problem of his parents. He wanted some way out. He was not ready to bow to either of them. He would prefer to choose his own dates and—if he *had* to work—his own job.

As he took another bite of the sandwich, he decided that the thing he most wanted was that massage. He wanted Emma Gray's hands on his body.

* * *

Emma knew she had not heard the last of Max's question about massage. An unanswered question just wasn't a possibility for him. *Where does this road go? How far does it go? If we started now, how long would it take us to get there? Why are so many cars going the same way?*

She had taught herself to answer the hard questions in the lightest of tones, as if there were no real mystery or concern about missing dads and frequent moves, and as she prepared their supper and shepherded Max through his nighttime routine she thought about how to answer the massage question when it surfaced again. They had talked about Max's body and the differences between boys and girls a few times, the questions returning as Max grew in awareness. They had even talked a couple of times about where babies came from, after the mom of one of Max's classmates became pregnant and a new sibling arrived midway through his kindergarten year.

The question returned in the middle of Max's bedtime story. "What's a massage?"

Emma closed the book. "It's a little like rocking a baby, something you do to make someone relax and feel safe."

She waited while Max thought about that explanation. At last he said, "But Josh isn't a baby, so you couldn't rock him."

"No. It would be more like pushing and pulling on his shoulders, like you do with Play-doh or clay. Or like a backrub…only for shoulders."

"Is it something girls do for boys?"

"No. It's not a girl/boy thing exactly. It's like a nurse or doctor thing for a patient. One person does it to help another feel better."

"Does Josh feel bad?"

"Maybe a little."

"Why?"

Because he's a self-indulgent prince of privilege who's never had to go without anything. "He doesn't have a job anymore." She was guessing, but that seemed the best explanation for the change in his pattern from moderate to total idleness.

"Why does he need a job?" Max asked.

"Well, he needs money to pay for things."

Max shook his head in the way he always did when he rejected one of her explanations. "Josh has lots of things, and his car is way better than ours." He gave her one of those looks she found hardest to take from a six-year-old, the look that said he'd figured something out without her help. "I think he likes you. You said people touch when they like each other. You said it's okay if two people like each other."

"That's right." She wasn't going to undo the talk they'd had about good and bad touching, but she didn't like the direction Max's questions were going.

"So, I think Josh likes you, too."

"Me? *Too?*"

"Yeah. Like he likes Annie. He touches Annie." Max flopped over onto his side and slid down under his covers. "G'night, Mom."

Right. Emma swung her feet down hard on the salt-and-pepper shag carpet that looked vaguely like an aging terrier that had rolled in dirt. It was a good thing she could count on her son to set her straight. She did not have to worry about Josh Huntington wanting anything more from her than some impersonal pressure on his delts and trapeziuses to release the tension generated by his indolent, expensive life. It was she who had in a flash misconstrued the situation by imagining her hands on him.

In the unlikely event that she ever owed him that particular favor, she would do her best Big Nurse imitation and get on with it.

Chapter Five

Emma never meant to eavesdrop, but the symmetrical architecture of the duplex was against her. The two units faced each other on the second story above the garage, across a narrow metal staircase that led down to the driveway; her open living room window faced Josh Huntington's across a mere fifteen feet of air and the two dark brown window boxes she'd planted when she first moved in, part of the deal made with him to lower her rent. She had done her best all morning to ignore his music, his aimless wanderings, his staring at the ocean.

It was Wednesday, her day without work or classes, so she had parked herself early at her computer. She was getting nowhere fast when the beautiful redhead came up the stairs and knocked on her landlord's door. Emma kept her head down over her laptop as he answered.

A quick glance told her that he actually had pants on, a pair of salmon-colored shorts suitable for yachting off Martha's Vineyard or Cape Cod. They should look ridiculous, but they sagged around his lean hips and exposed his long tan legs down to his elegant bare feet. The first breath of the afternoon breeze flattened a loose blue polo shirt against his torso, and butterflies of awareness fluttered in Emma's stomach. His eyes should not be so blue.

He turned the full force of his charm on his visitor. "Annie." His greeting was warm and genuine. "What brings you here? Tell me you changed your mind about marrying Sloan. You discovered that he listens to Garth Brooks and Loretta Lynn, and those green eyes and tech billions suddenly aren't enough."

He made the woman laugh, a lovely sound. "I came to deliver this, personally."

Emma glanced again but didn't see what the woman offered. "Coffee?"

"Sure."

The redhead disappeared into the apartment and reappeared at Josh's living room window opposite Emma, looking out toward the ocean. She offered a friendly wave, which Emma returned.

Emma tried to refocus on the paper she was writing. It was the last one of the term, the last one for her art major, but she'd lost the thread of her argument about light on color in a group of paintings by several contemporary Plein-Air artists. Across the way, Annie looked unaffected by Josh Huntington's dangerous charm—which made sense if she was marrying someone else. Emma should not waste a minute trying to figure out his relationship with the beautiful woman, but her thoughts kept straying to the conversation happening over there in her landlord's unit, and she looked up again when the pair returned to the entry.

Annie shifted her bag to her shoulder. "Will's going to call you this week. He has a favor to ask."

"Hey, I'm in no position to do favors for tech billionaires."

The redhead was silent a moment. When she spoke, the lightness had left her tone. "Josh, did something happen to your trust fund?"

"My trust? Nothing. I'm just trying to make it on my own. Self-reliance. Thoreau and all that."

"Emerson, actually." Annie laughed. "So, in the spirit of self-reliance, can you do Will a favor? I'd be grateful if you would hear him out."

"No fair. You know I can't turn you down."

"Good. And Ulysses and Tyler want to talk with you, too. The boys are bringing the C-Notes to our party, and they're working on their solo or duet or whatever."

Huntington shook his head. When he spoke, he sounded amused. "You still think I'm a nice guy. After every underhanded trick I played to bring you and Sloan together?"

"You did bring us together. I'll be eternally grateful, and you don't know yourself if you think you're not a nice guy."

In spite of her best intentions, Emma lifted her head from the computer screen and caught a glimpse of the redhead leaning close to kiss Huntington's cheek. It was a friendly kiss, almost maternal. Josh stood with his hands in his pockets as if indifferent, but Emma saw the posture of a man defending himself from loss.

The redhead left, and as her hand trailed down the stair rail a significant diamond on her finger flashed in the sun. So, Emma's landlord was attracted to a beautiful woman who was in no danger of being misled by his charm. That had to be a first for him, and Emma felt an odd sympathy. He'd apparently lost his trust fund, and now there was something else that he would never have. The two facts explained a lot. She knew what a shock it was to leave Planet Privilege behind.

She chided herself for being soft. Her landlord could probably use a dose of toughness. He did not need her sympathy, and she had things to do: a paper to write, a concert to get into, a kid to take care of. That was her agenda, dealing with the unfinished business of her life, so she could get on with the future. She had promised Max a house and a dog, and she had to deliver.

* * *

Within an hour after Annie left, Josh had a call from Will Sloan. Given the state of Josh's love life, it was depressing how in tune Annie and Will were.

Josh had called Sloan dozens of times in his months-long effort to bring them together, but it felt odd to have Sloan calling him. In high school they had never been friends, if they had played football on the same team. Josh's role had been to stand in the pocket and toss the football downfield to wherever Sloan got himself. Sloan, a rare financial-aid student at Canyon, had been the one taking the hits most of the time—on and off the field it turned out. Hence the anger Sloan felt toward Canyon, which, now that Sloan had won the love of Annie James, was gone.

At the tender age of twenty-seven, Sloan and his partner Beau Lassiter had gone from being college football buddies with a start-up to being tech billionaires. That made them older than some start-up geniuses, but selling their Z-Text security concept put Sloan leagues ahead of most of his former Canyon classmates no matter the size of their trust funds. A non-competition clause in the deal required him to return to L.A., where he had reunited with his first love. Josh had taken a modest hand in the thing by throwing the two of them together at Canyon events for six months in spite of Sloan's insistence that he wanted nothing to do with Annie. Josh had been betting the other way the whole time: that once Sloan saw Annie James again, the man would be a goner. And he'd been right.

So, now Sloan had a favor to ask of him?

Yes. Sloan had a meeting set up with Jack Joyce, and apparently he wanted Josh there. That gave Josh pause. Jack Joyce had been "the invisible man" of their Canyon class, and he'd kept up his reputation by being the guy impossible to locate as Josh planned the school's big centennial gala. It turned out that Joyce was hard to locate because he'd been a mercenary in places the State Department warned tourists not to go. He'd also been the holder of the school's unpaid bond, the man who threatened to close the place down until Sloan simply bought the whole debt.

Josh supposed his job at this meeting was to provide the social grace the other two lacked. A conversation between Sloan and Joyce would be blunt and short on tact. The other odd thing was the meeting location. It would be at Canyon, in the Hall of Canyon Men. Like Sloan, Joyce had hated Canyon.

When Josh put the date of the business meeting in his phone calendar, it was kind of lonely. Another sign of his declining fortune.

* * *

Emma gave up on finishing her art paper after she collected Max from school. Between her landlord sprawled in his big armchair and Max, who had reached the limit of his capacity to be self-entertaining, her concentration was shot.

She proposed an outing to the park, and while Max scurried to find his sneakers she packed a snack and some water in her backpack and stuffed her keys and her phone in her pocket. She got a call as she and Max stepped out of the apartment into the entry at the top of the stairs. It was Leo asking her to work an extra shift. She immediately said no, but Leo wasn't listening. Instead, he was explaining that he'd just fired another employee, a guy named Eddie who had a real following among the usuals at the store. Leo hinted that Emma needed to show some loyalty to Daddy Rock if she wanted to keep her job, and right now keeping her job meant holding on to her chance to meet her father.

"Leo, I can be there in an hour."

Leo didn't like that idea at all. He reminded her in no uncertain terms of the nature of boss-employee relations, which she knew well. It was one of the fundamental laws of Planet Ordinary: If you took money from someone, you played by their rules.

Emma looked down at Max, who tugged on the sleeve of her free hand. Her unfinished paper lay inside, in all its chaos of note sheets and open references, Leo was waiting, and she also had a little boy who deserved her undivided attention. And she had no sitter.

Max tugged on her arm some more.

Her landlord opened his door. His glance took in the situation and he said, "Sounds like you need a...massage-sized favor."

Emma said a very bad word, the sort of word she had banished from her vocabulary when Max was two and in the habit of repeating whatever she said. Max froze, and Leo started swearing at her from her phone, threatening to fire her for her insubordination.

Her hand went limp. Huntington took the phone. Emma knelt and took Max in her arms and apologized to him while above them Huntington introduced himself to Leo and explained that Emma's expletive had been directed at him. When she stood, Huntington handed the phone back, and she apologized to Leo and agreed to do the shift.

She hung up, took a deep breath, and faced Huntington. "Okay. I accept your help this afternoon. Will you take Max to the park?"

"Sure."

"No junk food. No crossing the highway. No beach." She used her no-nonsense, obey-or-die voice that always worked on Max, and gave her landlord her toughest look.

"Your obedient servant, ma'am."

"Hah." He was no one's servant. He was just what his massage bargain suggested he was—a first-class manipulator with nothing but his own self-interest at heart—and she did not want to owe him a massage. She did not even want to think about touching him.

"I have to go." She looked at Max. "Be safe. Don't let Josh let you do things I wouldn't let you do."

Max nodded, but he was bouncing with excitement. Emma reopened her apartment and got out her death metal gear.

* * *

At the store, Leo put Emma front and center to man a display of Grindstone memorabilia. The *Toxic One* album was playing, posters from the 1990 tour hung from the ceiling, and the main counter display case held bass guitarist Rezford's guitar strap resting in a bed of bright-colored picks. On a black velvet-draped box was the famous two-page rider from the last tour with the list of the band's special requests for everything from which brand of condoms, Scotch, and underwear they required, to their Grey Poupon mustard, to of course the stage setup for the final act of their show.

The concert was apparently now official—though still private. Customers who wanted a chance to attend the invitation-only benefit could put a sales receipt with an email address into a large ceramic guitar next to the display of memorabilia. Leo told Emma to make sure the thing was full when she left, and there were plenty of customers to make that happen. The word had spread not only among metal fans, but among gamers as well. Apparently Leo was not above using the buzz to generate more traffic to the store.

Brandon stepped up next to her. His hands were shoved deep in the pockets of his black overcoat. "Thought you'd be here."

Emma shifted to her right. "It's called being a store employee."

"So, what's the deal? Do we have to buy something?"

"With any twenty dollar purchase you get a chance at a ticket."

"That sucks, you know," Todd said, appearing next to Brandon. He picked up the ceramic guitar and gave it a shake. Realizing that Leo was watching, Emma retrieved it.

"You want to see the show, don't you?"

"Anarchists don't pay to see shows. We're against the whole commercial music establishment."

Apparently Brandon failed to see the irony in his position.

"Music should be free," Todd said.

Emma stared at him. "Pretty much everyone who has an album in one of these bins would disagree."

"Yeah, it still sucks though."

"We want *you* to get us into the show."

Brandon was now officially standing too close to her, enveloping her in his trademark taco scent, and Emma shook her head. "I don't know that *I* can get in the show, let alone help you two."

"We should work together. We could come up with a plan. Like, you could let us in after the warm-up band."

"Why do you care so much about Grindstone?"

Brandon and Todd looked at her and then each other.

"The axe," Brandon said, referring to Grindstone's signature stage moment of grinding a double-bladed axe to shrieking sharpness against a giant spinning wheel. "They're Vikings. They're unstoppable. They pillage and burn. *We* need some Vikings. Everything's too commercial. It's all bought and sold like"—he indicated the ceramic guitar—"this thing."

Emma stared at them. "You think that's Grindstone's message?"

Their two heads nodded. Across the floor, Leo gave her a look that suggested she lose them. He was all about the number of units sold per shift. Helping Brandon and Todd would get her exactly nowhere. It was going to be a long afternoon.

Emma saw her chance to move them along. "I think you should listen to the latest Entombed album."

Chapter Six

It was just getting dark when Josh and Max headed back to the apartment. Josh had no complaints about the afternoon they'd spent. The kid had a thousand questions, but Josh was getting used to that. He'd also listened to what the boy didn't say. Again there was no mention of a man in Emma's life, and no mention of a family. Taking the kid to the beach hadn't been the original plan, but the park had been overrun with some lavish kid birthday complete with a bounce house shaped like a castle.

What Josh had to do now was remain cool about the massage. Emma owed him, but she would be tired and ready to pay attention to Max when she returned. It was unlikely that she would be free before nine. He could wait, and it would probably be better for her to give him the massage after Max was in bed. That way she would not be distracted, and whatever happened they would not be disturbed. He supposed that she would have to give him the massage at her place so that she could keep an ear tuned for her son. She had no couch and only a pair of wooden chairs for the table where she did her work, though, so Josh would have to think of something he could put down over that questionable carpet.

The duplex was in sight when he realized that Max's steps were dragging.

"Tired, buddy?"

"Mom's going to be mad," Max announced.

"Why?"

"The beach."

We won't tell her, flashed in Josh's mind, but he rejected it at once. He really could not encourage a six-year-old to lie to his mother. The kid would have to learn sooner or later when to share information with a parent and when not to.

"I have sand on me," Max continued. "She'll see."

"No big deal. Let's get it off of you."

At the foot of the driveway, Max started brushing at his clothes, loosening thin streams of sand. It had managed to collect in the pockets and folds of both his shorts and Josh's. Josh also had sand sticking to his toes. Emma wouldn't want to get it in her carpet. Old and worn as her unit was, she kept it super clean.

"Tell you what, Max. You wait here. I'll get us some towels, and we can wash the sand off outside."

He sat Max down on the bottom stair and sprinted up to his place for some towels. As he came out of the apartment, towels in hand, he heard the hose running. He glanced over the stair rail at the driveway below.

"Hey, Max, what's up?"

Max looked at him. He stood holding the hose to his chest, water running down his clothed middle. "I'm taking care of the sand," he said.

Josh nodded. He should not be surprised.

Max looked down at himself. His shirt and shorts clung to him, and his sneakers looked drowned. "Will Mom still be mad?"

Josh couldn't help nodding again. Still, he did not want to scare the boy. Maybe he could turn the situation around.

"Hold on, buddy," he called. "We can fix this." He draped his towels over the stair rail and emptied his pockets of phone and wallet. He headed down the stairs and spread his arms wide. "Hey, you help me next."

Max, the good boy, his mother's rule-follower, hesitated about a nanosecond. A look of sheer delight then sprung up in his eyes, and with a squeal he turned the hose on Josh.

Josh let Max spray him until he, too, was soaked and dripping. It felt crazy. It also felt good, and Max was laughing. They took turns blasting each other, ignoring California's persistent drought.

When the boy's teeth started chattering, Josh leaned over and turned off the spigot. "Time to get dry. Come on, Max, I've got towels at the top of the stairs."

They trudged upward. Max's sneakers squished with their water load. At the top, Josh helped the boy out of his wet shoes, and they stepped into the entry between the two units. Josh was just reaching for a towel when he heard quick light footsteps on the stairs and a gasp from behind them.

"What is going on here?"

It was Emma's no-nonsense Mom voice.

Josh and Max turned and froze. In her death metal gear, Emma looked seriously alarming. Water dripped from them, pooling on the entry tiles, but Josh had the presence of mind to say, "Water fight. It's a guy thing."

She glanced at him, and her eyes got round before she tore her gaze away to Max. He looked down and saw that his shirt and shorts were molded to his body with Speedo-like cling.

Max was shaking.

"Out of those wet clothes. Now." Emma stepped forward, flipped her son's arms straight up and stripped his soaked T-shirt over his head. In the next instant she shoved her hands like two wedges straight under the elastic band of his sopping shorts and skimmed them and his briefs off his shivering body, leaving the kid pink and naked.

Watching her, Josh's whole body came to instant attention. He wanted her to do the same him. He held himself very still and concentrated on not giving himself away. This was not the moment to mention the massage she owed him.

Not that Emma was looking at him. A gray-black line of wet sand circling Max's middle below his belly button had her full attention. He saw the realization hit her. She spun and said, "You went to the beach. I told you…"

Her outraged glance demanded an explanation.

"We built a sand fort under the lifeguard station. We did not go in the water."

He offered her a towel for Max. She snatched it away and knelt, wrapping her son tighter than a spring roll. She paused only to give the boy one of her brief fierce hugs before they disappeared into their unit. The door slammed behind them. Again, there was no thank-you for an afternoon of helping out. At least she blamed him and not her kid.

Josh released a long, slow breath. She was seriously weird about the beach, and seriously fierce as a parent. The contradiction made his head spin, and it made no sense for him to be turned on by her yet again. But he was.

He stripped off his own soaked shirt and shorts and wrapped himself Fijian style in the towel. He hung his wet clothes over the stair rail and headed for his fridge. A shower was not a good idea.

Standing naked under streams of warm water was not the way to stop thinking about what he wanted his tenant to do to him.

Six months of slumming had brought him to this. He was sexually obsessed with a prickly, fashion-impaired single mother who found him worthless even as a babysitter. He grabbed a beer, turned on some head-banging late Iron Maiden at a volume that would swallow up even Emma's knock, and settled down in the big armchair.

She didn't knock. She just came in and killed the music. She still had her fake tattoos and piercings, and this time a cropped top that bared her whole midriff and revealed a glittering stud attached to her navel. He realized he had been holding his breath in a way, waiting for her to knock for an hour or more. The music had been to summon her, not to cover up her knock. He had been more afraid she wouldn't knock.

He tried to contain a rush of satisfaction. She might not like it, but she was hooked, too. He knew as much from the guarded expression on her face, and the part of him that seemed to respond to Emma like a struck tuning fork uncoiled and stretched.

She was holding out the towel he'd given her for Max, and she gave it a little shake. "What is this?"

Not a deep question, but it troubled him nonetheless with that belly button piercing staring at him. "A towel?"

Apparently he had not offered the right answer. She dropped it on the arm of his chair. It smelled of laundry soap and dryer heat.

"My towels offend you?"

"It's from the Intercontinental in Bali. What's wrong with ordinary towels?"

He put down his beer. "The Intercontinental sells the towels. I picked some up the last time I stayed there."

She shook her head. Her look said he was nuts.

"I like thick towels."

He could see that she wanted to make a speech condemning his profligate ways, but she took a steadying breath instead and said, "I do not want Max near the ocean."

"I got that."

To be polite he should stand up, but her presence was having its usual effect on him and there was a real danger of embarrassing himself, or worse, her, with a tent pole under the towel. What he really wanted was to pull her down into the chair on top of him.

"There are rogue waves and riptides and sharks," she said. "It's too dangerous."

He nodded, but her gaze did not meet his. She had to be making this stuff up. This was the South Bay, not some dangerous coast where only nutcase, die-hard surfers braved the waves. He did not repeat that he and Max had not gone into the water. He could see that she wasn't rational about the ocean. There had to be a reason for that, and he would have to probe for answers later. He was usually good at getting people to reveal things they meant to conceal, especially women.

She tugged at her right ear, releasing the row of fake piercings that lined the lobe. Today she had tied her hair in dozens of knots all over her head, and just looking at her he knew she had a headache. So he shifted and stood. Whatever the towel revealed of his reaction to her nearness, he'd just distract her a little. Her anger couldn't be doing that headache any good.

Lifting his right hand, he reached out for her other ear and brushed his thumb over the clipped-on steel loops, removing them. The soft rim of her lobe was pock-marked with red dents. He turned her hand over and poured the metal bits into her palm.

"Are you into pain?" he asked.

Emma shook her head and pulled the stud out of her navel—before he had a chance to touch her there, too, as he'd hoped. She wrapped her arms around her middle. "It's just a look for the customers."

"Your admirers?"

"They are not my admirers. They are serious fans of Swedish metal. It's my job to help them find what they like."

"Grindstone, apparently," he muttered. He did not miss the sudden wary look that passed through Emma's eyes or the contradiction in what she said. His comment seemed innocuous, but Grindstone apparently meant something more to her than a cult favorite she could pitch to metalheads. Another Emma mystery to investigate.

"Headache?"

She nodded. Her gaze was focused on his chest.

"Then we can wait on the massage."

Her head snapped up. "The massage!"

"That was the deal for this favor. An afternoon of exceptional childcare."

"It's not a favor to expose my kid to a near-death experience."

"Don't weasel out of our deal, Emma."

"I'm not weaseling."

"You are. Max is fine. He had fun. Building a sand fort under the lifeguard station is not a near-death experience."

Her arms came away from her midriff. She drew herself up. He guessed she was a towering five-three. "He's my kid, so my rules. No beach. Max is having a time-out because he broke the rules. But he did it because you, you...talked him into it. You don't ever follow the rules, ever, do you?"

He shook his head no. "So, this apparently makes two things that terrify you: the ocean and touching me. Why are you so afraid of touching me, Emma?"

"I'm not afraid of touching you." She poked him in the chest. "I have no interest in touching you. There's a difference."

He took a step back and shifted to the right. "You owe me, Emma. And I know one of your rules. You always pay your debts, don't you? On time and without fuss."

She glared at him.

"It's true, isn't it?" She'd never missed or been late with her rent.

He moved again, angling toward the door. She nodded, turning to follow.

"Okay," he said. "No massage for now." He picked up Annie's invitation from the console by the door and completed his move. Now he was between her and the door. "Instead, come with me to this party."

The alarm in her face would have been comical, but he sensed he had touched a raw nerve. He had to wonder what made her afraid to go to a party with him. In spite of her tough exterior, Emma had some great big fears. Maybe her fears explained the need to encase herself in ink and chrome.

"It's an engagement party for a friend and her man at his mother's house in Redondo Beach," he assured her. "It's a barbecue, not an orgy. There'll be kids there, and a dog. We can bring Max."

He handed her the invitation, and she looked at the thing with all the suspicion in her nature, but there was nothing there except names, a date, and a time, and a reassuringly modest Redondo Beach address.

"This is red-headed Annie from the Center? The one who was here this morning?"

"She brought me the invitation. She's marrying an old classmate of mine from high school."

Emma handed back the paper. "I can't go."

Again, he seemed to have set off Emma's internal alarm, and he didn't know why.

"Fine." It wasn't fine. It was disappointing in some way he couldn't name. The idea of taking her had been the inspiration of the moment, but it represented a shift in the dynamic between them. He had given up his leverage...but he knew how to recover it. "The massage works for me."

Emma's glare was back. "Why even suggest that I go with you? Why not pick the most beautiful woman you know?" She closed the gap between them and poked him in the chest again. "To show Annie that you are indifferent, that you don't give a rap that she's marrying the other guy?"

Josh held perfectly still, caught off guard. How had she figured out that he'd had a thing for Annie James? She'd been more aware than he realized. He didn't love Annie, but she'd been a wake-up call about what he wanted in a relationship someday. Annie was the kind of woman who brought out the best in a man, as she had brought out the best in Sloan.

He shook his head and got back to the point. "You know, the party might be fun, but you're afraid of going for some reason. You're afraid to go out in the world among ordinary people without your hazmat suit."

"Hah!" She glowered. "You don't know any ordinary people."

"Mom?" Max's voice came from the other side of the door. "I finished my time-out."

Emma tensed instantly, caught in the act of having forgotten about Max for five minutes. Josh reached for the door and pulled it open, releasing her.

"Massage it is," he whispered, back in control as she slipped past him.

Chapter Seven

When she had classes at State, Emma drove Max to school. He could get an extra half hour of sleep that way. This Thursday she planned to skip classes and stay home an extra day to work on her unfinished paper, so she had cajoled him into walking the brief mile from their apartment.

He had lagged a few paces behind her most of the way, so they were barely going to make it on time. She knew better than to nag. Ahead she could see the cars lining up for the drop-off lane, and other kids approaching with moms, or in groups on bikes. Most of the kids were skipping or running, full of energy. Max was keeping his distance from her, walking along the inside edge of the sidewalk, dragging a stick he'd picked up along fences and walls, creating different sound effects. He had not asked her a single question.

She concentrated on moving forward, alert for any sign of his mood shifting. Huntington had managed to unsettle them both by breaking their no-beach rule. Emma had twisted and turned through a sleepless night. She'd punched her pillow into different shapes, tried sleeping on both sides and her back, and kicking off her quilt. Nothing worked. Every time her eyes grew heavy and she felt herself drifting off, her busy brain threw up an image of Max plunging into the ocean, black waves closing over him…or Huntington in his black boxers inviting Emma to touch him. She had lain awake in the dark, trying to will away her inconvenient interest in her landlord and her unreasonable fear of the beach.

By daylight, her fear of the ocean always looked particularly unreasonable. The long stretch of beach just blocks away from their apartment was dotted with lifeguard towers and not known for treacherous surf. But reason didn't matter at night. Reason didn't matter when you knew what loss meant. Emma had learned at an early age that her mother was dead. It was a fact. There was a lovely room in her grandparents' house that belonged to her as a child. On her mother's birthday each year in September, Emma and her grandmother would visit the room, and Emma would be allowed to touch her mother's hairbrush, and open her closet, and sit on her bed.

What Emma had not known until her senior year in high school was how her mother died. It was only with the school librarian's help that she found and made a copy of a newspaper article detailing how her mother drowned, trapped in a car she'd taken from her parents and driven wildly along an empty, winding stretch of the coast north of Malibu until the car missed a turn and plunged into the sea. There were times when Emma could not shake the images that came to her of her mother's desperate struggle as cold dark waters closed over her.

The thought of Max entering those waves triggered the same suffocating fear. Emma's brain's images of Huntington in his black boxers were almost comic in contrast.

This morning she had given up on her bed before dawn. She'd showered away the heat and stickiness of her restless night, had a cup of strong coffee, and roused Max early. Her daytime remedy for fear was action. Doing the next thing on her list had a straightforward immediacy that could easily put an end to a fear cycle.

She had intended their walk to be fun, to be a way to clear her head and restore her easy camaraderie with Max, but the plan wasn't working. They had reached the chain link fence that enclosed the schoolyard, and a boy ahead of them at the entrance spotted Max and called out to him.

"Hey, Max. We're going to play soccer. Come on."

Max dropped his stick and broke into a trot, his backpack bouncing with his stride. "'Bye, Mom. Gotta go."

"'Bye, Max. I'll pick you up at the Center."

She resisted the temptation to call him Maxie in front of the other kid, but as the boys turned to enter the yard, the other boy glanced over his shoulder. "Your mom's not a regular mom, is she? She's sort of freak, right?"

"Naw." Max did not look back.

"But she has tattoos and stuff."

Emma held her breath for her son's answer. He said, "Not all the time. Just for work. She works at a record store."

The boys turned and ran into the schoolyard. The teacher on duty waved at Emma, and she waved back then watched Max shed his backpack and dash onto the lawn with the other boys. He was safe, and he didn't think his mother was a freak. She would have to put letting go of her ocean fear on her to-do list…but it wasn't today's task.

* * *

Around eight on Thursday morning, Jack Joyce sent a driver, which pissed Sloan off because Sloan was the kind of guy who did everything for himself. Josh had no problem with it. The driver was competent and efficient, and even Sloan had to admire the way he maneuvered the black SUV through L.A.'s perpetually-on-the-edge-of-gridlock traffic pattern.

An earbud-and-shades-wearing hulk of impressive dimensions met the car and escorted them from the parking lot through the inner courtyard to the Hall of Canyon Men. Entering the old hall, Josh tried to catch Sloan's gaze and failed. Seven months earlier, former headmaster Chambers and his lackey Dunsmore, the school's development director, had tried to secure a three million dollar donation to the school by offering Sloan a place in this hall as one of the honored alumni, whose portraits lined the walls. The old alums were sober uniformed men that, as a student, Josh had never been able to imagine as boys. Sloan had declined and refused to give them a dime.

As they stepped from the heat and glare of the L.A. sun into the cool gloom of the old hall with its oak-paneled walls and high, chapel-like windows, Josh realized that Jack Joyce had a chance to look them over before they could see him. Joyce apparently liked to be first to see anyone coming his way.

Whatever the deal between Sloan and Joyce over the use of the hall, Joyce's people had taken full charge of the space, transforming it into an office area with scattered desks, laptops, a conference table, and a sitting area where Joyce and a black dog held court. The old portraits of Canyon men had been removed or covered over, and in their place was a series of slick, corporate-looking poster boards with album covers, photos of Grindstone, and images from a video game, apparently all explaining the purpose of the benefit concert to potential donors. Josh had time for a quick glance but not the full story. His main impression was of the irreverent pictures of the band that transformed the room from a dull shrine to duty and sacrifice into an altar to rebelliousness and excess.

Josh pushed his shades up on top of his head. His eyes still had to adjust, but he could see Joyce was no longer the skinny, glasses-wearing nerd other guys had picked on or ignored in high school. Except for the deep red hair, which he wore long to his collar, there was something military about him in the set of his shoulders, the chiseled angle of the jaw, the economy of words and motion. And in the tattoos—real ones, Josh suspected, acquired in places remote from the tattoo parlors of Venice Beach.

Joyce sat upright in a deep leather armchair with an air of intense concentration, like a man straining to hear a muffled conversation. He didn't stand to shake hands or offer water from the table beside him set with a pitcher and glasses. Even the black dog at his side didn't move.

They clearly had not been summoned to shoot the breeze about old times. Joyce waved Josh and Sloan into a pair of straight-backed wooden chairs under the high windows as if they were boys again sitting in rows to hear one of Headmaster Chambers's lofty but phony lectures on morals and manhood, chairs in which Josh hadn't sat since his first year at Canyon. He had been elected as a sophomore to be a caped prefect, one of the six head boys striding freely among his seated classmates.

The ironies piled up. Chambers's portrait was gone from its place over the door, and the class of 2005's least likely candidates for a place in the Hall of Canyon Men now sat on the room's hard chairs.

Sloan started the conversation. "You wanted to see us, Joyce?"

"I don't go by that name anymore."

If the guy were normal, he would have told them what name he *did* go by. Or Josh would have asked. As it was, Jack-the-mercenary-formerly-known-as-Joyce did not clue them in. Instead, he turned to Sloan.

"What's happening to Chambers?"

"The board is investigating him."

"Looking at the money?"

"Every penny."

Jack Whatever-he-went-by nodded.

"You still want the place shut down?" Sloan asked.

"Not if Chambers is going to pay for everything he's done. Did you tell Huntington about the concert?"

"You have to give the board something concrete on Chambers first, before the concert can move forward. That was the deal."

Trust Sloan to demand such a follow-through, even with Chambers already ousted and facing a board investigation and possibly criminal charges. Of course, Josh suspected that the man had supporters among the alumni and parents who would protest any tarnishing of their hero's reputation.

"I don't do public appearances. That's where Huntington comes in." Joyce didn't exactly turn his head. His gaze merely shifted to Josh. "You knew I burned the Canyon sign down, but you didn't turn me in to Chambers."

Josh shrugged. "No sense in bringing Chambers's wrath down on you when Annie James came forward to save Sloan's ass."

"Have you told the board what you know about Chambers?" Joyce asked.

"What do you think I know?"

"Who he slept with, how often, and where. His private building projects. What he did with our grades. Why he fired that college counselor. For starters."

Josh nodded, intrigued. For Jack Whoever-he-was-now, that four-sentence outburst came from an interesting starting point. Josh would not have guessed this guy knew what sex was in high school, or cared who was having it with whom. Joyce had been some sort of math whiz who doubled up in every subject, a science genius who also excelled in English and history classes. His Spanish and Latin teachers loved him. He seemed to remember everything a teacher ever said.

However, Joyce's father was a big Hollywood producer and his red-haired mother had been an actress cast as the seductive other woman in iconic seventies films before she disappeared from the screen into her marriage. His parents had hosted one party at their house for the class of '05 in the summer before their junior year. It had done nothing for their son's popularity with his peers, but it had created a buzz about Jack's mother. Apparently she'd mingled with her guests at the poolside in a bikini that changed their collective concept of "mom" forever. For the rest of their high school years, almost anyone could get an angry, impotent rise out of Joyce by singing the Fountains of Wayne song "Stacy's Mom" that had come out that summer.

Josh had missed most of the excitement, having spent the evening in one of the guest suites with an adventurous caterer's assistant named Tina.

He looked at Joyce directly. "Sloan has much of that stuff covered. As for Chambers's sex partners...they might not want their relations with him to be known."

The man in front of Josh retreated to some inaccessible inner space.

After a momentary awkward pause, Sloan spoke. "You want what we want, Jack. We won't let Chambers off the hook, and you can help us bring him down. Are you okay with that?"

There was the slightest nod of agreement. "Is Huntington willing to help with the concert? There are security requirements if so."

"You should ask him," Sloan said. "He's got experience and knowledge of the school, and I think he can get the permits you need. He made a conquest of Barbara in the city parks and rec department."

"Is that right, Huntington?" Joyce asked.

Josh shrugged.

The conversation turned suddenly to details about the timing of the upcoming Grindstone concert, the numbers expected, and Josh's role in organizing everything for the recent gala. The conversation was slow, and Josh had plenty of time to study the poster board story on the walls. The concert began to make sense.

Finally, Sloan signaled Josh that it was time to leave. Josh wouldn't have known, as their host didn't stand, just lifted his intent gaze to watch them do so. He rested one hand on his dog's black nape, and spoke just as they were at the door.

"I go by Ryker now."

Josh and Sloan followed the hulking security guard back into the courtyard. There Josh turned to Sloan and said, "You're going to explain this meeting to me, right? Did Ryker just hire me?"

"He did. I'll get you a contract."

"What if I don't want to work for him?"

Sloan looked solemn. "Look. I don't want the guy to burn the school down."

Josh nodded. Sloan had a point. The little actually said by Ryker had revealed that he too wanted Chambers to pay for his past misdeeds, and neither of them knew just how far Ryker would go. Neither Sloan nor Josh wanted the school to suffer for what the old guy had done in the past.

They crossed the familiar courtyard at the base of the sloping lawn. Josh glanced around at boys in Canyon khakis lounging on the grass and working on their perpetual tans, a group playing Wiffle ball, and the crowd streaming toward the cafeteria. Discarded backpacks lay in drifts at the base of several palm trees. He didn't see either of the two boys who had helped them uncover Chambers's wrongdoings, the two friends Ulysses Aristides and Tyler Dalton. In the past six months that pair's unlikely friendship and Annie James's love had changed Sloan's mind about Canyon and made him one of the school's biggest supporters.

"What do you think happened to him?" he muttered, thinking of Joyce, now Ryker.

"Besides war and imprisonment?"

Josh thought a moment. "The tattoos?"

"They disguise prison markings."

Josh nodded. Whatever the soldiers in the Hall of Canyon Men had suffered on foreign battlefields in the wars of the 20th century, none of those uniformed veterans bore any outward signs of the effects of war. Ryker did.

He said, "I'm betting that dog is a service dog."

Sloan was quick to say, "The guy's not blind, though."

No. Ryker's gaze had followed every shift of the conversation. "Not blind, but he has to concentrate super hard and he didn't stand up."

"A balance problem?" Sloan guessed.

"Could be. Ryker seemed to process the conversation slowly." They passed in reverse through the main reception area to the front parking lot and walked toward the waiting SUV. As they did Josh said, "So, what's the real deal with the concert? I mean Ryker's deal with it?"

"I don't know. I had to agree that he could use Canyon as the venue in order to get him to sell the bond. Maybe the request was a bit odd, but I needed him to sell, and I figured we could make it work somehow. And we will."

"You had to make it okay with the board, too."

Sloan shrugged. "They're okay with it. What's weird is, when I asked Ryker to speak about Chambers to the board, he closed up. That guy has to let go of some anger, whatever it is he's mad about."

Josh couldn't help asking, "You do see the irony here, don't you? You're one to talk about letting go of anger."

Sloan gave him a rare grin. "I am learning—and I've got help. Ryker is alone and locked up tighter than a bank vault."

"So, why sponsor the Grindstone reunion? Joyce doesn't seem the old school Swedish death metal type."

"You've heard of them?"

Josh nodded.

Sloan shrugged. "You noticed the concert is also to launch a video game? Apparently the game features a Grindstone track that no one's ever heard. Joyce—er, *Ryker*'s involved on the production side, and all the money goes to some brain injury support group for veterans."

Josh shook his head. "That guy does not strike me as the philanthropic type."

Sloan laughed, and they dropped the topic.

Getting into the SUV and setting off, the conversation lagged. Sloan checked his email, and Josh had plenty to think about. He remembered how Chambers had humiliated Sloan all those years ago when he was young and powerless, but now he had to wonder what the man had done to Ryker.

There was an awkward moment when the driver pulled up at Josh's place. Sloan cleared his throat and said, "Annie told me you might need a job after this Ryker thing. If you want to come back to Canyon, I can arrange it."

The last thing Josh was going to admit to Sloan, now that their positions were reversed, was the state of his bank account.

"No thanks," he said. "I'm good for now."

* * *

When Emma returned from taking Max to school, she found a sticky note pressed to her door.

Car wash.

Her landlord had obviously switched tactics. She didn't think for a minute that he was giving up the massage. He had just picked an item off her list of favors that he knew she had promised to do.

Snatching the thing off the door, she smacked it back up on the wall inside her front door. The main thing was to stay on track, focus and finish. Huntington had gone off in a black SUV, and she could finish her paper in his absence.

She pushed onward for several hours until the paper felt done, or as done as she could make it. She stored the document on a thumb drive to take to campus, where she could do the required electronic submission from one of the computers in the main library. She had until the end of the week to turn it in; she just needed a morning or an afternoon off from the store to get out to campus. Someday she'd earn enough to budget for Internet access, but she wasn't there yet.

Emma unplugged the little drive from her laptop and held it in her palm. It fit there. It was crazy to think that the device contained the very last work that she needed to graduate from college. She'd come a long way from where she'd begun, as a pregnant unwed teenage runaway. If her story sounded like a made-for-TV drama, it wasn't. She had simply refused to be helpless, had chosen her path and kept moving down it one baby step at a time, just as her friend Maria liked to say. Emma had wanted to keep her baby and own her life. That meant she had had to grow up and not take any more money from her grandparents.

A few more steps in her plan remained, including meeting her father, but she'd done it! Emma wanted to do a little dance and tell someone, but that would have to wait. She and Max would celebrate on their own for now.

She stuck the thumb drive into a pocket of her book bag and took a minute to stretch and flex her shoulders. When she got up out of her chair, her landlord's sticky note stared her in the face, a reminder that she owed him a favor. Huntington was no part of her plan, but he was a debt to pay—and Emma paid her debts.

She went to collect Max. By dinnertime, she and her landlord would be square in the favor count.

Life was good on Planet Ordinary.

* * *

There was no sign of his tenant when Josh returned. The note he'd left on her door was gone, so she had received his message.

Setting up his laptop where he could watch the stairs for his tenant's return, he stopped himself from thinking too much about a certain genre of Internet video featuring cars, sprays of water, and lots of slick wet female flesh. He wanted to check up on Jack Joyce, now Jack Ryker, and so he'd open his computer and do just that.

Most of what he found came from government agencies investigating abuses by private security companies. Josh had traveled the world with little thought that he needed protection, but protection was apparently big business provided by private armies with multi-million-dollar contracts and hardened soldiers. Possibly the most infamous of these private security companies operating around the globe was Blackwater—they had a new name, actually, Academi—but they were not the only player in the game.

Every outfit seemed to have a niche: guarding Afghan governors, guarding oil company installations, guarding the UN. Some offered training. Others required prior military service in elite groups like the Special Forces or even the French Foreign Legion. Josh couldn't connect Ryker directly with any of them until he found a picture of the International Defence Exhibition and Conference, IDEX, in Abu Dhabi in 2011. There, surrounded by military hardware, standing between an African general in fatigues and a stocky Eastern European president in a business suit, was Jack Ryker. Producing video games struck Josh as a much healthier lifestyle.

He took a break for a quick check of his email. It showed an Evite to the Glen reunion with a breezy note from Mackenzie Burke about seeing him there, and a more formal message from his mother's assistant reminding him of his mother's deadline—and offering him the first of his opportunities to earn a month of his trust. There was also an email from his father's executive assistant.

He returned to the one from his mother's assistant. To earn his first check, he could take out a philanthropic former deb named Bethany Elaine Douglass, whose charity provided prom dresses for poor girls. Attachments included the dress code for the black-tie event, a brief bio of Bethany, and a picture. His mother's assistant also indicated that she would need a routing number for his bank account.

Josh went back to digging into Jack Ryker's past.

Chapter Eight

When Emma and Max returned home, her landlord sat with his computer open at the table in his dining area. It was more effort than she'd seen him make in days.

He waved. Max saw him and waved back with happy enthusiasm.

Car wash his note read. *You owe me,* was the subtext.

She let Max into their unit and got him a snack of apple slices and peanut butter. While he ate and talked about his day, she stared down at the two cars in the driveway. The contrast between them, her squashed, faded, mustard-colored wreck that she didn't even own, and his gleaming green, super-charged machine made for off-road adventures, said everything about why she and her landlord should not mix. He might visit Planet Ordinary once in awhile, but he didn't live there. More to the point, he didn't *want* to live there.

For the moment he seemed to have backed off on his insistence on a massage, which was good. Even thinking about that had unsettled her and interfered with her sleep…which made no sense. She *couldn't* be attracted to Huntington. She couldn't afford to be. He came from the life she'd abandoned when she chose to keep Max, and he clearly had ties to the world she'd left behind. Of course, she should not owe him a massage after he broke her rules and took Max to the beach. There was no way she was going to explain the beach thing to him. That was private and personal. He already thought she was some kind of nutcase.

Emma did owe him a carwash, however. She had offered it, and it was best to get that over and done with. She left Max to finish his snack, crossed the entry, and knocked on her landlord's door.

He answered, dressed for once, in khakis and a jade-colored Hawaiian shirt with black pineapples. His sockless feet wore elegant loafers. Emma wore jeans and a gray workout T-shirt from a defunct gym franchise.

"You got my message."

He had Grindstone playing, and she momentarily forgot why she'd knocked. Then she held out her hand. "Got a key? I'll get started."

He didn't move, just looked at her jeans and T-shirt. "No work today?"

"Tomorrow. Your key?"

He still didn't move. The music's aggressive rhythm and dense power chords filled the entry, but she heard the door to her unit open behind her and turned to see Max looking at them.

"Hey, Max," Huntington said, which was all the invitation her son needed. He came forward to exchange some kind of handshake. "What's up?"

"At school today, we built a tower out of cups. Our group made the highest one."

Huntington nodded.

Max's glance shifted between Emma and their landlord. "What are you doing? Is Mom going to give you a massage?"

"She's going to wash my car. Inside and out. Basic car wash stuff."

"Oh." Max's eyes got big. "Can I help?"

"If it's okay with your mom."

"Is it okay, Mom?" Max bounced a little on his toes.

Emma nodded, but it was annoying how easily a little attention from her shameless manipulator of a landlord restored Max's mood. "Go put on some trunks and flip-flops."

She turned back to Huntington, who held out his car key.

"This is all wrong, you know. You make my kid think I'm some kind of servant. You make him like you. You teach him your secret Canyon handshake."

She knew as soon as she said it that she'd made a mistake. He hadn't connected her with Canyon before because she'd never given him a reason to do so. Now she'd been careless, and his sharp blue gaze reminded her that there was nothing slow about Huntington's brain.

"My secret Canyon handshake? What do *you* know about Canyon?"

Emma shrugged. "No magic powers of deduction here. You went to some reunion thing, didn't you? It's a guys school. The handshake is a guy thing, right? By the way, in case you hadn't noticed, the music's really LOUD."

His glance shifted, and she turned for the stairs. When she reached the driveway, Max was standing with the hose in his hand. She told him to wait but gave him Huntington's key to try while she wrestled the old-fashioned garage door open.

Inside was like a sports outlet; the garage was filled with Huntington's toys, his skis, snowboard, surfboards, wetsuits, and fins, golf clubs, tennis rackets, and camping gear. Plus there was a baby grand piano of all things, an oversized sofa, deck furniture, and dozens of mover's boxes stacked to the ceiling. Only one corner was reserved for practical items that real people needed in their lives—like brooms and buckets and her box of car tools.

Emma gathered some car-washing rags and gear and wheeled her canister vacuum out to the base of the stairs. Max was busy clicking the Range Rover's doors open and shut and making the hazard lights flash.

"Look how cool this is, Mom."

She smiled grimly. Her car might have a distinguished Italian heritage, but she always carried a box of fuses to fix the irregularly functioning electric system. She tried not to have car envy where Huntington was concerned, but it was a very cool car.

"Have you got all the doors open?"

Max clicked again and grinned at her.

She reached out her hand for the key and tucked it in her pocket. "Great. Let's go to work. First we're going to clean the inside."

Emma opened the driver's side door and slid into the seat. Luxurious, soft, almond-colored leather cupped her body. There was still a slight hint of new-car smell, but mostly the car smelled like Josh Huntington—a warm lazy male smell like tanning lotion or sun on skin. It made her want to close her eyes and sink into the upholstery.

She scrambled out and marched back to the open garage, where she searched her own things for a shoebox that she handed to Max. He would be in no danger of a mind melt from the car's interior scent, so she told him to find all the loose things in the car and put them into it.

Max climbed up into the cab. "It's like an airplane, Mom."

"Sort of." She felt her jaw tighten. "Just find everything, okay? So I can vacuum." That Josh Huntington could impress her kid with his rich boy toys made her slightly crazy. He could carelessly undo her efforts to teach Max that what she gave him—a mother's love—mattered more than...*things*.

She hooked up an orange extension cord and positioned the vacuum cleaner. Out of the corner of her eye she could see Max on the floor of the passenger side reaching under the seat. She heard things hitting the inside of the shoebox.

"How's it coming, Max?"

"I found six things so far. I'm going to do the back seat now."

The box went onto the center console, and Max climbed between the front seats into the back, disappearing momentarily. She heard more things land inside it. Then her son's head popped up in the back window.

She opened the door. He held the box close to his chest. "I found fifteen things. Look!"

She did look. She couldn't help it. Among other things, she saw three pairs of dark glasses, each of which exceeded her food budget for several months, a tube of sunscreen, and a sand-crusted yellow disc of Dr. Zog's sexwax. An empty Vanilla Bean blended-drink cup stuck up from one end of the box next to a disposable pink pedicure flip-flop from a nail salon. In the middle of the box were two strings of LifeStyles condoms in their red and blue wrappers, a one hundred dollar bill, and some kind of remote. Her landlord's car was guilty of oversharing.

She took Max by the elbow to help him jump down from the car. He was looking at the items in the box as if they were treasures.

"Josh is a lot like you, Mom."

Emma almost choked. "What makes you say that?"

Max picked up items from the box. "He likes coffee. He pays for things with cash, like you do. He uses sun lotion like you want me to, and"—Max pulled out one of the strings of condoms—"he keeps bandages in his car."

Her outrage died. Bless her son.

She heard Huntington laugh behind her and spun, looking into the late afternoon sun so that all she could see of his face was the light on his golden hair. She wanted to tell him everything that was wrong with his careless, privileged, useless lifestyle, but he was taking the box from Max and thanking him for his help.

He was a polite worthless person, she had to admit that. She flicked the switch on the vacuum and let the angry whine of the machine express her feelings. She wanted to hold on to her anger, but she had to admit that Huntington was neat, too. Other than some sand on the floor mats, there was little to vacuum. At least he respected his car.

When she finished the vacuuming, she found Max and Huntington, barefooted, leaning back against the stairs, arms crossed over their chests in identical poses, watching her through matching pairs of dark glasses. Her fair-haired son looked like a mini-Huntington.

Max burst out laughing, but Emma went still. How effortlessly Huntington's charm seduced her son—but Huntington knew nothing about what it really was to care for a child, to be there with the constancy required. To him Max was a fun temporary companion. To her, Max was the person she would die for.

Max offered her the third pair of dark glasses, but she declined. She took a calming breath. Her paper was written. Her time at Daddy Rock would end soon. She and Max would leave the beach, and *they* would be the ones to walk away. She would remind Max tonight that they were going have a house and dog. That was the promise.

Carefully she put away the vacuum and turned to get her window-cleaning gear. Closing herself in the car, she removed any hint of Josh Huntington's presence with a long wet squirt of sharp, nose-tickling window cleaner.

* * *

Josh watched Emma turn away from the offer to play, unwilling join the light moment he'd shared with Max. If anything, he would guess that he'd offended her somehow. She was bent on being in control, spraying and scrubbing the insides of his car windows with savage efficiency.

He suspected that work was Emma's way of blocking out unwelcome thoughts and circumstances. She'd be finished in minutes while, irrationally, he wanted her to linger and move with slower strokes.

He could see her determined face through the glass. Not going to happen.

Yet.

He turned to Max and pointed out how fast Emma was working and suggested a race to see if the boy could put away the things in the shoebox before she finished. The kid's eyes lit up at the challenge, and Josh held up the empty coffee container and the pink flip-flop.

"Recycle bin and trash."

Max dashed off with the items.

The next thing that caught his attention was the remote. Josh had left it on the seat after his visit home, and he explained to the boy that it opened the gate to his parents' house. The question he got was not the one he expected.

"You have parents?" Max pressed the remote button.

"A mom and a dad. I have a sister, too."

"My mom has no parents," Max replied, not taking him up on the topic as he hoped.

Josh glanced at her. No parents? Another Emma mystery. "Does that make her sad?"

Max shook his head. "Mom says it's a fact."

A fact. Josh couldn't help but feel bad for her. Realist Emma apparently had some hard facts to deal with. He took the remote from the boy, handed over the surfboard wax and showed him where to stow it, keeping an eye on Emma the whole time. She had moved to the back seat.

"Your mom's almost done," he said. "Most of these things go back in the car. I'll take care of the rest." He put the shoebox on the foot of the stairs. Emma was finishing the last side window when he used his spare key to make it descend and asked through the opening, "Are you hiding in there?"

"Not at all. I'm done now." Her cheeks were flushed, and strands of her fine brown hair were coming loose from her ponytail.

He opened the door and she climbed out. He flicked the window closed and signaled Max to grab the hose.

"Okay, wait," Emma ordered. "I'm in charge of this car wash, and I say how we proceed."

Josh gave her a mock salute. Max, glancing at him, offered one, too.

"Do you want your car washed or not?" she snapped.

"Hey, just waiting for your orders."

"Fine, I'll ask you"—she pointed at Josh—"to turn on the water in a minute." She turned to Max. "First we do an overall rinse. Then we wash the roof, rear, hood, and sides. We use lots of suds to float the dirt away."

She positioned Max on the driver's side of the car, facing toward the rear, and guided his hose hand before nodding at Huntington to turn on the water. She let Max do one side mostly by himself. Then she took the hose and, moving around the vehicle, finished the work.

When she had the car rinsed off, Emma gave Max a soapy sponge and told him he could work wherever he wanted. She positioned a footstool on the passenger side and climbed up to begin work on the roof, leaning against the car to extend her reach. Josh felt a jolt to his system the first time she straightened up, her T-shirt dark and clinging to her ribs from contact with the wet car. She concentrated on moving her sponge in long sweeps over the car's wet roof.

Getting the view of Emma that he'd wished for earlier did nothing for Josh's state of mind. He bent down to Max, who was pushing his sponge into the chrome vent flutes on the driver's side.

"Are these gills? Like fish have?" the boy asked.

"Sort of. They let the engine breathe when it gets hot. Do you want to help your mom with the roof?"

Max nodded, and Josh hoisted the boy up onto his shoulders.

"Hey, Mom, look at me," Max called. "I'm helping."

Emma glared at Josh. Unfortunately his sunglasses offered little concealment, and he was sure that his roving gaze made her conscious of her wet T-shirt. So he swallowed and said, "You'll get done twice as fast with our help. I might have to go out."

"Fine."

He hoped she would not need adult orthodontia from clenching her teeth so tight.

There was no slowing her down. In a few minutes she motioned them away and took over the hose to rinse the roof. She started to work on the rear of the car, inviting Max to join her.

The boy with a sponge in his hand had questions. He asked Josh about the lights, the license plate letter sequence, the number of license plates in the state of California, and how fast the car could go, how far he had gone in it, what Idaho was, why he'd gone there, whether the car ever broke down and if Josh could fix it himself and why not. They had come to the question of why Josh had three pairs of dark glasses in his car when his mother interrupted to give him the hose then stepped aside to scrape her escaping hair back into its ponytail. Josh thought about that hair. At first it had seemed to him the color of wet sand or indistinguishable little birds, but now it made him think of the dark flavors and colors of Mina Street in Oaxaca where they ground up cocoa beans. He'd ended up there once on his way to the famous surf spot at Puerto Escondido on Mexico's west coast.

Max happily sprayed the rear of the car. The flow of questions had stopped while Josh watched Emma fix her hair. She had her hands behind her head, looping the ponytail holder in place. He tried to pull his glance away, remembering that he hadn't answered Max's question about his pairs of dark glasses, and started to answer.

At his first words, Max swung around with the hose in hand and caught Emma in the chest with a full blast of water. She sputtered and shook and pulled her sopping gray T-shirt away from her body. Bright beads of water ran down her neck and arms. Her look blamed Josh.

He couldn't help himself. He knew he was looking at her as if she were some wet T-shirt fantasy, not his prickly, no-nonsense, plain-brown-wrapper tenant. Something was seriously wrong with his hormones.

"Don't be mad, Mom," Max pleaded.

She turned. "Right. Not mad at you, Maxie. Just let me take the hose."

Max handed it over, and Emma banished both him and Josh to the stairs with a wave of her hand. Josh didn't want to desert the boy, but he didn't want Emma angry with the kid for his misstep, either, and he figured his absence would help.

"Hang in there, Max," he told the boy. "It's me she's mad at."

He took himself off up the stairs. She didn't seem to notice. Emma just turned off the water, twisted her T-shirt semi-dry, and went back to work as if he didn't exist. So Josh went back to his computer and Jack Ryker, weapons consultant to third-world warlords.

In surprisingly little time she knocked on his door. Max was nowhere in sight when Josh opened up. Her clothes were still damp and clingy. She fished his key out of her jeans pocket.

"We are even. We are fair and square. Done."

"We are not even. You owe me a massage."

He extended his hand for the key, and she slapped it into his open palm. "When I think of the things I want to do to you, massage does not come to mind. I have not ripped you to shreds with my mother fangs only because when my six-year-old pulled two strings of condoms out of your car, he thought they were bandages. And what are you doing with a hundred dollar bill on the floor? On the floor! It's not loose change for heaven's sake.

"And as for your sneaky trick of getting Max to blast me with the hose, what were you thinking? I'm no Victoria's Secret catalogue model. You hose me down and all you get is a blip on the electricity bill when I dry my jeans."

"Are you done yet?"

"No." She took a shuddering breath. Her expression turned grave, and he went a little cold waiting for her to speak. "I want you to stay away from Max from now on. I will make other arrangements so that we won't trouble you, but I do not want him around you."

"Why?" Josh asked.

"Why?" Her body shook a little. "Because you're irresponsible, idle, self-serving, manipulative. You don't *do* anything; you just look good and have stuff. That's not life. You're supposed to be a grown-up."

Josh stepped forward and shook his head. "I don't think that's it at all. I think you want to avoid me because you like me."

She looked seriously steamed. "Your ego is more supercharged than your car. I'm a mom. Max is what matters to me. I can't… I don't want…what you want."

She smelled like wet laundry, and he felt his usual inexplicable attraction to her.

"What do you think I want?" He wanted her to say it.

Whatever her anger might have betrayed her into saying, she gathered herself to make a measured reply. "Nothing. I'm sure you don't really want anything from me or my kid except our rent on time, which we will manage. I am sorry I've imposed on you in these last couple of days. It's best if we keep out of each other's way."

"Is that best for Max?" Josh asked. "Whatever you think I am, I know how to be a friend."

"You don't need a six-year-old friend. You have your…limo friends and women. Like that woman Annie."

Josh felt his jaw tighten. She'd summed up his character again based on the contents of his car. Well, she could use a bit of her own medicine. "But Max doesn't have a lot of friends, does he? Why is that, Emma?"

"That's low. I won't let you take Max up like some kind of toy and then drop him when you go back to your real life. I won't let that be his experience."

"My *real* life?"

He watched her make a quick mental recalibration. She'd apparently said more than she meant to say.

"Your un-boring life, when you do things and go places. When you again live someplace with room for your oversized chair, your toys, and your grand piano."

"You think I pay attention to Max because I'm bored?" Josh said, genuinely puzzled that she couldn't see his fondness for the boy. "I like Max. I won't let Max think I don't."

Emma was looking at her feet again. Josh resisted the impulse to reach out and make her look at him.

"What?"

"Don't be nice. You are not nice."

She didn't meet his eye as she spoke, and he gave up on being Mr. Nice Guy. "Fine. Believe the worst of me if it helps you keep your distance, if you're too afraid to face what you really think. Believe I'm 'not nice, not decent, not up to your friend standard.'" He leaned forward, getting past the smells of wet clothes and cleaning agents to find the disturbingly natural scent of her, which only made him madder. "So, here's the deal. I'll leave Max alone the day after you give me that massage."

Her stubborn chin came straight up, and her eyes flashed. "That's despicable."

"You want me to leave your kid alone? That's my offer. Go get dry, Emma, your not-a-Victoria's-Secret-model shape is showing."

* * *

He'd shut the door in her face, and Emma stood at the top of the stairs looking down at the driveway. The cement was drying fast, and her wet clothes were heavy and cold against her skin. A slant of late-afternoon sunlight caught the front window of Huntington's car and lit it up with a glow while her own car sat squashed and primer-mottled like a toad in the Rover's shadow.

Josh Huntington was the kind of low, sneaky scum that offered impossible choices. She was right to separate Max from him.

So why did she feel so mean?

Chapter Nine

He'd made a classic exit. He'd zinged her and shut the door—and abruptly his apartment felt as narrow as a prison cell.

He'd spent the night in one once in San Diego. He had been crashing with Nate Fletcher in Ocean Beach and there was this blonde female professor full of passion at Nate's school. They'd followed her to a protest where Josh was arrested and spent a night on a metal frame bed in a gray cell courtesy of the city. His father had deducted the time billed to his lawyers from Josh's trust.

Low in the sky, a shaft of sunlight shot in almost horizontally through the front window like some kind of laser beam, lighting up the big leather armchair and ottoman that took up most of his living room. The leather was a rich dark caramel color. Originally he'd picked the chair to go with some Navaho rugs he'd inherited from his grandmother, a great collector of Native American art. There was no room to hang the rugs on the walls of the duplex, however. The chair looked oversized and trapped.

Josh felt trapped. He couldn't spend the evening sitting in his box of an apartment thinking about a massage that was unlikely to happen. He definitely had to get back to his real life. The Rover key was in his hand, and the c-note Emma had retrieved from his car was in his pocket. That wasn't much, but he could get in the door somewhere: a club in Santa Monica, a restaurant in Korea Town. And wherever he went, he was sure to find someone he recognized, someone who knew who he was and why he mattered on the planet.

He changed for clubbing and was down the stairs in minutes. Next to Emma's squashed bug of a car, his Rover gleamed in the driveway. He pressed his key and popped the door locks, but when he slid into the driver's seat he was annoyed to find the interior smelled of window cleaner. He opened all the windows and the sunroof and started the engine.

His usual route took him inland behind the first hump of house-covered dunes along the old rail line, now park land, to the end of the beach towns and the wide-open stretch under the LAX runway, nothing between the road and the sea except a wide beach. The setting sun turned a few long furrows of cloud bright gold, and the wind ruffled his loose shirt against his chest and blew away the last of the cleanser smells. Planes taking off overhead drowned out

Green Day's "Boulevard of Broken Dreams" from his car's sound system…and the thoughts in his head.

On the 405 Freeway, the slightly elevated height of the driver's seat and the maneuverability of the Rover made shifting from lane to lane wherever he spotted a gap in traffic easy, like a slalom run. The Rover handled the seams and cracks and rough patches of the bleached asphalt surface as if it were all glassy smooth. He felt his mind clear. He needed to forget about his tenant and think strategically about his mother's proposition.

His mother. She had the idea that she could hand her wayward son over to some Trustafarian princess who would manage him with hot sex and a packed social calendar, keeping him from embarrassing the family. There had to be a way around that list, other than taking a long term job he didn't want from a friend of his father's. Neither plan put him in charge of his own life, and he definitely wanted to be in charge, not taking orders from anyone, least of all from his demanding tenant.

The traffic ahead of him slowed abruptly, closing in on one another like people fleeing a fire but forced to use one exit, brake lights flashing, a ripple of red. On his right a double-trailer rig braked with a squeal and a sway of its bouncing second trailer, and for no good reason Josh pictured the rooftop of Emma's car not quite level with the upper rim of the semi's wheels. It occurred to him that Emma took the 405 headed south for school three mornings a week, and her rent-a-wreck would jolt over the rough parts. She would be hemmed in by huge trucks and endure long slow stretches of the commuter crawl. He didn't know whether her car even had a radio, and he hadn't looked at her tires, but he could imagine the worn tread on them.

It would be an act of kindness to let the air out of those tires. Then she'd have to depend on him to drive her to school.

The idea was pathetic. He was pathetic, and he'd never been pathetic, but he was in no state to go clubbing and he had no patience for another minute on the stalled freeway. Malibu was out of the question. At the first forward lurch of the mass of cars, he saw a jagged path of spaces open up and swung the Rover into first and then the next. An off-ramp dumped him on Sawtelle, and he headed south.

He broke the hundred at the bar in the Power Plant microbrewery and walked over to the corner reserved for Canyon men, drink in hand. His three oldest friends were always here, guys he'd known from grammar school, and they'd be the least likely to care about his lack of funds.

"It's the 'loser,'" Trevor Lynch greeted him. He and Greg Shields were partners in the microbrewery enterprise, having finally learned some chemistry after college in the service of brewing a great IPA. Lynch's traffic-cone orange hair had not dimmed one watt since high school. "Did you get your trust back yet, buddy?"

Nate Fletcher, who was perfecting his tan and keeping his watch on the waves as an L.A. County lifeguard until his own trust kicked in, wore one of his usual red-and-white chick-bait T-shirts. "Huntington, you effing cost us a bundle."

Josh slid into their booth. "I told you Sloan would give big. You chose not to believe."

Greg Shields spun his Porsche key on the table. "You tricked us. You conned us into betting against Sloan when you knew he would give anything to be with Annie James."

Josh shrugged. "Did you guys pay up yet?"

They had each agreed to donate a thousand bucks to Canyon if Sloan gave the school a million. In the end, of course, Sloan had gone way beyond the one million mark by buying the bond and saving the place. Getting those donations had all been part of Josh's original plan to meet his father's conditions for keeping his trust. It had almost worked.

The guys started in on him. Josh drank his brew and listened to their abuse. His favorite blonde waitress, Melissa, in her Power Plant uniform of a yellow hardhat, black T-shirt, and cutoff overalls, came over and leaned against Lynch's shoulder instead of against Josh as she once had done.

He waited. His friends would come around. That's what friends did. They might be angry about the bet he'd conned them into, but the money wouldn't matter to them in the end. Soon they'd all be laughing together like old times.

"You know what Sloan wants to do to the school?" Shields asked.

"What?"

"He wants to make it *coed*."

Lynch spoke as if announcing the most egregious violation of anything ever. All three of the men were looking at Josh, who said, "I don't think Sloan, by himself, can make that call. There's a board, you know, and an alumni association."

"But what if it's true? What if the board and all are going along with him because he gave the big bucks?" Lynch persisted.

Josh looked at them, really looked. Did they not do irony, at all? For Sloan, who had hated Canyon, to become its most generous supporter while Canyon's more privileged alumni grudged the school a few thousand bucks struck Josh as irony in all caps.

"Shall I call him?" he asked. Without waiting for a response, he pulled out his phone and punched up Sloan's number. When the guy answered on nearly the first ring, he asked, "Sloan, are you in the middle of a romantic evening with your beloved?"

Even the noise in the Power Plant could not disguise the typical unprintable Sloan reply.

"Apologies for interrupting. Give Annie my love, and answer one question. Are you pressing for a coed Canyon?"

This time, he got a laugh out of Sloan. Then a serious reply.

He clicked off and took another swig of India pale ale as the crew watched him before saying, "Sloan says there's a board member pushing the idea, but he's against it."

"Well, I heard it was a done deal," Lynch said. He was well-connected. His father had been the board of trustees chair when they were in school, one reason he had always preferred to do his partying at someone else's house.

Josh nodded. He imagined there were lots of rumors and resentments circulating about the school now that Headmaster Chambers was gone. The man's mistreatment of scholarship students and misuse of the funds supposed to go to them had been made semi-public by the media, but not everyone could completely dismiss the spotless public persona Chambers had worked so long and hard to perfect. He had made himself synonymous with the Canyon brand of elite preparatory school for young men of character.

"You know something that is true?" Josh said, wanting to move to another topic. "Jack Joyce is back."

"What is he?" Shields asked. "Some kind of professor or something?" He'd always had contempt for brains.

"Actually, he's a mercenary. He's a weapons consultant to small private armies in the Middle East, Africa, and Latin America." Josh chuckled. "If you're looking to buy some serious hardware in Abu Dhabi, Ryker's the guy you want to meet."

The others gaped. He understood their doubt. They only knew Jack Joyce, the short, frail nerd with the usual nerd accessories like glasses and a graphing calculator. They had not yet seen what he'd become.

"He calls himself Jack Ryker now."

"You're lying! That guy was a total weakling in high school." Nate Fletcher had personally stuffed Jack Joyce into various trash receptacles on campus until Dr. Archer intervened.

"Yeah, but remember that party at his house?" Shields spoke up. "Remember his mom? She was hot. Kind of your type, Huntington."

"So what does an arms consultant do in L.A.?" Lynch wanted to know.

Josh shrugged. "Exactly what he wants, I suppose."

Shields pulled out his phone and read a text. "Hey, guys, it's time." He stood, and Nate joined him. "We're outta here. Later, Huntington."

Lynch stayed put. At the table, he twisted his glass in his hands and stared at the foam residue. He said, "They're off to a party, and I've got to get back to work here. Melissa will bring you another on the house if you want it."

"No thanks," Josh said. "I'm good." He recognized a brush-off when he saw one.

Lynch turned back, as if suddenly ambivalent. "Look, man...you're just too tight with Sloan. You're supposed to stick with your friends, not with some *nobody*."

Josh nodded. He would have agreed with that once, but he'd always respected Sloan's toughness, and he knew Sloan better now. Sloan without a giant chip on his shoulder was a stand-up kind of guy. "No worries. I've got plans of my own."

Thinking fast, he sent Sloan a quick text. The guy might be taken by Annie, but his friend and business partner would be dancing the night away in some club and with any luck would pay the freight. *Sloan. Where's your buddy Lassiter tonight?*

When he got the answer, Josh tossed his usual tip on the table and took off.

* * *

At bedtime Emma scooted back against the wall with one of Max's pillows at the base of her spine and their current book on her knees. Max had borrowed it from the Center, where Annie James read aloud in the afternoons. It was the story of an orphan and her friends trapped by a pair of evil schemers in a Cinderella-like existence in the basement of a grand mansion in old San Francisco. Emma worried that the orphan plot would raise old questions.

Max had been quieter than usual for most of the evening, and she realized as she settled next to him that she had not been paying attention, trying to sort out her thoughts about Josh Huntington.

He put his hand on the book before she could begin. "Mom, are you mad at Josh?"

Emma closed the book. She believed in being truthful with her son, but she was careful about which truths he was ready for. She tried to think of what honest thing she could say about her feelings for their landlord. "I'm annoyed with him."

"Because he took me to the beach that time? Other people go to the beach. Some kids I know go every day."

"Because he broke our rules without asking."

"So, if he asked you, you would let him take me to the beach?"

"I would rather take you to the beach myself."

"But you don't go to the beach."

"So, I do other fun things with you." Someday he would be old enough to hear why she didn't like the beach.

"But what if *I* really like the beach? Would you go because *I* like it?"

"Sometimes you are ready to do things before I am ready as your mom to let you do them, like climb a really high tree or swim in the ocean. The beach will always be there, so if you can wait a little longer I will try to be ready for you to go there."

"I can wait till summer."

Emma ruffled his hair. "That would be good. Now, are we ready to read?"

She opened the book, but again Max put his hand on the page. "One more thing, Mom."

"Sure."

"If I wanted Josh to be my dad, could I ask him?"

Her heart jolted painfully. She wanted to protest, *You have a mom who loves you, isn't that enough?* Aloud she said, "It doesn't work that way. We don't get to choose our dads."

"No? How does it work?"

Emma closed the book. She and Max had talked about dads the way some people binge-watched old episodes of their favorite TV shows. The explanation she had most often relied upon came from the stiff cardboard picture books they read when Max was very little. His favorite was *I Am a Bear*, in which a mama bear and her cub fished and played and slept in the woods of summer as the cub grew. Emma had told him that some dads were like the bear dad, one-timers who helped to make a good baby and then left. Max knew that he had the one-time kind of dad.

Emma had loved that story, too, because the mama bear had been enough for the cub. The baby bear never missed the dad he didn't know. But Max was past the bear story now. Emma wished she had a new explanation handy for the hole in their family, but she was going to have to make it up as she went along.

"You must like Josh a lot," she said.

"I do. He's my friend."

She made herself admit that Max could be right, at least partly. "Josh probably likes being your friend. But a dad is different."

Max looked up at the seriousness of her tone.

"Being more than a one-time dad, being an all-the-time dad, is a big job. A person has to decide for himself if he wants that job."

"So, Josh could pick me for his kid?"

Emma felt her eyes sting. Her son's attraction to her landlord was worse than she had imagined. Max was dreaming and wishing for something that would never happen.

She swallowed the lump in her throat and shook her head. "Well, Josh couldn't take you away from me, you know. We have to stick together—and Josh might not pick us both."

Max was silent. He pinched his quilt into folds and made spines of fabric from his knees up to his tummy. Something clearly troubled him about her explanation.

"Do you understand?" she asked.

He nodded, but his fingers kept making folds of cloth. In the face of his silence she tried again.

"Why do you want Josh Huntington for a dad?" She knew that Max would say Josh was fun and had cool things, and she had her arguments ready to counter such dad-selecting criteria. At six Emma would have taken any dad. At seventeen she had been willing to accept Steve Saxon, a man who didn't even know she existed. She did not want her son to make the same mistakes.

"Josh teaches me things. And he answers my questions like you do. And he's not too old to do stuff."

"I like that list, Max," she said, surprised and pleased at her son's good judgment, but no longer sure of her counterargument. "Those are good dad qualities, and I'm glad you told me what you've been thinking. But I would like you to think about it some more and give me a chance to think, too, before you ask anyone to be your dad. Will you promise to wait until we can find the right dad together?"

"You mean, until we have our house and our dog?"

"Yes," she said, taking what he offered. "It would be good to wait until then. Promise?"

"Promise."

Relief made Emma a little giddy. By summer they would be across L.A., far from Josh Huntington.

She opened the book again, and this time Max settled against his pillows to listen. Emma began reading, and at last her son's eyelids drooped and his hand fell open on the quilt. She closed the book and whispered goodnight and let him slide down under the covers.

Emma pushed herself up off the bed and couldn't resist straightening the room a little. Everything was second- or third-hand, a thrift shop buy or a kind donation…but she reminded herself that Max had the most important thing a kid needed: a present parent who loved him. The hard thing was that he was also missing a parent, and no matter how happy the storybook bear mother and her cub were, a human kid needed to make sense of a missing dad over and over again. A missing dad was a broken record. She had a promise from Max, but she did not trust her charming landlord. Without meaning to, without making any deliberate effort, he could easily break a person's heart. She did not want Max to pin his hopes on such a man.

At Daddy Rock, Emma answered almost daily emails from people whose favorite record made a backward skip, endlessly repeating the same 1.8 seconds of sound. She knew from the purists at the record store that what most people called a broken record was really a locked groove. When a record was bumped while playing, the needle could carve a path through the soft vinyl—and for some deep gouges there was no fix. Emma and Max had the same deep gouge.

Of course, Emma had also lost her mother. Her grandparents had tried to pretend that was her only loss, and they'd tried to fill the void with objects and wealth. When Emma was six, her room was a palace of pink frills, her dolls fabulously dressed and given appointments at doll salons to have their hair styled. Emma's grandfather had taken her on all the rides he loved, from his antique cars to theme park extravaganzas and classic carnival rides. But neither of them had ever offered Emma the truth. Her dead mother's room had been a shrine, but questions were not permitted. In particular, queries about her missing father received cold silence and stiff disapproval.

She had tried to do better by Max, and when he was older Emma would tell him the whole story, but for now her job was to love him and keep him from hurt. She bent over to pick up a tiny sharp-edged yellow Lego stuck in the shag carpet.

"Mom...?"

She turned to Max. His eyes were open, but he did not lift his head.

"I think Josh would pick you."

Her sweet son yawned, and his eyes fluttered shut again. Emma straightened and turned off Max's light.

Pick me? Huntington? Not in a million years.

But Max's comment made up her mind.

* * *

Both units were dark except for the entry light when Josh returned from the club, and it along with a streetlamp on the corner lit his way up the stairs.

His footsteps echoed hollowly. The usual din of LA had quieted to a low rumble like an idling engine, and it was impossible not to glance at Emma's unit though he knew she would be fast asleep. It was past three.

Her door ajar made him stop and caused his pulse to kick up. The overhead fixture of their shared entry threw a faint shaft of light across her unit's interior wall, and he listened for any sound of movement from within but all he heard was the crack of a sizable wave breaking a hundred yards away. The open door puzzled him. Emma wasn't careless. She would never leave her door open.

Maybe she'd waited up to apologize. He knew that was unlikely, but the door wasn't visible from the street, so it was equally unlikely that an opportunistic intruder had climbed the stairs of their rundown duplex.

He was the landlord. He should check it out.

He pushed gently, and the door came up against an obstacle. He heard a small exhalation, like a sleeper waking.

"Huntington?"

"Yes."

He heard a rustling of fabric and the door swung further open. Emma stood there in a pair of blue and white plaid PJ bottoms and an oversized white T-shirt. She had a blue flowered quilt around her shoulders, and her eyes looked huge in her pale face.

"I'm ready to give you that massage now."

Just what he wanted, but the words felt like a stinging slap in the face. There was only one reason for her to give in now, after their previous conversation. She wanted to separate Max from him. So Emma Gray apparently had an even lower opinion of him than his mother did.

He tried to shake off his annoyance. The car wash that he'd hoped would build friendlier landlord-tenant relations had ended in Emma's rejecting any relationship with him at all. He'd worked all night to rid himself of the sting of that rejection. In a popular club through an unmarked door where bottle service was a requirement to gain entry, women in shimmering silk tops and skintight jeans had pressed and ground their bodies against his in a friendly way, acknowledging that he was hot. For hours he'd been pretending to forget Emma Gray, mixing in that bouncing, smiling crowd, living in the moment under the influence of a locally famous DJ, while she'd been plotting to separate him from her son.

Under his gaze, Emma squared her shoulders and lifted her chin. "I don't want to think about it anymore."

He leaned against the doorframe. He hadn't had anything to drink except water for two hours, but he felt as reckless as if he'd been throwing back twenty-dollar tequila shots. "Why is that, Emma? This *isn't* because you want to separate me from your son, is it? It's because you secretly want to touch me and anticipation stokes the fire. You're tired of waiting and wanting."

She shook her head, but she pulled the quilt more tightly around her shoulders. "Of course not."

"Liar," he said.

"Listen. You've been the one insisting on a massage. You offered to trade a neck and shoulder massage for your promise to keep away from Max. That's what I want. I want what you said originally. I want you to leave Max alone."

Josh no longer felt any malice. He could see that she was lying, could tell that for some reason she was curious and afraid in equal measure. Part of the puzzle of Emma was how she'd come to be a mom without figuring out her feelings about sex.

He straightened and pushed her door so that it swung fully open. "Here? Now?" He stepped into her living room, shrugged out of his jacket and tossed it over the back of a chair at the table. The room was dark, but not dark enough to make him forget the questionable state of her floor.

"Can you put that quilt down over the carpet?"

He felt the glare she shot him, but he decided it was probably better to have her angry than frightened. She thought she was going to win this round. She thought she could touch him and walk away unmoved herself, her resistance intact. He knew better. He had advanced degrees in the signs of female interest and coaxing women a step or two further than they'd intended to go. Emma didn't have a clue what she was up against, especially because she wouldn't admit to herself that this thing between them wasn't just a one-sided case of irrational attraction.

When she spread her quilt like a picnic blanket, Josh said, "I need something for under my neck. Can you roll up a towel?"

She nodded as he emptied his pockets and put his watch on the table.

"And you might want to put some lotion on your hands."

She disappeared down the short hall to the back of the unit. He saw light spill from the bathroom and heard her open a cupboard. Then she was back, moving with her usual quick energy.

She wanted to get the whole thing over with. *Good luck with that, Emma.*

He took the rolled up towel from her and settled on the floor with it behind his neck, his phone handy.

"Twenty minutes," he said. "I'll start the timer when you begin."

Chapter Ten

Emma knelt at her landlord's head, her fists closed and resting on her thighs. He lay on his back, stretched out long and lean from his golden head to his ankles bare and disappearing into his expensive loafers.

She had seen him in black boxers, so she should not find him sexy now when he wore jeans and a T-shirt. He'd draped a loose jacket over her chair. His white V-neck T-shirt clung to the swells and hollows of his chest and abdomen like a second skin, and he smelled warm and male from exertion. She suspected he'd been to a club somewhere. The inside of his left wrist bore a faint red stamp.

He rested his right hand lightly on his phone, ready to time her efforts if she could bring herself to touch him. His hair fell away from his wide brow. His eyes were closed, his lashes made slivers of shadow on his cheeks. She could look down his straight perfect nose at his closed mouth and dented chin. He did not have to move or speak or even smile to be a temptation, simply lying there open to her touch tempted her, stirred feelings she dimly remembered.

At State she rarely drew even a glance from classmates, though that was mostly because she wanted it that way and because she was older than the usual student and tied to Max's schedule. Her whole sexual experience other than making Max went back to high school. The available boys had been Canyon boys, and her friends Olivia and Megan had led the way to Canyon basketball games and the after-parties. Emma remembered one night ending up in an eternal slow dance, clasped warmly against the chest of a tall, solid boy in a red sweater named Nick whose face she could not now remember. He was older, a junior, and both less awkward and more masculine than the other boys she knew. She had not dared to move in his hold. The hardness of his chest against her cheek and the slight abrading of their bodies made by their shifting feet had been exciting. In the end Nick had kissed her rather passionately, but in a disappointing, unsatisfying way, his face rough against hers.

For a few short weeks Nick had been her boyfriend, though they hardly spoke, and he'd continued to kiss and grasp her in his determined way while Olivia insisted on hearing every disappointing step of the relationship. Nick had wanted her to do things to his person that she had not wanted to do, and something Emma wanted from Nick had not been there. Of course, the memory of this struck her as a random trick of her tired brain that had nothing to do with the real male body in front of her.

Emma tried to think of a safe place to touch Huntington, but no touch seemed safe. That was probably what he wanted her to think: that he was some irresistible sex god. Which he wasn't. She could resist him.

She reminded herself to be Big Nurse and studied her landlord again, looking for a way to begin. The whole massage business would be easier if he were lying on his stomach—and as soon as she had the thought, she realized he had chosen to lie on his back deliberately, counting on her ignorance.

"Turn over," she told him. She might not be a match for Josh Huntington in experience, but she didn't have to give him any extra advantages.

"What?" His eyes opened.

"I want you to lie on your stomach so I can reach your neck and shoulders better."

"Hey, my massage, my rules."

"You don't have a single knotted muscle in your body."

"You have no idea of the tension I'm feeling."

"Turn over."

He rolled lazily to his left, came up on his elbows, grinned at her, and adjusted the towel under him, his face turned to the side. She stared at his back. Better, but not a whole lot better. He had a nice back. His torso tapered from wide shoulders to a narrow waist and hips. Still, she could do this. It would be like washing his car or kneading bread dough, just her hands doing a job. And it was all for Max, who lay sleeping in his bed. This was all for Max, who wanted a dad and was looking in the wrong place. She knew how dangerous it could be to look for a dad in the wrong place.

She came up on her knees, took a deep breath, and pressed the flat surface of her fisted knuckles against the top seam of his T-shirt. At the first contact, her body shuddered all over. The little hairs on her arms stirred. Her skin entered an altered state of hyper-awareness of cool air and soft PJs and warm man, and with a brush of his thumb, he started the timer on his phone and let his hand go slack on the quilt.

"Ten minutes a side," he said.

She knew it was to provoke her.

Emma started pushing her knuckles against the sloping ridge between his neck and shoulders, in an alternating rhythm, not opening her hands. She tried to keep her fists closed, to think of her hands as feet stomping on grapes, or baby elephants trampling on grass. When she reached Huntington's shoulders, she opened her hands and gave a slight squeeze, pressing the heels of her palms against the curved bulge.

He made a noise in his throat, like a stifled groan.

With her hands open, Emma worked her way back toward his head, her thumbs and fingers pressing deep into the long corded muscle. At the place where his neck met his skull, she cradled his head in her hands and pulled straight toward her knees. She rubbed her fingers in circles over the warm places behind his ears. It was then that she noticed his freckles. A light dusting of them ran across the upper edge of his cheekbone.

She swallowed. So, Josh Huntington had freckles. A few freckles could not melt her resistance. She remembered having a conversation with Max about a playmate's freckles. Emma had told him they were sun kisses, but Max objected that kissing was gross, so she had suggested instead that freckles were the sun's cinnamon sprinkles.

Huntington's phone gave a cricket's chirp, and the screen flashed. Abruptly he shifted under her and was once more on his back.

"Part two," he said.

She closed her eyes against the image of him lying on her quilt. When she opened them, he hadn't moved, so she tried to think of what came next. There was no way she was going to touch his chest, as he was clearly inviting her to do.

Emma went up on her knees, leaned forward, and pushed her open palms down his arms. She felt the warm exhale of his breath against her chest, and her breasts fell forward, suspended in the cups of her bra as if they wanted his touch. She drew her hands back along his arms, her knuckles brushing his ribs, and heard his quick intake of breath. His abdomen clenched and relaxed again, and from somewhere deep in her body came an answering clench of muscles she couldn't name, and a hot tide of sensation.

She lifted her hands from his shoulders, breaking the contact, panting a little.

"Don't stop."

Her landlord's voice was a low, husky plea that sent an aching bolt of awareness through her girl parts. She returned her gaze to his face, where two small frown knots puckered his brow directly above his nose. They weren't hot or sexy, just little nubs of puzzlement.

What did he have to be puzzled about?

She pushed them flat then ran her thumbs across his eyebrows and smoothed his forehead with her fingers, which she drew down along the outside of his face along his jaw. The faint friction of his beard against her fingertips sent another wave of sensation through Emma, and she could feel her body warming despite the night air. Her breathing sounded loud in her ears.

Emma stopped, steadying herself, her hands resting on his collarbone. Huntington reached up and grabbed her right wrist, pulling her hand down over his chest. She balled her hand into a fist, resisting, but he pulled harder, tugging her forward, off balance, so that she tumbled across him, her chin colliding with his left hip. He slid his left hand under her and pulled her upright, turning her in his arms so that she lay on top of him; then his arms encircled her waist, pinning her in place.

They were face to face in the dark, breathing unsteadily.

"Just so we're clear. Just so you know what I'm thinking and what I want," he said.

"The deal was a neck-and-shoulder massage," she reminded him. "I did my part. You agreed to keep away from Max."

Huntington nodded, his mouth closed in a grim line. His eyes were a bright glitter in the light from her hallway. "I'll stay away. But you can change your mind any time, Emma. Knock on my door when you figure out what you really want from me."

He rolled them over so that he lay on top of her, a weight different from anything she remembered. He didn't hide how the massage had affected him, how *she* had affected him, and she experienced a brief moment of pleasure that she quickly subdued.

She thought he might kiss her then, but he didn't. He just pushed off of her and stood.

She heard him scrape his things off her table and shut the door quietly as he left. Emma lay on the floor waiting to feel triumphant. She'd done it. She'd won. Max was safe from him. But her heart raced, and her body felt as if it were stretched taut, straining for something out of reach.

It was just adrenaline, she told herself. Once it stopped she would feel great. But the other half of the red-sweatered Nick memory returned, and her plain-speaking friend Olivia advised her, *"If a guy doesn't turn you on, dump him."*

Emma had recognized the truth of it then: Nick did not turn her on. So she had summoned her courage and told him she did not want to see him anymore. Within a week Nick had become Olivia's boyfriend, but Olivia's betrayal was not the point of the memory. The point of the memory was the forgotten lesson of wanting to be turned on, of her body wanting something and being denied.

That elusive craving had been awakened tonight. Emma was turned on; that's what the swollen achy restless feeling was. She was turned on by her landlord, by a careless, idle Canyon boy with a man's body, a garage full of toys, a pricey car, and no purpose. He would make a terrible dad for her kid, and now her quilt smelled like him.

Chapter Eleven

Josh woke tangled in his high thread-count sheets but clear in his head. There was something wrong with his hormonal wiring at the moment, and he needed to get it right. He'd apparently miscalculated in accepting a massage from Emma, thinking that he'd come out satisfied and she'd be the one left wanting. The girl had him going. He was stuck in an old Kinks song. *"You got me so I can't sleep at night."* The ache of his Emma-induced erection was gone, but he needed to put some distance between himself and his tenant.

He left the apartment in record time, grabbing a passable cup of espresso from Java Jack's, but in spite of the caffeine kick his brain had to work hard to keep certain recollections at bay. He knew he'd tempted Emma—and he'd betrayed Max. Whatever Emma thought, Josh didn't want to hurt the kid's feelings by staying away. But she was the mom; she got to decide what was right for her kid.

He liked that protective fierceness in her, so he would keep his promise. The hard part would be staying away from Emma now that he'd made a tiny crack in her armor.

He tried not to over-think the thing, but he was sure Emma had been tempted. She'd begun with closed fists, but her hands had opened around his shoulders and arms. Her purposeful pace had slowed to a more sensuous rubbing of her fingers over his skull, and she'd been into it, and into him, before the thing ended. Which meant he'd been right all along. She was into him.

He squelched his feeling of satisfaction. It was crazy to feel good about a mild seductive triumph over Emma Gray. When he thought about it, really *thought* about it, she was a complete novice and not his type. And she had a kid. She was behaving with good sense to end their trading favors routine, knowing that whatever they found together couldn't last.

He was pretty sure there was no handbook for the kind of landlord-tenant relations they were having, but he wondered if he could evict her.

* * *

Max spotted the jacket on the chair when he put his cereal on the table. Trust Huntington's carelessness to cause trouble. He'd promised to stay away, but his presence lingered.

"Who was here?"

"Josh. He left his jacket."

Max slid into his seat. "Did he come for his massage?"

"He did. Now, eat." Emma put a glass of milk next to her son's bowl. Nothing wrong with his memory.

"Did you touch him?"

"Yes." She held her breath waiting for the next question.

"Can I take him his jacket?"

Her boy was up and out of his chair and at the door before she could think of what to say. She heard Max's knock on their landlord's door, and then Max reported back from the entry, clearly deflated by not seeing his idol.

"He's not home. His car is gone, too."

"Oh well. We'll keep his jacket safe until he gets back." Emma took it from Max and nudged him back to the table.

"Can I keep it in my room?"

"Let's leave it right here, so we don't forget it."

"I won't forget."

"Maxie, concentrate on your breakfast. We leave in five minutes."

"Okay, Mom."

Emma sighed. It was going to be harder than she'd thought to separate her son from her landlord. She had to think of way to tell Max they were going to see less of Josh without making a big deal of the change.

* * *

At Canyon, Josh noticed for the first time the sign on the door that indicated the Hall of Canyon Men was closed to students temporarily. One of Ryker's hulking, bouncer-like security people reinforced the notion with his presence.

While Josh waited to be given an official badge and admitted, he considered Canyon's layout. He had never thought of it before, but the grounds were oddly suited by design to be a rock concert venue. The wide, shallow "V" of the main buildings opened onto a brick-paved courtyard, and the outer wings of the classrooms cupped the sloping hillside, wooded at the top, like a mini-Hollywood Bowl. It was easy to imagine fans crowded in the courtyard in front of a stage while the music blasted up the hill. Of course, there were sound ordinances, and the music could only blast until ten p.m. He'd dealt with the city when he'd planned the gala.

The security man let Josh in. Passing from the sunny courtyard to the dim interior, once again he reflected on the strange workings of fate that brought the three of them—Sloan, Ryker, and himself—back to Canyon. He had no answers at the moment, and the questions faded as he faced his new employer.

The hardest part of the work, he found, was the extraordinary concentration required to listen to Ryker putting together an idea. The lightning-fast mental processes Josh remembered from their high school days had slowed to a painful crawl. He never saw Ryker stand or move, and most of time the guy's hand was on the steady black dog by his side.

Ryker was trying to explain that he wanted the guests to have food, but for security reasons he didn't want any caterers in the school kitchen. The guy was intense about security, so they had already discussed the advantages of the school's gated entry and the disadvantages of its distant perimeter of bushes and chain link fence.

"Food trucks," Josh said as soon as Ryker managed to finish his thought.

In response he got one of Ryker's long, slow stares, and as he waited for his suggestion to register fully, thoughts of Emma invaded his mind. He concentrated instead on brightly colored food trucks, picturing them lined up along the drive from the gate to the main entrance: Korean BBQ, fusion burritos, Brazilian gourmet, vegetarian crepes, and ice cream sandwiches that were architectural masterpieces.

He waited for Ryker to get his point. The part of his brain that wasn't taken up with thoughts of Emma calculated first the take and then the costs of the concert plans. Ryker wanted a couple thousand guests to pay $500 a pop to attend the benefit. A few selected tickets would be pricier still for those who would meet the band afterward. But a few brain-injured veterans would be admitted free, and there would be passes for some old friends of the band. In addition to the gate fee, the organizers planned to auction some famous items of memorabilia collected by Daddy Rock. In all, Ryker expected to raise over a million bucks.

Eventually, Ryker gave a nod. Josh was on the phone half a second later lining up the best gourmet food trucks in L.A.

By late afternoon he'd lined up seven of the area's finest and briefed Ryker's security people on the campus weak spots, especially the long arroyo that separated the east side from the pricey neighborhood that surrounded the school. He was done for the day, but if he was going to keep his promise to Emma he had to go someplace other than home. He texted his mother's executive assistant, Margot Miles. Maybe he could get more information about the other women picked out before he agreed to his mother's vaguely insulting deal. If he could see the whole lineup, maybe one intriguing woman would make it worth his while.

Margot texted him in reply. She would meet with him whenever he chose to send his bank routing number.

It took him less than a second to decide his next move. He texted Sloan's friend Lassiter to see where the evening's action was going to be and got a reply that he was welcome to join in a party up on the Palos Verdes hill. He texted back, I'M IN.

* * *

Emma's ears hurt where the fake piercings pinched. She had worked for hours in the back of the store at her usual task of finding albums for Daddy Rock's online customers, but then Leo summoned her to work the death metal section late in the day.

She was still in the dark about the particulars of the Grindstone concert, which was coming up fast. Working in back, she'd had a chance to eavesdrop whenever Leo took a phone call, but so far she'd heard nothing that gave her a clue to a location. She'd done some research, and the usual venues—Club Nokia, House of Blues, Epic Lounge, and the Viper Room—were booked solid for weeks. That probably meant the concert would happen on some private estate. It would help if she knew anything about the backers of the concert or the cause they planned to support, but without that information, Leo remained her best bet for scoring a pass.

She kept herself busy, trying not to think about Huntington. Whenever thoughts of her landlord did surface, she reminded herself that Max mattered most, that she had given Huntington that massage for Max, that no matter how it had felt to touch Huntington, the main thing was her son. But she felt edgy, stirred up, restless. The turn-on hadn't turned off.

Emma was not dumb. She knew she was attracted to Huntington. Her body's restless discomfort was a big sign. The earrings were just one thing that bothered her. Her whole body felt tight in her skin. Her waist felt warm and damp under her wide leather belt, and her fishnet stockings chafed her thighs. Her fake tattoos itched like drying scabs. And sometimes her body remembered lying pressed to Huntington's long lean warmth, and her stomach took an odd dip as if she'd caught air going over a speed bump.

The attraction was doubly unfortunate, because it was both the wrong time for one and Huntington was the wrong man. She had become a mom before she'd intended, and she wasn't going to rush any other part of her life. She and Max had each other. Being sexy and playful did not give her landlord the right to be part of their little family. Huntington could not walk in on them now just because he knew how to have fun. Maybe Max did need a dad, but Emma and the new dad would pick each other mutually. After all, she was the one who knew what caring for a kid really meant. She was the one who had been there for all the sleep-deprived nights and cramped apartments and second-hand baby gear, all the fevers and spit-up, all the thousand and one judgments a parent needed to make a kid both strong and loving. If Max was going to have an all-the-time dad someday, Emma wanted that dad to be wise and good and strong and funny and…a grownup.

And the sexual attraction she and Huntington felt, it was probably just proximity and lack of other options. She didn't know why he felt it, but she was probably susceptible because she was tired and worried about getting into the Grindstone concert. She wasn't spending enough time with friends. She missed Maria, her friend and sometimes babysitter who would tell her to take one step at a time, to tough it out, to stick to the plan and keep out of Huntington's way as much as possible. But she *had* taken every hard thing one day at a time. The turned-on feeling would fade, and she'd get over her desire for Huntington like getting over a cold.

Emma took a deep centering breath and straightened the records in the Amon Amarth bin. The unmistakable odor of tacos made her look up.

"Hey," Brandon greeted her. He flashed her the sign of the horns.

She nodded.

He leaned toward her left ear, breathed salsa her way, and whispered, "We've got a plan."

"A plan?" She leaned away from the taco smell.

Todd appeared and started shuffling the records in the Amon Amarth bin she had just straightened. "To get into the Grindstone concert."

Emma regarded them warily. This could not be good. Their notion of being anarchists came down to not wanting to pay for anything and feeling entitled to go anywhere they wanted without benefit of tickets or passes.

"Good luck, then," she said.

"Don't you want to hear it?"

She shook her head. She would not encourage the madness.

"It's simple really. We should have thought of it earlier."

She glanced up and saw Leo watching them. He probably recognized Todd and Brandon as non-buying regulars. He was not at all fond of perpetual browsers, in spite of the store's stated policy of encouraging vinyl buffs to explore the collection.

Holding up Evergrey's *Recreation Day* album she said, "What do you guys want to buy today?"

"Jeez, not Evergrey," Brandon complained.

Todd immediately took the album. "Why not? Tom Englund has one of the best voices in metal."

Brandon shook his head. "Too progressive. I'll stick with Amon Amarth's classic Viking stuff."

Emma glanced over at Leo. He had a customer now, so she relaxed.

"Hey, chill, your boss isn't looking," Brandon confirmed. "So, here's the deal. We followed Leo. We know where he went yesterday afternoon, and it's gotta be the place. It's a little weird, but we're going to check it out tonight. Once we're sure, we'll scout the best way in."

"If you don't get a pass out of Leo, you can go with us," Todd offered.

She had to admit there was some intelligence in what they'd done, at least regarding gathering information. "Where is this place?"

Brandon wagged a finger at her. "Not saying yet."

"We're still confirming," Todd added.

Emma shook her head. Even if they were right, they were nuts to try to crash the thing, especially given how secret the producers were being about the show. Whoever was behind it wasn't exactly welcoming the public. "You do know that there will be security, and wristbands, and all the usual checks in place. You could get kicked out or arrested."

Brandon shook his head. "Don't be a chicken, Emma. Fake wristbands. No big deal." He snapped his fingers.

"Thanks for thinking of me, guys," Emma said quickly. Leo had finished with his customer and was coming their way. "I'm touched, but I'll take my chances on another way in."

"You two buying anything today?" Leo asked, appearing beside the Amon Amarth bin.

"Thinking about it," Brandon said, holding up the band's *Fate of Norns* album.

"Think harder or take off," Leo advised.

"Hey, we're your best customers," Todd protested.

"Cash is king, boys. If you're buying, you're customers. If not, move on. Emma, see if you can make a real sale before you leave today. And plan to work the floor all day tomorrow."

"I can't...," she started to say but stopped. "Sure."

Chapter Twelve

On Monday, three days into her deal to keep Huntington away from Max, Emma discovered another downside to getting what she wished. He had disappeared over the weekend, but now his Rover was back in the driveway, which meant that at least half of her son's daily quotient of questions was about their landlord. Emma had read that the average six-year-old asked over three hundred.

Why is water wet? Where does the sky end? What's the biggest number there is? Where is Josh? When will he come back for his jacket? She reminded herself to be patient. Something or someone else would catch Max's attention. She hoped it would happen soon. She'd kept them both busy over the weekend, even taking Max with her to the record store, keeping him out of Leo's way, and giving him a stack of price stickies to apply to Daddy Rock T-shirts.

As she walked up through town to the Coast Highway and the Center, she braced herself for an evening of more questions. She had been putting Max off his Josh questions with a steady string of answers to the effect that their landlord was busy with his work, but she felt like a hypocrite. She was acting the way her grandparents had acted with her.

As a child, she had asked hundreds of questions about her grandfather's cars and her grandmother's paintings. Her grandparents had patiently answered those, but every time Emma veered away from asking about things to asking about people, she met silence. They steadfastly refused to answer the questions that consumed her: *Do I have a dad? Who is he? Why don't I live with him?*

Long before high school she had stopped asking those important questions aloud. But when she and her friends began taking biology as high school sophomores, the desire to know came flooding back. When the class got round to studying genetic inheritance, Emma's friend Olivia began urging her to get information from her grandparents. She insisted that Emma did not really know who she was if she didn't know who her father was.

"What if they're not telling you because you have some genetic disease? What if you have, like, hemophilia?"

For weeks their biology course fueled endless speculation on Olivia's part and revived the desperation that had lain dormant in Emma's heart. Still, she had not asked those questions of her grandparents until she discovered the truth of her mother's accident.

At seventeen, when she realized that her mother had died alone and that her father might be alive, she confronted her grandparents at the dinner table. She'd stormed at them, pouring out accusations of their deception. Her grandmother had gone rigid with anger and hurt. After all they had done for Emma, after they had protected her from the unforgivable monster who had destroyed her mother, how *dared* she ask about the man?

Emma refused to give up. The urgency of her need to know consumed her, and her grandparents were suddenly strangers who had lied to her all her life. In the end, just weeks before her high school graduation, her grandfather cracked. Her father's name was Steve Saxon. According to her grandparents, Saxon was a flamboyant, outrageous rocker, infamous for lewd behavior on stage and even more excessive behavior off stage. Her mother had left him to return to her family and have Emma, but Saxon had called her back and she'd died trying to reach him.

Young as she was, Emma had recognized the narrative was one-sided, and she desperately wanted to know her father's side of the story.

In the following weeks Emma had read everything the Internet had to offer about Steve Saxon. Most of it was tabloid headline versions of her father's life: stories of salad bowls of cocaine, sex with anything that moved, the trashing of hotel rooms that led to arrests. But he was alive and coming to L.A. with his band Grindstone for a reunion concert at a private party. And while her high school friends were emailing their prospective college roommates, Emma was writing her father a letter, her first letter to him. Above all she wanted to see him, to see if she felt any connection at all. She wanted to give him the letter she had written with a picture of herself, and she desperately wanted answers to her questions. Had he loved her mother? Did he know that her mother died trying to reach him?

She'd imagined it would be an easy thing to buy a concert ticket and find someone who would help her get backstage. She had never expected that her attempt to see her father would give her Max.

Emma pushed the pedestrian crosswalk button at the intersection and waited for the light to change. A glittering stream of cars rumbled past, spewing exhaust and blaring random radio sound bites from open windows. When the traffic slowed, the occasional driver gawked at her metal attire. A kid with a leather jacket and a ridge of gelled hair down the center of his head flashed her the horns.

The light changed, and she crossed. She did not want to mislead Max about his father the way her grandparents misled her about hers, but she understood their silence better at twenty-four than she had at seventeen. She had learned a series of life lessons since she'd left home, most of them from being a mom. Emma called them her Max lessons, and the number one Max lesson was that to lose Max would be unbearable. Everything her grandparents had done came out of the loss of their daughter. She knew that now.

At the Center she found Max with a group of older kids huddled around a whiteboard where a tall, skinny, dark-haired kid in shades was explaining a math problem. She had seen the kid working with what looked like middle-schoolers a different visit.

She stepped up to Max and tapped him on the shoulder. "Hey, ready to go home?"

Max shook his head. "No, Mom. I want to stay with the Bookman."

"Who's the Bookman?"

The kid leading the group stopped and turned. "Hi. Ms. Gray?"

Emma nodded.

"I'm the Bookman—Ulysses. I help kids with math here."

Emma smiled at the youth and turned back to Max, surprised. "You want to stay? Are you learning math?"

Max shook his head.

Ulysses faced him and said, "It's okay if you have to go, Max. You can come again tomorrow."

Max folded his arms on the table and put his head down. He mumbled something into the tabletop.

Emma squatted down so that she and her son could be face to face. She tapped him on the shoulder again. "Tell me. Why do you want to stay?"

"I want to see Josh."

"Josh?"

"He's coming here."

"Is he? When is he coming?" Emma looked at Ulysses.

The older boy shrugged. "Not until late. Too late for you, Max. Josh is coming to help some kids with their college stuff, but it won't be until after dinner."

Emma knew she faced a stubborn little boy who was about to dig his heels in big-time. He was tired and probably hungry. When had Josh Huntington become her kid's hero? How had he won Max's affection with his careless affection and a simple beach outing?

She stood and crossed the room to retrieve Max's backpack from its cubby against the wall. Reaching in to check for his afternoon snack, she found his cheese stick and apple slices untouched, so she perched beside him to see if he wanted them.

When she nudged him, Max lifted his head from his arms. "I don't want to go home."

"I know. Here, eat your snack."

She let him eat until the Bookman's math lesson came to an end. The other kids thanked Ulysses, gathered up their things, and headed off. But after Ulysses said goodbye to Max, Emma glanced at her son.

"Max, it's going to be lonely here for awhile. Everyone is going to go home to eat. We should, too."

"But I'll miss Josh."

"You will, this time," she admitted, "but it sounds like you should share Josh tonight with the big kids. We can see him anytime because he's our neighbor, but the big kids need him tonight for important stuff they're doing."

"But we *don't* see him anymore."

"He's been busy, but we'll see him soon."

"Can I knock on his door later?"

Emma did a quick mental calculation of the likelihood of getting Max to bed before Huntington returned.

"Sure."

* * *

Josh had found a great way to keep his word and avoid his tenant and her son. He'd spent the weekend partying with Sloan's buddy Lassiter and his friends up on the hill. With the start of the new workweek, he would have to leave his place early and come home late to avoid Emma and Max. That was the plan. And at the end of the week, he'd be putting his first Ryker check in the bank. Then he could think about some serious evening entertainment.

On Tuesday he was late getting up, however, and he found Emma with her car hood up doing something to the engine while Max sat glumly with his backpack at the foot of the stairs.

"Josh!" The little boy leapt up and extended his hand for the Canyon handshake. "Mom's working on her car."

"So I see." Josh kept moving toward the Rover. He'd made a deal.

"Where are you going?" Max asked, trailing after him.

"Work, buddy." Josh swung open the driver's side door.

"Are you still my friend?"

He turned. "Sure, Max. I'm just busy."

"Will I see you later?"

"I might work late. You have a good day at school."

Max looked at his mother, who stood with her hands on her hips, staring at her car engine, her expression plainly defeated. "Mom can't get her car to go."

Josh glanced at the thing. It had passed its use-by date years ago. He'd watched her keep it alive for months with almost daily adjustments to its inner works, but maybe it had finally died.

"Emma, can I help?"

"No." She didn't look at him. "My car is *not* dead. It's just having a bad moment."

For a realist, she was kidding herself big-time. Josh turned back to Max. "Your mom's resourceful. She'll figure something out."

He climbed into the Rover, closed the door and started the engine, turned on his music and got Outkast's "Hey Ya!" Perfect. He focused on feeling good and pulling out of the driveway.

At the corner, he glanced back in the rearview mirror and said a word he almost never said—loudly, and several times. Emma had now joined Max on the bottom stair, hugging him like a giant stuffed animal as if the boy could comfort her. So Josh reversed the Rover down the block and into the driveway.

He got out and stalked over to the pair on the stairs.

"In the car, buddy," he said as Max looked up at him.

Emma opened her mouth, instantly ready to protest. He shook his head at her.

"Forget it. Max needs to get to school. Where do you need to go?"

"I can take a bus."

He wanted to shake her. "At least a bus would be safer than this wreck." He dislodged the hood rod and let the hood slam down over the dead engine. "Get your stuff."

"I don't need your help."

"Unfortunately, you do, and I'm helpful. Get your stuff."

She stood there, stubborn and torn, all scrubbed and ponytail neat, all signs of death metal washed away, and he wanted her very badly. It promised to be a long, frustrating day.

"I have to turn in a paper today on campus."

In other words, only desperation would make her consider accepting his help.

"Fine," Josh said. "Let's go."

At last she moved. She retrieved a backpack from the backseat of her wreck and locked it. He shook his head at her, and she walked toward his car. He turned the engine on but killed the blast of music.

Max wanted to know what it was. "Is it metal? Mom is a metal expert. She knows lots of bands. What bands do you know?"

Josh answered Max's questions on the quick trip to his school. Emma said nothing. The Rover fit right in with the other vehicles in the drop-off line, as her car never would.

Mostly moms did the morning carpool duty. Dressed for work or working out, they greeted one another, phones in hand. Emma looked more like a babysitter than a mom in her jeans and oversized gray pullover state college hoodie. She delivered Max to the crowd of children playing in the yard, and Max went off without a backward glance.

She climbed back into the Rover and buckled the seatbelt. "You were going somewhere."

"Canyon," he admitted. He caught her brief start as he pulled out of the elementary school driveway and headed south. "You object to Canyon?"

"No."

It was too quick a denial to be honest.

"Are you working there?" she asked. He heard the note of caution in her voice.

"I can work by phone," he said. "Where are we headed for you?"

She told him. "I need to use a computer in the main library on campus to submit a paper electronically. It should take half an hour."

"Any classes?"

"Not today. Just the paper due."

"What's it on?"

"Some contemporary painters and how they use light."

He must have looked skeptical, because she added, "You object to art history?"

"I thought maybe your interests would be like engineering, or accounting, or something practical."

"Art history works for me."

He put the music back on and tried not to think of all the places on a college campus where he might get Emma alone—empty classrooms, library stacks, or convenient landscaping.

The 405 Freeway was its usual sluggish river of gleaming metal. He used the Rover to advantage to move in and out of the carpool lane whenever he spotted movement there, and he knew he was showing off a bit. Even when her car had been running, she had been stuck in the slow lane. Her car had been incapable of quick acceleration. Now it didn't do acceleration at all.

On campus she directed him to a visitor lot. He told her to text him when she was ready to leave and went in search of coffee. Over an Americano on a patio where students lingered he checked his email and answered a text from Ryker. He ignored one from his mother's executive assistant asking for his bank routing number again. Maybe he had a hang-up about the thing, but he just didn't want his mother making direct deposits to his account as if he were a kid getting an allowance.

An hour later he exchanged a couple of texts with Emma to establish his location. She told him to wait where he was and showed up ten minutes later, accompanied by a short, round, graying woman in a gauzy purple tunic over jeans and sandals. With some reluctance Emma introduced him to her art professor.

"Your friend Emma has a remarkable eye for the effects of light on color, and she picked the perfect private collection to write about. It's rare for students to pick living artists, and a local American artist, as well!"

"Emma's full of surprises," Josh said.

"Well, we're proud of her in our department and expect her to land a great internship or graduate fellowship right away." The professor offered Emma a quick hug and Josh a wave and then left.

"All done?" Josh asked Emma.

She nodded, squinting up at him in the bright sun. Behind her two palm trees leaned toward each other against a deep blue sky.

"Home?"

She nodded again. "Thank you."

"Sure."

He let Emma lead him across campus back to the car. The day had warmed up, but she still wore the oversized gray sweatshirt. At the car Josh popped the door locks, and they climbed in.

He reached to turn the engine on but stopped. Emma huddled on her side of the car, not moving to secure her seatbelt.

"What?"

"You've done me another favor."

"It's not a tragedy. You said 'thanks,' so we're done. You can't even the score all the time."

"But I don't..."

"I know. You don't want to owe me anything."

He pushed the lever that reclined his seat back from the steering wheel and reached for her, pulling her slowly but inexorably up over the console and into his lap. She was shaking her head, murmuring a protest, but her body yielded to his pull.

Her left knee bumped the steering wheel. He swung her legs to the side and nestled her bottom atop his crotch, against his straining erection where he'd wanted her to be for weeks. He pulled her in against his chest, tucking her head under his chin, his arms tight around her, her shape muffled by her sweatshirt.

Her breath made warm puffs against his throat as she spoke. "We don't even like each other."

"Maybe not," he said, "but we both want this."

She was shaking her head. "We're in a parking lot."

"The windows are tinted, and we're fully clothed."

"You have an answer for everything, don't you?"

"You know what I think? I think you don't like this because you're not in control. You like to be in control at all times, don't you, Emma?"

She stilled in his arms. "I'm just sensible and responsible, that's all. I do what needs to be done. My job is to be Max's mom. I don't get...distracted."

"And I'm distracting you?" He *was* trying to distract her, trying to get one hand inside the thick sweatshirt without her notice so he could feel her spine and warm, damp skin.

"Yes."

"Good. I'd like to distract you a whole lot more, but you can decide how much, Emma."

"Sex is overrated, you know."

She shifted slightly in his lap, and he swallowed hard at the pleasure of it. "Is that a long term position, or a temporary one?" His hand was on her back where the band of her bra made a ridge under her thin T-shirt. Her bra had no fastenings that he could detect.

"It's my position right now."

"Bad experiences?" He waited for her answer, holding her lightly, thinking about her secondhand lifestyle in a new way. The car, the cash, the readiness to move, the absence of family and friends were signs of an escape from someone or something.

Where were you seven years ago, Emma?

"Yes," she said.

"I can change your mind."

She twisted, pulling back in his arms to look accusingly at him, recovering her resistance, her face flushed rosy pink. "You are ridiculously sure of yourself."

"I won't do anything you don't like, Emma. Let's get you out of this sweatshirt."

He pulled the bottom of the garment up so that she had to lift her arms, momentarily trapping her in its softness. She squirmed, trying to get free.

"Where did you get this thing?"

"The lost and found. They give away unclaimed clothes at the end of each term."

Her voice was muffled by sweatshirt. Josh took a brief glance at her breasts and slim rib cage before he gave a final yank, freeing her from the garment. She was leaning back against the steering wheel watching him. Her thin white T-shirt with its puckered seams had the look of the lowest rung of the retail food chain, but it made the design of her bra visible. She didn't need much support, just a band of white stretchy fabric that could be pulled on or off.

She regarded him with a mixture of wariness and longing.

He tossed the sweatshirt onto the passenger seat and nestled her head under his chin, her left shoulder against his chest, her hands clasped together on her knees. He knew what her problem was; she was turned on, ready for him in ways she didn't even know how to name. It had started with the massage, and she didn't know how to stop it. Unpracticed as she was, she had no defense against her own body.

"You survived the massage, didn't you?" he murmured.

"It was a mistake."

"It can't be undone. Now you know how you feel."

"But I don't want to feel this way about you."

He fought back his annoyance at those words. Trust Emma to be frank and open about her feelings, but he guessed that her real complaint was more about her own weakness in the grip of desire than about her objections to his character. And her protest said a lot about how strong that desire was. "You might try to think of me as useful for your education. It might be good to get over those bad experiences."

Emma said nothing. Josh put his hand on her ribs, tugging her loosened T-shirt free of her jeans. Now he could put his open palm directly on warm, moist skin, and he slid his hand up the smooth arch of her back and slipped the tips of his fingers under the band of her bra. He lifted them, pulling back on the band, so that she could feel the pressure of the fabric against her breasts.

She gave a little moan and squirmed in his lap. He waited for the wave of pleasure to subside then slid his hand around her, his fingers following the line of the bra until they made contact with the soft underside of her breast.

"You're so soft." He said the words against her hair, which smelled of vanilla. He waited, savoring her expectation, communicating by his delay what he wanted. Then he slid his hand upward, taking full possession of one sweet, soft breast.

Her body shuddered in response. She pressed her face deeper against him. He could feel the rising heat between them, and he took hold of her nipple between his thumb and forefinger and tugged and teased it into a tight bud of arousal. When her hands clutched his shoulder and she pressed her forehead harder against his chest as if she could contain the sensation, he stilled his hand.

"Is this what you majored in? The female sexual response?"

He half smiled. "Always my favorite subject."

"I'm sure I'm not a very interesting example."

Josh shifted her against him so that her breasts flattened against his chest. "Emma, believe me, you have my full attention."

She didn't answer. For a brief mindless moment he thought she might yield to the perfect fit between them. Instead she freed herself from his hold, scooted back over the console, and buckled up, her moment of need, or vulnerability, or whatever it was, over. "I won't keep you from your plans any longer."

Josh gave a mock sigh, like a teacher impatient with a reluctant student, but he couldn't help his grin. It was her loss, but she'd come to her senses eventually. What she felt wasn't going to release its hold on her any time soon. "Okay, but I want you to make an agreement with me that you'll tell me if I do anything you don't like, anything that reminds you of past bad experiences."

She gave him a look he could only describe as tolerance of his idiocy. "You think we're going to do more of this?"

"Lots more if you want to overcome those bad experiences."

"Maybe I'll try therapy later, thanks."

He took her home on surface streets, up through the harbor over the soaring bridge to the Palos Verdes peninsula where a shifting ribbon of road ran along the edge of crumbling cliffs above the ocean. "If you get that wreck of yours to run again, don't take it on the freeway," he warned.

"You don't have to worry about me. I've been on my own for—"

"Seven years? Since you were seventeen?"

"Yes, as a matter a fact. I left home…after high school, like most people do."

"Who's looking for you, Emma?" he guessed, and he did not miss her swift start.

"What makes you think anyone is looking for me?"

"You. You're hiding. You must have had a home and parents at seventeen. Did you leave home before or after you got pregnant? No one helped you. Right?"

"No one's looking for me," she said. He noticed what she did not deny, but they did not speak again.

In the driveway, next to her wreck, she thanked him again for his help. Josh made himself leave after she got out of the Rover. He'd done her a favor, and she was grateful. She'd let him hold her, and she'd almost admitted her attraction to him. He had briefly seen the softer side of Emma she tried so hard to conceal. And there were other benefits yet to come. He knew Emma; she couldn't tolerate depending on anyone. She'd want to pay him back, and he'd be ready for the moment. He'd be ready to make her as crazy with wanting as he was.

On the drive to Canyon, he texted his mother's executive assistant. He'd bet they could work something out if he agreed to see the first of his mother's hand-picked women. Maybe he could get a cash advance in exchange for attending the charity event with the ex-debutante without giving in about the bank routing number. Maybe the ex-deb could even help him get Emma out of his mind for a night.

It was a plan.

Chapter Thirteen

As Emma saw it, she had two immediate problems—her car and her landlord. The two were related. If her car did not run, she could not run. She could not pack up and disappear in a single hour as she had done in the past. She couldn't even get to campus for her finals.

Huntington was a much bigger problem than her transportation woes. She needed to stop relying on him. His kindness made her do dumb things like climbing into his lap and letting him hold her and promise her great sex, which, she suspected, he could give her. But really great sex, even if she believed it existed, was not part of her plan. It would be irresponsible to get side-tracked by him, especially when she was so close to attaining all of her goals.

Somehow in that parking lot she'd lost her focus, and now she needed to get it back. Getting ready for work would be a start. It was payday, and today she was going straight to Leo with her Grindstone pass request.

She opened her closet and began assembling her death metal look, putting on every piece of hardware in her collection. *You're so soft.* That's what Josh Huntington had said, but she needed to be tough and hard and invincible. Where he was concerned, she needed to be as spiny as a sea urchin.

Her phone rang while she was applying the day's tattoos. Out of the blue, she heard her friend Maria's familiar voice explaining how sorry she was to have let Emma down. Maria's mother had suffered a stroke, and Maria was in San Diego caring for her. Emma listened sympathetically to her friend's tale of a week of coping with difficult news in the unfamiliar world of confusing medical options and family angst. Maria apologized for her lack of communication. It was only today that she'd gotten her head together enough to call people like Emma outside her own family. When Maria abruptly ran out of breath and laughed at herself, it was Emma's turn to remind her mentor and friend to take the baby steps Maria herself always recommended.

Emma thanked her for the call and wished Maria's mother well as she recovered. Immediately, Maria was her old self, talking about arrangements to cover Emma's weekend sitting needs. Maria reminded Emma that Maria's cousin—Claudia, in Lomita—could be available if Emma needed help on the weekend. Maria would have her cousin call as soon as possible.

Just hearing Maria's voice boosted Emma's confidence. Tough situations could be faced and overcome. At Daddy Rock, she went directly to Leo's office and knocked on the door.

He looked up, gave her outfit a quick scrutiny, and nodded her in.

She would let him pay her before she made her request.

"How much do I owe you today?"

She told him and watched him count out her hundreds, a down payment on her rent at best. He went back to looking at his computer.

"Leo, I want a pass to the Grindstone reunion concert."

He didn't look up. "Why?"

"You know I know everything about them."

"I doubt that. You were a baby when they were big."

"I was seventeen when they had their last reunion gig. I was there."

Leo skewered her with a look. "No way you were there. It was a private party."

"I had a…date with a guy in the crew."

Leo's bushy gray brows met in a doubtful "V" over his nose as he studied her. He jerked his thumb to indicate the large framed black-and-white portrait of the band members and roadies from the 2008 Reunion Tour that dominated the wall behind his desk and that Emma studied every chance she got. At the center was Steve Saxon.

"You were there? With one of these guys? Who?"

"It doesn't matter."

Leo picked up a stack of black-and-white photos from the clutter on his desk. "These are some shots from backstage at that party. We've put together a retrospective on the band for this concert and tracked down the crew. Should I be looking for you?"

Emma shook her head, swallowing hard to control an unexpected roiling nausea. She would not be in any of the pictures with the band because she'd never actually made it to the party. "So, will they all be here for the concert? The crew, too?"

"You want to hook up with an old flame?"

"No."

She would not appear anywhere in those pictures, but Max's father was in several of them. He was on the wall in front of her, bottom row, second from the end. From the first time she'd come to Leo's office she had confronted his image. It was almost familiar now. He was a short, wiry young man with a head of blond curls who'd told her that his name was Ron.

In her head she'd had a thousand conversations with Ron, working out how she felt about his actions. He had taken advantage for sure. He'd spotted her eagerness or her desperation and her total lack of experience with the rock scene, and he must have realized that she was alone. He'd promised to get her into the part of the hotel where the band members were partying after the concert, offering weed, which she'd refused, and then a drink, which at the time she thought she could handle. She'd been to parties, after all. He had been hot to have sex and assumed that she wanted it, too. He'd told her as he pinned her flailing body down on a huge sofa, "Listen, baby, I know what you came for. You'll like it."

She hadn't, but her arms and legs had been too rubbery with alcohol to push him off of her. Then, when he finished, he'd made that devastating remark about rich girls.

Emma believed that she'd faced the facts of that night squarely. Max was the biggest fact. He existed, and he was good; she'd known it from the moment she held him against her, skin-to-skin. She and Ron might each be at some fault for their actions, but whatever was messy, ugly, or selfish in his making, Max was none of those things.

She had promised herself that if she ever met Ron again she would stomp on him with her heavy metal boots, but Emma also owed him her most precious possession. She believed he must have some good in him, too, because Max was good. She had even practiced forgiving Ron for Max's sake, but the one thing she was clear on was that he could not have any part of the boy. He had given her child some DNA, but he did not deserve to be Max's father.

It was possible that Ron would be part of the Grindstone reunion. To reach her father, Emma would risk meeting her son's father again. As long as he did not recognize her, as long as he did not want any part of Max, she would be okay.

She took the hundreds that Leo offered her, and counted them carefully. "Leo, I want a backstage pass because I want to meet Steve Saxon."

"Sweetheart, you don't exactly fit the profile of a Saxon girl."

"A Saxon girl?"

"He had a type, you know—blonde, built, and willing. There were hundreds of them."

"I heard there was one special girl."

"Ah, you've looked at that rider then?"

Emma fought down the pounding of her heart. "Well, the rider says there must be an empty black chair on stage at each venue. Saxon puts a single red rose on it for his lost 'Helen of Troy.' Didn't he write a song for her? Did you ever hear the track?"

Leo stared at her. "Now you do sound like a fan. Every loony thinks he's going to find that lost bit of rock history that changes everything. Not going to happen. You buy the story of the mysterious rich girl? You think she was real? Saxon and Rezford and Dalton and Phillips were like all the rest. They wanted to be rock stars. They didn't want to create music. If they wrote a 'girl' song, it was because girl songs sell. Were those guys ever in love with a groupie? Never."

Leo's annoyance gathered momentum. "Saxon liked more than one partner at a time. He liked to line them up. The band wanted to snort, smoke, or shoot everything that could get them high, they wanted to trash every hotel room, and they wanted to screw every woman who flashed a tit at them."

Emma tried to cut him off. "Leo, I don't want to sleep with Saxon. I want to *meet* him."

Leo stared at her for a moment then shook his head. "Those concert tickets are big bucks."

"But a backstage pass from you is free."

Emma saw her mistake at once. In Leo's mind nothing was free. His bushy brows shot up. "It's like an extra five hundred bucks for nothing. Do I look like Santa Claus or something? I'm paying you too much anyway."

"Didn't I sell more of the limited edition Metallica demo tape than anyone else? And didn't I get sales no one expected on Stone Sour's cover tracks?"

"Not enough. Volume, that's what counts. Get your sales up over fifty this week and I'll see what I can do." He went back to staring at his computer screen.

For the first time in seven years, Emma's father would be in the country. In the *state*. Her chance to connect with him was now, but Emma knew better than to plead or to give Leo any hint of how much was at stake. She'd met plenty of people like Leo on Planet Ordinary, people with a little power and a big sense of grievance who liked to lord it over anyone under them in the pecking order. Emma had learned not to trust such people and never to show weakness around them or you'd end up in a worse position than before.

She turned and left Leo's office, making sure not to give herself away by glancing again at the photos on his desk.

* * *

In between making calls for Ryker and meeting with city officials, Josh tried to locate Emma on the Internet. She was not Emma Gray the hockey player, Emma Gray the sheep farmer, or Emma Gray the distinguished journalist. Her version of Emma Gray did not seem to have an identity anywhere in cyberspace, and her absence there confirmed exactly what he'd guessed about her. She was hiding. She had run away from something.

But if she was not Emma Gray, it would be harder to figure out where she had been living seven years earlier.

He gave up his Internet search briefly for a trip to city hall to meet Barbara, the woman handling the city's end of permits for the concert, and to go over the paperwork with her. He'd met with her many times in the winter about the Canyon gala and knew how she liked things organized. On paper Grindstone's reunion concert looked as much like the gala as he could make it, a classy event at which a small music group, a quartet, was playing for a well-heeled audience in support of medical care for veterans. There would be music and food provided by properly licensed vendors. Valets would manage parking on the school's practice field. The school groundspeople would direct traffic. The event would begin at five, and all music would end by ten. Beer and wine would be served inside only and only to adults. The neighbors would never know the thing had happened.

He thanked Barbara for her help and returned to campus. Waiting for Ryker, who was talking with one of his security people, Josh again studied the enlarged photos of Grindstone that covered the walls in the Hall of Canyon Men. He was staring at them when Sloan called.

Sloan cut straight to chase, as he always did, and it was sweet to have the guy who'd once hated Canyon now worried about the place. Josh was tempted to mess with him, but he settled for giving his honest opinion.

"I don't think Ryker's going to blow the place up or anything. I actually just think he has some twisted sense of humor that's tickled by bringing Grindstone here, giving these bad boys of rock center stage, covering up all the old farts in the hall with pictures of shirtless guys in animal skin pants humping their guitars."

"He never smiles, Huntington," Sloan said.

"That's possibly the brain injury." Off to his left Josh could see Ryker's rigid profile. "Isn't there some condition that freezes your face? Bell's palsy or something?"

"Could be something like that, I suppose," Sloan allowed. "But if you see anything suspicious you'll let me know?"

"Hey, 'be true to your school.' Yeah, of course I'll let you know. I wouldn't want our young friends Ulysses and Tyler to lose their place of education."

"Thanks," Sloan said. "And come to the engagement party. Both Annie and my mom want to see you."

Josh smiled to himself at his friend's perpetual lack of tact and clicked off.

Ryker's security man soon signaled that the boss was ready to talk again—which remained an interesting exercise. No matter what idea you sent Ryker's way, you waited while whole bureaucracies of synapses processed the words individually behind the guy's eyes. It gave Josh time to study the man's tattoos, his stillness, his hand on his dog. Josh had yet to see the guy move or walk, and yet Ryker looked to be in top physical shape. Also, for a man who took his time speaking, Ryker seemed to miss nothing that was said, and Josh couldn't shake the feeling that the guy was amusing himself here. Well, that and atoning for something.

Step by step, Josh went over the plan he'd put in motion for the benefit concert. Because the band was coming together after years apart, there were lots of extra arrangements to make. It was all happening, though, both with personnel and equipment, including the famous grindstone and axe. By phone Josh had connected with the band's past manager, Leo Grant from Daddy Rock. Grant had no recollection of their previous brief conversation the day he'd almost fired Emma for not working an extra shift. Josh wondered, talking to him, how Emma handled working for the guy. It couldn't be easy. Grant had to be right all the time, and he didn't take kindly to anyone else's ideas. Still, Grant had connected Josh with a theatrical outfit that worked on Grindstone concerts and knew the band's preferred stage plot and requirements for sound, special effects, and lighting. Leo might be a grumpy old cynic, but he'd known whom to call…which was lucky, because he was apparently one of the few old rockers associated with Grindstone who had not fried his brain on drugs or poisoned his liver on booze.

As much as Josh could tell, Ryker approved of the arrangements. The guy never blinked at the cost, and he didn't look like someone who planned to blow the place up.

"So," he asked, probing a little, "why Canyon for this concert?"

The question seemed to catch Ryker off guard, and for once something happened behind that unblinking gaze of his; his glance took in the hall with its life-sized photos of Grindstone in place of the staid and modest war heroes of Canyon's past. Still, he said nothing.

Josh tried again. "Is this a secret plot to have Grindstone trash the Hall of Canyon Men?"

He thought he detected a muscle twitch at the corners of Ryker's mouth, like some vestigial smile. Ryker's dog sensed something, too, and lifted its head under the guy's hand.

"They won't." Ryker's gaze shifted from Josh to the wall. "Pictures."

Josh nodded. He got it. Ryker was actually protecting the hall from destruction by covering the walls with images that these premier narcissists of the rock world would not destroy. The largest picture, the one Josh had been studying most recently, featured the whole band and their roadies and manager backstage at the 2008 concert in what must have been a rare moment of sobriety and harmony before the band's big breakup.

"Nice move," he said. "Works for me. It would also piss Chambers off."

He watched the effect of the ex-headmaster's name on Ryker. The hand tightened on the dog then actually lifted, and Ryker pointed at a portion of the wall not covered by band pictures.

On either side of the hall's Old Spanish style doors, the oak wood paneling concealed closets where the ceremonial objects of the school and some of its historical items were kept. The trappings of an all-boys school with a hundred-year history were like something out of Harry Potter. As a prefect, Josh had had access to the closet where the prefects' long black capes hung alongside a heavy oak podium, the school mace, and a rolled up banner for graduation ceremonies.

He crossed over to the panel Ryker indicated and pressed the concealed spring that opened the door. The familiar ceremonial objects were there next to shelves crammed with old exam books and numbered dictionaries with gold lettering that Josh recognized. Before every kid had a computer or a tablet, Canyon boys had been issued these, and it had been part of the study hall routine to take your dictionary out of the cupboard before you sat down. Every guy had one. You put your name and class year in yours under the names and years of guys who had gone before you.

As far as Josh knew, most guys had never consulted the well-worn dictionaries in order to figure out the meaning of an unfamiliar word—except maybe Jack Joyce himself, when he had been Jack Joyce, or maybe Brian Drosafarian, another classmate of theirs who had been terminally earnest and sincere. The goal had been to find and mark words with sexual content, often adding commentary or an illustration to share with other bored classmates.

Behind him, Ryker spoke. "On top. Mine. Letter P."

Josh picked the top dictionary off the pile. As promised, he found the name Jack Joyce was written inside the cover. Josh found the appropriate half moon indentation in the pages and let the dictionary fall open in his hands. The letter P had kept them all busy, but he innately knew the word Ryker had in mind.

He found the page and reference easily enough: ***Priapism*** *(pri a' piz' m), n. [L., fr. Gr.* Priapos*] a condition of persistent erection of the penis.* And he had to laugh. In Ryker's old dictionary was a very good cartoon drawing of Headmaster Chambers in his academic robes with what every ad for erectile dysfunction cures warns its users is a very dangerous condition.

When Josh looked up, Ryker's expression had darkened—if such a thing were possible. Headmaster Chambers's sexual activities were clearly a matter of anger and frustration.

Josh knew how he himself had learned of Chambers's sexual activities. As a new prefect in his sophomore year he had been in and out of the headmaster's office on school business countless times. It hadn't taken him long to figure out that Chambers and his executive assistant had more than a working relationship, or that the large private bath that Chambers added to his office suite had other uses than the occasional quick shower for a busy head of school. At the time Josh had shrugged off the discovery. He hadn't wanted to judge the guy on whatever private arrangements he made to satisfy his sexual needs. Chambers's talks on morals and manhood had struck him as phony anyway, so Josh hadn't minded the guy having a mistress. It would have been different if Chambers's partner was unhappy. Her name had been Melanie, and she had never said anything to Josh about being unhappy.

He closed the dictionary. Ryker radiated extraordinary tension, even for him.

Josh didn't expect an answer, but he asked anyway. "So, Ryker, how did you learn about Chambers's…extracurricular activities?"

On the dog's nape, Ryker's hand closed into a fist. Josh stood and returned the dictionary to the closet, giving the other man time to think.

Ryker's mind might work slowly, but with a jumble of memories from that long ago time Josh felt his own brain move into the fast lane. The thing that had made Sloan so angry at Canyon had been Chambers's abuse of power, his taking advantage of Sloan's helplessness and isolation as a scholarship student. Unlike Sloan, Jack Joyce had a wealthy powerful father. So, Josh's instinct told him, if Chambers had wronged Jack Joyce it was through his mother.

Chambers had always been friendlier with the moms than the dads, anyway.

When Josh turned back, Ryker had recovered himself. The hand on the black dog's nape had relaxed, and the conversation turned back to the business of the benefit concert. It was clear that Ryker was going to keep his old wounds private and that the question about Headmaster Chambers would not be answered yet.

* * *

When he left for the day, Josh headed to his mother's house. He'd done some financial calculations, and he definitely needed his trust back. Ryker was paying him well, but the job would end.

Thinking about his finances as he pulled into his parents' estate was sobering. A thought hit him as he cut the Rover's engine. Ryker and Sloan were both calling the shots in their own lives, while he, Josh Huntington, was trying to get an allowance out of his mother. Things had certainly changed for the three of them: the loner, the invisible man and the golden boy. But only for him did the trend seem to be a downward one. His old nickname meant nothing without his trust, and his cape-wearing days were definitely over.

He found his mother on a chaise longue by the pool, wrapped in a white robe, her pale golden hair wet from her swim and coiled at her nape. She was sipping water and studying something on a sleek tablet device.

"You've had over a week."

"Sorry," Josh said. "Did I miss the deadline? I've got some things going."

"Who is she? A waitress?"

He sat opposite his mother and kicked off his shoes. A cold swim would feel good. Food would be good, too. His stomach reminded him that he missed his favorite food spots. "Actually, I'm working on another Canyon event. Do you remember a boy from my class, Jack Joyce?"

His mother spoke without reaction. "His father was that producer who married a brainless starlet, cheated on her repeatedly, and left her fifteen years later."

"I doubt she was brainless. Jack Joyce was the valedictorian of our class."

"Well, he did not marry that woman for her intellect. She didn't fit in his world."

"Joyce Senior dumped her?"

"She was a liability to him."

"Do you know what happened to her?" Josh asked.

"She had a breakdown of some sort."

"Where did she end up?"

His mother put aside her tablet. "Santa Barbara, somewhere decent and discreet I'm sure. You're not raking up this sort of thing, are you?"

"Just thought you would know."

"You're straying from the subject is what you're doing."

"Am I?" Josh asked. "Is there some kind of rush? Are you hoping to get a grandchild out of this project or something?"

His mother's face assumed an expression that he could only describe as horrified, but she made a quick recovery. "Your bank account must be hovering on empty, darling. My assistant says you have not provided her with a routing number. I assume that's because you are meeting your needs in other"—she made a moue of distaste—"less acceptable ways."

It's called working, Mom, he thought. But he didn't tell her about his job for Ryker. Instead he shook his head and flashed her a grin. "You know me too well, Mom. But I'm game. I can start work on your list this week if you can float me a little loan. Who's first? Bethany?"

"Very well." His mother gave a tight smile, reached for her phone, and sent a text. "Margot will set you up tomorrow."

Josh couldn't help giving her one last nudge. "By the way, are you okay if I check out Dad's offer? I mean are the parental offers mutually exclusive?"

"Don't push me, darling."

"Just asking for clarity." He rose, scooped up his shoes, and crossed the flagstones to drop an air kiss on her unblemished cheek. "You don't mind if I have a swim before I go. Do you, Mom?"

She waved him away.

* * *

When Josh returned to his place, light was fading from the sky and Max sat huddled on the bottom step of the stairs with a few of his toy trucks. Emma, still in full death metal gear, was leaning over the side of her car, reaching deep into the engine. Josh tried not to notice her bottom or remember it pressed against him earlier in the day.

When she stood up, her expression was bleak. Her hands were grease-covered, and her makeup made deep smudges under her eyes. A row of padlock-sized safety pins covered each pocket of a sleeveless denim jacket she wore like a vest over a midriff-baring cropped T-shirt. He'd never seen her wear so much metal. She looked awful, and yet the effects of his cold swim evaporated instantly.

Next to her open toolbox on the driveway was an old plastic dinner tray covered with Disney characters. She'd filled the tray with neat rows of bolts, screws, and parts that she'd obviously removed from the engine. It was almost nine, and he wondered how long she'd been pursuing this lost cause.

Mother and son spotted Josh at the same time. Max jumped up with smile as Emma gave Josh a warning glare.

The kid stuck out his small hand. Josh looked aside and shoved his own hands in his pockets.

"Hi, buddy. Looks like you're busy helping your mom."

Max let his hand drop. "She won't let me."

"Next time," Josh said. He went by the boy and up the stairs, surprised at how hard it was. As he unlocked his door he heard Max asking, "Mom, are we gonna eat soon?"

"Just as soon as I finish, Maxie."

Josh pulled his phone out of his pocket. Some things he hadn't promised. With his last working credit card, he texted a pizza delivery to one Max Gray.

Chapter Fourteen

She was not a woman to give up easily. At eleven she knocked on his door, and when he opened it she stood unchanged, covered in grease and streaks of makeup and TSA-nightmare-inducing metal gear. If he let her in, he was going to make every effort to get her soft and naked instead.

Her gaze skimmed over his bare chest and away from his boxers. "You ordered my kid a pizza."

"It was a plain marguerite—that's Italian for toasted cheese, basically. It even has basil on it."

He waited while she sorted out the demands of her parenting principles and her politeness. "Thank you."

"Did you get the car running?"

"No."

Josh had known the answer. He would have heard the motor turn over if she had.

"Take a shower. Go to bed. Get some help in the morning."

He couldn't get more heroic than that, but she didn't move. She didn't flee. She fixed her gaze somewhere over his right shoulder and asked, "How do you make it stop?"

Josh drew in a slow breath. Emma Gray was asking him about the wanting, about being turned on by a glance. She had apparently tried to bury her attraction to him in her futile attempt at auto repair.

"Working on the car for hours didn't help?"

She got that stubborn look and folded her arms across her middle, hugging her elbows, still avoiding his gaze. "I just want it to stop."

He straightened. He could help her, but not in the way she wanted. She wanted some mind trick, some form of magic self-control, a shutoff valve for her inconvenient feelings. He, on the other hand, was just the man to help her discover where those feelings could lead, and what she was admitting sent his mood from cautious to unreasonably hopeful in an instant. Nonetheless, he gave her one last out. "Take a brisk walk or a very cold shower."

She looked doubtful. "Is that what you do?"

He laughed. "I'm self-indulgent, remember. I don't try to make it stop."

He wasn't being entirely truthful. He had done his best to tire his body out in the pool this afternoon after agreeing to date the first of his mother's picks. Whoever she turned out to be, she'd be the opposite of Emma, easy on both the eye and the ego, wholly accepting of his toys, his towels, and his lifestyle. She'd be a better match for him. He could therefore help Emma by staying strong for one night and shutting his door. She wouldn't need super willpower if he did that, and she'd have nothing to regret. He was pretty sure that Emma would regret letting herself enjoy sex.

"You know," he muttered, "we're living the marshmallow experiment."

She stared at him. "What are you talking about?"

"A psychologist put little kids in a room staring at a tiny marshmallow, the kind you put on hot cocoa, and told them they could have more if they could just wait and not eat it. Most of them caved, ate the marshmallow and ruined their lives: bad grades, low SAT scores, no college degrees, no success."

"You made that up," Emma accused.

"I've been a marshmallow-eater from the start. I know how it works."

"You think I ought to walk away," Emma realized.

"Right now."

She looked so confused and so totally let down by his answer that he had to reach for her. If she could admit the attraction, why should he deny it?

"Come on."

He got a palm full of studs sticking out of one of the leather cuffs she wore, but he pulled her into the apartment and down the short hall to his bath. He opened the door, flipped on the light, and gave her a little push.

She stepped over the threshold and looked back at him over her shoulder, her eyes wide. "You redid this bath, didn't you? I have that crummy bath in my unit with rust and mold and drawers that stick, and you have this gorgeous pristine shower. You should lower my rent."

He laughed. "Have you had any illusions about me from the beginning? Just take a shower. And enjoy the towels."

"I don't have any clothes to put on."

"Go home in a towel," he replied.

He immediately thought of how she would look emerging from the steamy bathroom wrapped in one, and he imagined peeling that super-thick, oversized bath sheet from her body and pressing her flesh, warm and sweet, to him. But it was clear that she knew nothing about foreplay. She looked like she still thought the shower was going to help her resist the pull between them.

She had enough sense to shake her head. "I need clothes."

"I'll bring you something," he promised.

Okay. So there were limits to her wanting. He stepped back, closed the door, and went by his bedroom to pull on shorts and a shirt. If they weren't going to get naked, he needed some armor.

Josh heard the water start up as he pulled a Polo shirt over his head. Resolutely he crossed the entry between their two units and slipped into hers. He checked on Max, sound asleep in his bed. Emma's room was like an indoor campsite, with her blue and white quilt on top of a sleeping bag spread along one wall. The view reminded him of the night she'd moved in. She had taken the key from him and apparently unloaded all her worldly possessions from her car. She and her son could be gone just as quickly.

He found her PJ bottoms and the oversized shirt with the state college logo hanging on a hook in the closet. Grabbing the shirt, he returned to his unit, but he stopped at the entrance to the hall. The water was still running, which meant she was still naked in his shower.

Great.

He'd had flashes of this exact situation for weeks, but always under different circumstances. Now would be a good time to get a grip, to remember that this woman regarded him as a waste of space on the planet and did not want him near her child. Now would be a good time to walk away, to leave her a note, to get in the Rover and head right back to his favorite club, to call an old friend, to do anything other than wait patiently for her to finish her shower.

He knocked on the bathroom door and spoke over the sound of running water. "Your shirt is hanging on the doorknob."

No answer. His brain had time to imagine water streaming over Emma's body, but she did not speak or open the door.

"I'll be in the living room," he called.

He stood at the window and listened for waves breaking, for traffic, for any sound that could drown out the shower and the heavy pulse of desire beating in him, but his ears were tuned to the water going off, the silence that followed, and then the opening of the bathroom door. Warm, soap-scented air reached him. He turned from the window and caught his breath at Emma without makeup, her sweet bare legs peeking out from beneath the hem of the oversized T-shirt.

"I've ruined your towel." She clasped a lumpy, streaked bundle of terrycloth to her chest. It clinked when she set it down beside his door, and he imagined her metal gear rolled up inside the thing. "I'll wash it tomorrow," she promised.

Whatever. He felt a demented urge to grin. She hadn't walked directly out. She'd put the bundle down. He'd regained the advantage.

"Feel better?" he asked.

She nodded.

She made no deliberate move toward him, but she was alert and watchful—and she did not flee.

"Come here," he said, gambling. He held out a hand. "We're going to finish what we started this morning."

Her head came up, her eyes startled. But again she did not flee or say no.

"You can stop whenever." He hoped he could stick to that. Her edgy need was turning him on in ways he could not remember being turned on in the past. But she had to acknowledge she wanted this before he acted, and waiting for her to accept his offer was taking all his self-control.

A car pulled up across the street. Doors opened and closed. Male and female voices mingled, laughing and exchanging goodnights. The car drove off. Josh was still waiting for Emma to choose.

At last her hand came up to meet his. He pulled her with him to the big leather chair, settled in and pulled her down into his lap, nestling her in the V of his legs and wrapping his arms around her ribs. He could look directly across his apartment to her unit, but no one else could see in.

She smelled like soap and slightly aroused female. With his forefinger he caught a drop of water from the wet ends of her hair as it rolled past her collarbone, and she shivered in response to his touch.

He could tell she was thinking furiously.

* * *

Emma tried to contain her shivering, to get control of the situation. If she had not been half out of her mind with feelings she'd never had before, she would be asleep in her own apartment, but the feelings had taken hold and wouldn't let go.

Josh had so much more experience than she did. He knew how to touch her and drive her to distraction, and she didn't have the same knowledge about him. Her relative naivety was embarrassing.

"You've showered with women before, haven't you?" she asked.

Josh's fingers pressed her ears lightly where she'd removed the chrome clips. He ran his hands down her neck, over her shoulders and down her arms, stopping to squeeze her elbows and fold her arms across her middle. He took her hands in his. He was going to touch her breasts. That's where they'd left off in the parking lot earlier.

"My piano teacher in the pool house was the first."

She tried to imagine him inexperienced or awkward. "How old were you?"

"Fifteen."

His hands found and cupped her breasts through her T-shirt. The sensation streaked down through Emma, following some crooked pathway of nerves that led from the tips of her breasts to her womb and beyond to the girl parts at the juncture of her thighs. He brushed his thumbs over her nipples until they stood up for him, and she pressed her lips together to contain the sounds in her throat.

"Tell me if you don't like this," he said.

"How long"—her voice sounded airless in her ears—"did you study piano?"

"Never stopped really."

He was making her crazy. She couldn't hold back anymore. She let out a whimper and arched up into his touch, and he lifted the edge of the T-shirt and put his large, warm, very dexterous hands on her breasts. The skin-to-skin contact made her head swim. He stilled for a moment as if he were as dizzy as she was, and she could feel his heart beating crazily against her shoulder blade. When he moved again, she gave in to the pleasure of it and moaned.

Then he whispered, "Turn around."

* * *

Josh helped Emma twist in the chair, letting their bodies brush and press—a few seconds of contact but a dozen slo-mo frames of sensation—until she lay on top of him, her face inches from his. He told himself not to kiss her. They weren't in a relationship; they were mutually afflicted by a pretty hot sexual attraction. It wouldn't do to confuse her with kissing.

He reached behind her left knee and pulled, showing her how to come up on her knees, straddling him. She braced her arms on the chair, keeping her distance, and her eyes showed her new awareness of being open to him. He had no doubt that she'd be a quick learner, but in this area he was the expert. He could teach her things that apparently she'd missed while being Max's mom and a student and a bread-winner and an auto mechanic.

With her T-shirt hanging loose over his belly, he took her hips in his hands and pushed her gently down across his thighs. He wanted to touch her, to move her a few inches forward, to settle her against him in the fit they were meant to have, but he didn't want to startle her. Looking up into those hazel-gray eyes, wide and dark with arousal, torn between wanting whatever came next and needing to stay in control, he saw she was fighting the sensations.

He let go of her hips and reached up to run his thumb across her lips, tugging and pushing until she parted them for him, her breath ragged, her arms trembling.

"We have to quit now. Unless you want to get naked," he added.

Her eyes widened comically. "No."

"I'd like to get naked with you, Emma."

"No."

Josh swallowed a sigh. Apparently he could rouse and stir her till she was mindless with wanting, but she wasn't going to budge on the boundaries she'd set. Emma would have resisted the marshmallow. She would have gripped the table hard and stared the thing down for as long as it took.

134

He might have to rethink the kissing thing. One kiss would distract her while he gave her the release she needed. Then he could send her back to her unit. In the morning she'd be hostile again, but at least they'd make it through another day of staring down the marshmallow.

"So, you want to keep your clothes on…?"

She nodded emphatically.

"But you want to stop being turned on. So, let's try a kiss."

She gave him a skeptical look but didn't refuse.

Josh took her face between his hands and pulled her to him, kissing her with a long, slow, open-mouthed kiss, no invasion, just invitation. She opened to him with a simple acceptance that floored him, and he had to pull away to clear his head.

"Again?" he said when he could speak.

She made an almost imperceptible nod.

This time, when he pressed his mouth to hers she answered, and it rocked him so hard that for a moment he forgot the plan and went on kissing her. Sometime later it came back to him that he was the one in charge of this particular seduction, and he slid one hand along the sweet soft inside of her leg to the juncture of her thighs where the elastic band of her underwear made a boundary. On one side was the silky skin of her leg stretched over taut straining muscle as she held herself above him. On the other were the curls and folds of her, concealing sensitive, aching flesh. If he touched her, even through the scrap of cotton and lace she wore, he knew she would come.

He kissed her again and again, keeping her distracted long enough to shift his hand and cup her sex in his palm. Through the soft, thin fabric of her panties he pressed and squeezed and circled until she broke the kiss and with a sharp sweet cry sank down against his hand and began to shudder. She pressed her face into the hollow between his jaw and shoulder, and he did not let her go until the last tremors of her release died away.

His erection throbbed with unfulfilled desire, but Josh felt oddly pleased and happy. He pulled Emma close to lie spent and warm in his arms, on the edge of drowsiness, her body slack.

It made him smile to have rendered her idle for once. Emma at peace, Emma not busy, Emma not in charge, not struggling or resisting. He let his hand drift up and down her back.

The air cooled around them. A distant wave broke with a sharp crack, and she shifted in his arms, lifting her head. "You meant this all along, didn't you?"

"I told you it wouldn't be about kale salad."

She gave him a look that said she was back in control of herself, and she slipped out of his hold. "I've got to get back to Max." Pausing at his door to pick up her wet towel, she shifted the jingling, awkward bundle in her arms. She promised, "I'll wash this tomorrow."

He watched her go and finally knew exactly what he wanted from her. He wanted her to make love to him in the same competent, no-nonsense, take-charge way she handled her car or her kid. And he wanted her to admit what she wanted from him and to love getting it.

Chapter Fifteen

Late Friday afternoon Emma looked down from her living room as Tony Orlandi finished hooking her dead car to his tow truck. Technically, the car was his. Two years earlier she had talked him into letting her take it off his lot by proving to him that she could make the thing run and promising to bring it back if it ever failed. It was a lesser Italian make, but her grandfather had a similar, more costly version in his collection. Her first car had been Italian. Her grandfather had given it to her on the condition that she learn how it worked and how to do its routine maintenance.

Tony was sixty-something, with a cloud of white hair around his long lean face, a smoker's teeth, and a wiry build covered by loose dark blue coveralls. He was a connoisseur of vintage Italian vehicles with an encyclopedic knowledge of parts and where to get them. He kept dozens of old cars on his lot and did business with hundreds of classic car enthusiasts, and that was how Emma had known where to find him when she'd needed a car. He had not recognized her in her death metal gear as the girl who had grown up visiting his shop over the years with her grandfather.

As Tony finished rigging the car, Huntington pulled up in his Rover. The red and blue tow truck blocked the driveway, but Josh simply pulled up farther along the block. Emma tried not to watch as he parked in a tight spot with his usual effortlessness and sauntered back apparently undisturbed by the inconvenience.

It was the first time she'd seen him since he'd kissed and touched her, and seeing him started the wanting again. Just watching him move in his careless way threw a secret on switch somewhere inside her that set her nerves humming.

In the three days since she'd asked him to help her stop feeling turned on, she'd had time to do some serious thinking—mostly about the pickle she'd got herself into by trading that massage for his promise to keep away from Max. She reviewed the facts of what they'd done. Emma knew the names of the acts and of her response, but when she said those words in her mind, they lacked some content that the experience contained. Naming an orgasm and having one—two different things. She could dismiss sex as overrated when it was just words and a humiliating memory from the past, but now she was not sure she could resist it so easily, not now when sex meant Huntington.

He glanced up at her unit, and she thought about his mouth. Just that. Huntington's mouth. It was a mouth like any other, but he had kissed her with that mouth in a particular way that she was not likely to forget. A fact she now knew about him was that he was very good at kissing.

It was just a fact, though. It shouldn't matter to her at all.

She gave a little wave from the window. Huntington didn't come up the stairs. Instead, he nodded to Tony, who wiped his hands on a red rag and stopped to chat, the door of his truck cab hanging open, the big engine idling.

In a minute the two were talking. Huntington shoved his dark glasses up on his blond head and got that look he wore when he was *noticing* things. Emma's pulse picked up, but she was being paranoid. Huntington wouldn't care who took away her wreck. He considered it an eyesore. He would never figure out the connection that linked her to Tony; even Tony had not figured out how she'd found him.

The conversation ended, and Tony hopped in his truck. Huntington stood looking at the door panel with Tony's phone number in bright blue numbers until the vehicle pulled out and drove off. Emma's car disappeared down the block. Now she had no car, and *that* was the thing to worry about, not Huntington standing at the base of the stairs tapping something into his phone. He looked up again and caught Emma's gaze. From where she stood, she could see his big leather chair.

She was definitely remembering too much from their Tuesday night encounter.

Emma retreated to her kitchen and pulled a can of cleanser from under the sink, but the facts as she knew them played in her mind like one of those endless loops on the TV screens in an electronics store. Huntington admitted that he "ate the marshmallow every time." Huntington couldn't be interested in her ordinary, broke, child-rearing self other than as a convenient partner for sex, and they hadn't had sex exactly, at least he hadn't, so he could not have felt that desperate longing she did. He was probably texting some beautiful woman even now, not taking Tony's number in order to learn more of the truth about his tenant.

She heard him come up the stairs and enter his apartment but went on reviewing the facts. She had believed herself tough and strong and immune to sex. She had wanted to believe she could give Huntington that massage and remain unaffected by his long, lean body, but no. It hadn't mattered that she'd worked on her car until her back ached and she felt dizzy with hunger. She had not been able to eat or sleep, only to think about wanting to be near him, to touch him. It hadn't mattered that Max was asleep in his bed. Emma now realized that no one had ever locked her alone in a room with a marshmallow before. She'd never been tested.

So, Huntington was right about sex and she was wrong. She had stood in that shower, her whole being focused on him, wanting him, imagining him beside her, around her. She hadn't thought about Max once. She hadn't even thought about Max while sitting in that big leather chair, at least not until her body recovered from feeling so good. Apparently her brain could not focus on her child and Huntington at the same time.

Huntington. He had held her and touched her and pressed his long, lean body to hers. He had known what she wanted and how to give it to her with practiced competence, and she'd melted like an ice cream cone on a hot day on the pier. But he was also a man who had been showering with women since he was fifteen. A few touches were a big deal to Emma, gallons of water in the drought of her experience. To him those touches were meaningless drops, throwaways in an endless series of shower partners and who knew what else.

One part of her wanted to take charge and make him feel as crazed with wanting as she was. But that was nuts. She had plans and goals that did not include her sexy landlord.

Max. Max was supposed to be her surefire strategy for staying on track, for getting the work done, for sticking with the plan. His existence reminded her of all that she wanted and needed in life. Unfortunately, the deal she'd made with Huntington for Max had a really big downside, and now she was breaking her own rules big-time.

Emma shook off the thought. Huntington was staying away from Max, and she would have to stay strong even with her sex god of a landlord living in the next unit. She turned to the stove and sprinkled blue-white cleansing powder around the wells of the burners, took a wet sponge, and started scrubbing. Josh Huntington could wait until she got her stove clean, really clean.

* * *

Josh stepped into the shower and adjusted the nozzle head to a spray like hard cold needles.

Tonight he had a date with Bethany Elaine Douglass, the first of his mother's picks. He would be escorting her to a fashion show at a grand dame of an old hotel in Beverly Hills, and he had little doubt he could be escorting her to something else afterward. That was just what he'd wanted, just what he'd intended when he agreed to go along with his mother's plan. The problem was, taking a shower meant thinking about Emma.

Just turning on the water started it, thoughts about what they had done the other night…and what they hadn't. The water was cool, the pressure hard. Josh hurried the process. No sense in fantasizing about what might have been. He'd helped Emma over a hurdle, and they'd gone back to keeping their distance for three days. If Emma had decided that she and her son needed a responsible man in their lives, he couldn't blame her. Not that he was going to tell her that he'd lost his trust and was now willing to take his mother's money to date socialites.

In fact, he didn't know why he'd told Emma anything about himself, including that little bit of his sexual history, about his showering with his piano teacher. He didn't usually share anything of his past with a woman. Maybe he'd wanted to level the playing field because he'd guessed more of her history. Most single women her age would have had several partners and a long-term relationship or two, but Emma, who had become a mom young without much experience apparently, was set up to lose this contest they were having. Deprivation and lack of experience made her vulnerable, and he knew exactly how to use that weakness against her. The slightest stimulation hit her hard. Even now he'd bet she was staring cross-eyed at the marshmallow. Well, when she wasn't beating herself up for letting him kiss and touch her.

He turned off the water, reached for a towel, and remembered that she had his other one—which of course she'd return some day, which meant that she'd knock on his door. So, maybe he needed to give her some advice, some way to resist. One of them had to have a plan. Otherwise they were going to eat the marshmallow, and both of them were going to regret it.

* * *

He knocked on Emma's door on his way out. She answered with a can of cleanser in one hand and a sponge in the other. She took in his tux with a single sweep of her gaze then leaned her head out the door to look down at the driveway.

"Where's your limo?"

"No limo tonight, but I am seeing someone." He held up his phone with a picture of Bethany.

She glanced at it. "Are you trying to warn me off in case I had any illusions about your intentions?"

"I think I made my intentions perfectly clear, but I'll do my best to stay away, keep busy—"

"Sleep with someone else?"

"—let you have your own life."

"Thanks."

"Listen, you might try it," he continued, trying to ignore her dry tone. "Try seeing someone else that is. I know a responsible, unattached guy, late twenties, local, funny, didn't go to Canyon." Of course, he knew as soon as he said it that he would never introduce her to Beau Lassiter. He would never introduce her to anyone. Not like that.

"You think I'm going to give in to you, don't you? You think I don't stand a chance against your charms, that I'll knock on your door and eat the marshmallow. You are *so* full of yourself."

She stepped back and grabbed the edge of the door with the hand that held the sponge, but he put up one palm to stop her before she slammed the door in his face. "Just to be clear, Emma. If you knock on my door again, you will eat the marshmallow."

* * *

From the moment that Bethany Elaine Douglass slid with practiced ease into his Rover, Josh knew she was used to getting her man. She was also everything he had often sought: tall, blonde, fit, and flawlessly made up. She clearly had never lacked for male attention, and it occurred to Josh that Bethany might be expecting his mother to make a sizable contribution to the prom dress charity.

She checked him out thoroughly. "So, I hear you are something of a legend…" She let the word hang in the air between them. "…as an event planner."

"Am I?" He glanced at her. She fingered a heart-shaped, diamond-studded gold pendent nestled between spectacular breasts.

"Everyone is still talking about how you pulled off the Canyon gala in spite of the scandal. I'd love to hear how you did it."

"Lots of alums and their families are very loyal to the school."

Bethany smiled, clearly not interested in the details. "Maybe. But the real legend about you is your eighteenth birthday. Apparently that was one amazing Aloha party. I heard that everyone in your class got 'lei-ed.'"

Josh laughed, remembering his friends wearing leis to Canyon after that particular birthday. "Where did you hear that?"

"A woman has her sources." Across the Rover's front seat, Bethany gave his thigh a friendly squeeze. "I definitely want your opinion on the event tonight."

"Glad to share trade secrets. But you'll have to fill me in on your organization."

Bethany was happy to do so. Did he know that the average cost of prom attendance in the United States was easily nine hundred dollars? For some girls, that cost put the prom of their dreams completely out of reach. Bethany had set out to change that, one prom dress at a time, and by the time they arrived at the hotel Josh had to wonder whether his mother expected him to go to bed with Bethany or join the board of her charitable organization.

At the entrance to the ballroom, a young reporter with a TV mic and a hovering cameraman asked Bethany to explain what she was wearing and why she had devoted herself to the cause.

"I was a prom queen, so I enjoyed all the fun and all the glamour of that special night in a girl's life, and I just want to make sure that every girl has a chance to feel the same thrill. Each year our organization gathers over five hundred gently used dresses to donate to girls in the greater L.A. area who couldn't afford a dress otherwise. With the funds we raise from tonight's fashion show, each girl that Prom Perfect supports will have her hair and makeup done and receive a voucher for a safe ride home."

"I notice your unusual pendent." The reporter pointed her mic at the diamond-studded pendant.

"A gift from my parents for getting this project going. I wear it to all our events." Bethany leaned in to Josh and whispered, "Remind me to tell you what's on the back."

They both smiled for the flashing cameras and passed into the ballroom.

A master of the air kiss, Bethany knew how to work a room and never leave a lipstick-smudged cheek behind. Josh's role in these encounters was to smile and nod and accept a Bethany touch as she explained her views on entrepreneurship for good: "Social media is changing philanthropy, but there will always be a need for someone who can throw a great party." Josh had to give her points for knowing her world, and for a prodigious memory for personal details about others. She reminded him of…him.

L.A.'s elite schools were well-represented in the crowd. Bethany introduced him repeatedly as the man who pulled off the Canyon gala in spite of the school scandal, and Josh saw a fair number of Canyon donors he'd tapped in the past year. Whenever he met someone who knew him, the question was always about what he was doing now. But as Bethany conferred with the head of catering, Josh stood in a circle of familiar faces and felt oddly out of touch with them, as if in the months he'd spent working at Canyon the whole world had passed him by.

"Still planning parties? Did you help Bethany with this one?"

"She's amazing. I think she did it all on her own."

"I heard you'd dropped out and gone south or something. You in Cabo now?"

"I'm still around—doing another event, actually."

"So you're an event planner? I thought your dad set you up in business."

Josh excused himself to head for the open bar, but even there he found no escape. A guy he'd gone to camp with asked, "So, you and *Bethany*. Dude! You always did know how to score with women."

She was beautiful, but as the evening wore on Bethany treated his person like an accessory that needed constant adjusting.

She straightened his black tie or shifted him from one side to the other as they moved. In his head he heard his mother calling him "an agreeable piece of eye candy."

After the brief runway show and the longer dinner, Bethany leaned across him to speak to another guest and the chain of her necklace became caught in one of the studs of his shirt. As Josh reached to help her untangle her jewelry, his hands brushed her chest. Her perfume enveloped him.

"You know, if you turn the pendant over you'll find my initials."

He reached for the pendent and turned it over in his palm, his fingers inches from Bethany's magnificent attributes.

"My initials spell BED," she whispered.

Here it was, the answer to his months-long drought brought on by taking the Canyon job and trying to do something meaningful with his life. What had he accomplished? He'd lost his trust and ended up living in a stucco box connected with people whose net worth could hardly keep them in vanilla lattes. His sexual GPS had malfunctioned to point him in the direction of his ink-and-metal-wearing, don't-mess-with-me tenant in Viking battle gear. Tonight he could say yes to soft, silky-smooth Bethany and get right back on track.

He smiled and settled the diamond pendant back into its perfect nest. If Bethany wanted to extend their evening beyond the Prom Perfect benefit, he was game.

As he drove her home, he complimented her and she opened up about the food, the table décor, and the program. She was a little drunk, maybe, and a lot satisfied with the evening's success, but she deserved a decent amount of credit for that and he knew how much work it could be. Her hand roamed his thigh.

On the porch of her neat bungalow in Larchmont Village, he gave her a kiss to get things started. He turned her toward the door and got it open, but when she turned her back to ask for a little assistance with getting her zippers down, it all felt too easy, like a path he'd been down dozens of times with his eyes closed. Worse, the evening flashed through his mind leading up to this moment, and he saw himself as the icing on Bethany's cake, something she could have because she was used to getting whatever she wanted.

Abruptly he needed an escape and saw his chance to engineer one. Bethany was definitely feeling a post-party high, and her mind was working more slowly than it had been. He warned her not to let any man take advantage of her tipsiness, and with a gentle shove he sent her inside. Then he turned and sauntered back to his car, yanking off his black tie. With the Rover's capabilities and a few well-timed lights on Wilshire Boulevard, he thought he had probably hit the 405 before Bethany figured out that her offer had been refused.

His mother was going to be seriously unhappy with him.

Chapter Sixteen

Max dawdled over a bowl of oatmeal and walnuts, his usual
Saturday morning breakfast. With his spoon he pushed the walnuts
down into the cereal and watched the milk fill in the holes, and
Emma checked on him in between putting on her death metal gear
for the store. She was scheduled for extra hours today, and Maria's
cousin Claudia had called and was coming to take Max.

"Why can't I go to the record store with you?" Max was
making his reluctance to go with the woman clear.

"Because I can't pay attention to you in the store, and there's
nothing for you to do there."

"But I don't want to go away."

Claudia was from their first neighborhood. She worked
weekdays as a nanny/housekeeper for a family on the Palos Verdes
hill.

"You aren't 'going away.' You are going to our old
neighborhood where you know lots of kids. Eat."

"I don't like oatmeal."

Emma walked away. This wasn't about the oatmeal, she told
herself. Her kid wasn't going to starve. He would have a good time
once he got to Claudia's, and Emma would earn the last of the
month's rent and with luck a pass to the Grindstone concert, which
was now only a week away.

She stood in the bathroom and concentrated on applying a set
of fake tattoos to the side of her neck. Right now she and Max were
having a low time. Josh Huntington had done nothing to encourage
Max's interest in him except to exist, and Emma had done her best to
hustle Max off to school each morning, and to occupy him between
dinner and bedtime, but their conversations had come around to the
beach and their landlord almost every day, with Max insisting that he
wanted to see Josh.

She would have to make it up to Max this summer. Once she
met her father she would be moving on. She would quit the record
store job and leave this apartment. She would square things with her
grandparents—she owed them that much—and then she and Max
would start their new life with no more fears. The past was over. For
seven years now she had made her own way; she was a grownup, not
a teenager, and she'd earned the right to make her own decisions. If

her grandparents wanted Max in their lives she would be glad to reconnect with them. She could forgive them now, especially because she realized her grandparents had lost a child. That loss had shaped the way they raised Emma, the decisions they'd made for her, the control they had insisted upon—

"Mom!"

A shout from Max brought her running, and she heard male voices on the landing before someone knocked on her landlord's door.

Max scrambled down from his chair. "It's the Bookman!"

"Max, stop!"

It was too late. Her son flung the door open on two teenaged boys in blue and gold striped ties and blue Oxford cloth shirts, the shirts hanging out over their khakis. Huntington clones. Emma realized the boys were from Canyon, though what they were doing so far south she couldn't guess.

The boys turned to them.

"Hi, Max." The taller of the two boys, dark-haired and skinny with drug-dealer dark glasses, stuck out his hand, and he and Max did the Canyon handshake thing. "This is my friend Tyler."

"Hey, Max." The blond boy also shook Max's hand; then both boys offered Emma nods and polite smiles that hid any surprise at her death metal look.

"Hi again, Ms. Gray," said the dark-skinned boy. "I'm Ulysses. We met at the Center."

Her landlord's door opened. Huntington stood there in his black boxers, gorgeously unshaven, his hair uncombed.

The older boys faced him. "Hey, Josh, sorry to wake you. Annie said you'd help us with our song before the party today."

Huntington gave an easy grin and opened his door wide. "Sure. Let me get some coffee."

The boys moved, and Max bolted forward as well. "Can I come, too?"

His six-year-old voice boomed in the tiny entry.

Huntington looked at Emma over Max's head. His neutral expression said it was her call. She shook her head.

He squatted down to face Max at eye level, his hands clasped lightly together between his knees. His whole focus was on Max. That was the danger and the charm of him. He freely gave his attention to the other person. She didn't know when he'd come in from his date the night before, sometime long after midnight. He should look awkward or haggard, but he didn't. His version of bed hair and stubble was just as appealing as his dressed-up self.

"Sorry, buddy," he said. "Your mom's got plans for today. You've got to do what she says."

"I don't want to go with Claudia! Can't I stay here with you and the Bookman?"

"Come on, Max," Emma said to her son's back, "you've got to get ready to go."

Her boy didn't move, and Emma pulled him into a hug and drew him back into their unit.

Huntington closed his door.

Max flung himself out of her arms and spun to face her. "We don't ever do what I want."

"This summer—"

"That's what you always say, Mom. I want to do something fun now. I know those boys. The Bookman helps kids. He knows Annie. Why can they go to Josh's and I can't?"

"They are his friends."

"Josh is my friend, too."

"Not today, Maxie."

He crossed his arms over his small chest and stalked to the window. "Someday I'm going to do what I want."

From Huntington's unit came the sound of male voices harmonizing. They sang the Beach Boys classic, "Good Vibrations," and Max stood at the window listening. Emma could hear Huntington's deeper voice going over a part of the song, teaching the boys how to do it. He was explaining key changes and telling them how to hit the right notes with confidence. There was laughter and more singing. Emma moved the cold oatmeal to the sink, and she put an extra slice of cheese on Max's sandwich. Her kid would be okay.

Claudia arrived while Emma and Max were fighting over shoes. With practiced-mom cool, she coaxed Max out of his bad humor and offered to take a load of wash with her. Relieved and grateful, Emma buckled Max into one seat of Claudia's minivan and told him to have fun.

Unfortunately, she left for work with the Beach Boys' lyrics stuck in her head. *"I'm pickin' up good vibrations. She's giving me excitations."*

* * *

At five, when Josh stepped out his door heading for the party, he got a pair of texts. The first was a thank-you from Ulysses, and he halted at the top of the stairs in the heat of the still blazing sun to text a reply. The boys were already at the party, impatient for him to show up. The second text, from his mother's executive assistant, he deleted.

As he looked up from his phone, a dark-haired woman in her forties labored up the stairs, a little breathless. A substantial metallic gold purse sagged off one shoulder, and a white plastic laundry basket as wide as the stairs slowed her climb.

Josh took the woman's basket as she negotiated the top step. "Looking for Emma? She's at work, I think."

"I know." The woman smiled and pressed a hand to her chest. "I'm Claudia, the babysitter. Max is asleep in the car. I'm just going to deliver this laundry before I bring him in." She glanced down at the driveway. "I didn't block you in, did I?"

"Not at all." Josh held the basket while Claudia found the key in her purse and unlocked the door. "So, you're the woman who's known Emma and Max a long time?"

"Oh no. I am the cousin. It is Maria who has known Max from he is born."

Josh carried the basket into Emma's unit and set it down, and a few more questions earned him quite a story while Claudia dropped her purse and opened the windows to let in the afternoon breeze.

So, seven years ago a woman named Maria Felix had taken a pregnant teenage runaway under her wing and helped her to keep her child. Claudia's story explained a lot, but it didn't answer the question of Emma's past before Max, before she struck out on her own. Josh still didn't know why Emma had left her home at seventeen or who Max's father was.

* * *

Josh took a moment as he left the Rover and strolled toward the modest ranch house on a cul de sac in North Redondo Beach to reflect on his friend Sloan's amazing good fortune. The loner of the Canyon class of '05 had definitely done well.

At her door, Sloan's mother Mae welcomed him. He hadn't seen her since high school and not often then. Mae Sloan was as trim, dark-haired, and straightforward as Josh remembered. She'd worked as a waitress most of Sloan's life and, as Josh had learned from Sloan in the fall, she had rejected the villa on the Palos Verdes hill that he had originally purchased for her with his tech fortune. She was, however, wearing uber-pricey, high-heeled designer sandals that made Josh smile. At least she was spending some of Sloan's money.

A mutt of a dog with a wagging tail jumped on him until Mae called the animal off. "Josh, come in. No date?"

"I'm a free man tonight."

Mae laughed. "Well, free man, let me hug you. We owe you so much. I have been wanting to thank you for weeks for setting my stubborn boy on the path to happiness." She let him go and linked her arm in his, drawing him down a step across a small living room and out onto a crowded patio. "Come and meet everyone."

"Huntington, you're late!"

He heard his name shouted simultaneously by several people. Annie James came forward, kissed his cheek, and took his hand. "Don't listen to them. You're right on time. The boys are about to sing." She gave him a quick hug. "And be sure to talk with Louisa. She's going to beg you to take that job at the Center."

Sloan came up, shook his hand, and extracted his bride-to-be from Josh's hold. Josh looked around and saw the guests were not the usual Canyon crowd. No, Bethany Elaine Douglass wouldn't fit in, but without her death metal maiden gear Emma Gray would look right at home. She and Mae Sloan probably had a few qualities in common.

Beau Lassiter grinned at Josh and offered him a cold beer. As he took hold of it, everyone else on the crowded patio shuffled back to leave an open space in front of a small raised garden of olive and citrus trees that sloped upward to a vine-covered wall. Annie and

Will were pushed into the opening, and then the C-Notes filed in, wearing blazers, ties, khakis, and grins on their faces.

Josh felt a moment of pride for having been a C-Note back in his day. The fifteen boys in this group had been the ones to come to the rescue when old Headmaster Chambers tried to expel Ulysses from Canyon. Their protest had brought the TV news crews to the campus gates, and then Annie had written a story for the newspaper about the strength of the boys' unlikely friendship. That story had helped rally people to support Canyon despite the scandal.

The boys started right in with "Good Vibrations" and then worked their way through their set while people nodded and sang along when prompted. They ended with a serenade of Annie, a duet that got whistles and claps from the crowd. When it was all done, Josh gave both Ulysses and Tyler a thumbs up for getting all the key changes right.

Chapter Seventeen

Leo wanted to see Emma at the end of her shift.

Emma tried not to look at the clock. The sun was taking its lazy, blazing time descending. It still hung in the sky above the tops of the buildings on the west side of the Avenue, sending hot slanting rays down into the front of Daddy Rock, fading the old album covers lined up there. By now Claudia would have brought Max home and fed him. Emma would get home in time to read him a story and make him forget the spat between them that morning. She knew Max liked to have the last word in any mother-son conflict, but she also knew that angry words that troubled her for hours passed from his consciousness in minutes.

There were genuine worries she'd faced as a mom, and then there was stuff she just had to roll with like a bumpy ride over potholes. Max's threat to do what he wanted had probably faded from his mind as soon as he started playing with the kids from the old neighborhood. It might be hard to say no to Max, but she was right to keep him from their landlord. It was Parenting 101 to deny your kid the sweet treat or the shiny toy so that he could discover things of real value, and she reminded herself that she had lots of practice saying no to dazzling donuts with colored sprinkles or bright plastic toys with tiny pieces that would break in the first hour of play. Josh Huntington was a similar trap—for both of them.

She glanced up at Leo through the glass front of his mezzanine office looking for some sign of why he wanted to see her. The way he ate a crumbling burrito while peering at his computer gave her no clue.

The featured artists of the day were the Swedish death metal group Entombed. Emma was supposed to push a CD they had done with their rivals, Candlemass, the doom masters, where the two bands covered each other's songs. She was hoarse from making her sales pitch.

The customer listening to her at the moment turned the CD over in his hand and gave it back to her. "They're okay, but they're not Grindstone, are they?"

She could feel Leo watching her as the customer walked away. Daddy Rock employees were supposed to go after the customer three times and offer another product. *You might also like…*

When she looked up, Leo waved her up to his office.

The room reeked of burrito and dead coffee. Leo looked up at her from behind his desk as she entered. "How many Entombed units did you sell?"

"Six." She didn't blink. A fact was a fact.

"In five hours?" Leo shook his head. "I'm going to be straight with you, Emma." He leveled a frown at her from under his bushy brows. "You may look the part, but you're not holding your own on the sales floor. And you don't belong backstage at the Grindstone gig, so whatever you're thinking about getting close to Saxon, you'd better unthink it."

"Leo—"

He held up one slightly pudgy, be-ringed hand. "You're not the sort of bird Saxon looks at twice. You could flash your kumquats in his face and he wouldn't blink."

Emma shook her head. "Leo, I've explained that I don't want to sleep with Saxon. He's…well, he's old enough to be my father."

Leo's gaze narrowed. "You're not thinking of slapping Saxon with some kind of paternity suit, are you? Nobody's won at that game, believe me, and dozens have tried."

Emma's phone vibrated in her pocket. It could only be Claudia. She thought of the litany of reasons her babysitter would call: blood, vomiting, unconsciousness, visible bones… She put her hand in her pocket as casually as she could and said, "Leo, I have to take a call."

She stepped into the doorway with her back to him and got Claudia on callback.

The woman spoke rapidly, shifting from Spanish to English. She'd lost Max. She didn't know where he was. She had parked the car in the driveway and left him there asleep, taken the laundry into the apartment, and come back to the car to find him gone.

Gone?

Emma's stomach clenched and her knees gave way. She reached out and grabbed hold of the doorframe as she sank. Her heart thudded once hard in her chest and squeezed the air out of her lungs.

"Did you check my neighbor's house? The unit across from mine?" The words came out of a dry throat. Max knew the rules. He would not go willingly with a stranger, but he'd go anywhere with Huntington.

Claudia explained that she'd met the neighbor, who had helped her with the laundry, but that he had driven away in his car just before she discovered Max gone. There was no one nearby. She had knocked on the doors of the next buildings, and no one had seen Max.

Emma hoisted herself back up, her legs unsteady. If Huntington had taken Max, she would rip him apart with her mother fangs for breaking their deal and causing her such worry. If Huntington hadn't taken Max, she…she couldn't think what she would do.

* * *

Laughter had taken over Mae Sloan's tiny patio, a lot of it at her son's expense. The amazing thing to Josh was that Sloan, who'd had a boulder-sized chip on his shoulder at Canyon, didn't mind the ribbing. Sloan looked free of the past. His college buddies, his friend Beau, and his work colleagues could joke all they liked about his intensity and his pride at how much in love he was, and the guy's happiness was like a force field against any barb. He stood in the midst of friends, no longer a loner, no longer alone. How much things had changed since high school.

Again Josh thought of the moment he'd tried to get Emma to come to this party, and about her odd objection to Canyon. At the time he'd thought she was objecting to the excesses and privilege of the school. He suddenly wondered whether Max's absent father was an alum.

It seemed unlikely that Emma had any connection with Canyon in the past. Emma, with her frugal indifference to luxuries and her determination to earn whatever came her way, came from a world as remote as possible from the Canyon crowd Josh knew. Yet, certain encounters came back to him. Josh had hooked up with women who'd crossed his path as they waited tables or served drinks or did some other kind of work in the background at parties and school events, and it was possible that Max's father had not been

Emma's high school boyfriend at all but someone like Josh, someone thinking only of the moment, of giving and getting pleasure and moving on, of staying focused on his own life knowing another hookup would not change anything for him and unable to imagine it could change anything for his partner.

He wondered if Max's father had been a guy like him. Whoever he was, the guy had not taught Emma anything about good sex.

Josh almost didn't hear his phone through the noise of the party. He put his beer down and pulled it out, checked the number then slipped through the crowd back into the house. Moving down the only hallway, he fled the laughter and loud talk and swiped his thumb across the phone.

"Emma? What's going on?"

"I've lost Max. I think he went somewhere on his own—"

The rest was lost in another burst of happy noise from the patio outside. Josh cupped the phone to his ear, stunned by a rapid sequence of fearful possibilities flashing through his mind.

"Do you have him?" Emma asked. Her voice was hollow.

"No."

She hung up.

Josh swore and rang her back. "Tell me what's going on."

She could barely speak to fill in the details, but she did. "Where could he go?"

"The beach," Josh said. That was the forbidden place.

Emma said nothing in reply.

"Let me call my friend Nate, the lifeguard. Where are you?"

Emma told him.

"Stay there. I'll be there in ten minutes."

Josh headed for the front door, stopping only to tell Mae he had to help a friend find a lost boy. He asked her to save some BBQ for him, but she urged him on his way, and from the Rover Josh sent Nate a text to see if the guy was on duty or knew who was. Nate texted back that he was in his usual tower, so Josh called him and told him to be on the lookout for a blond six-year-old named Max.

The usual start and stop traffic on the Coast Highway gave Josh lots of time to veer between sympathy for Emma and anger at her continued low opinion of him. Max's wandering off was not his fault! Of course, he had probably distracted Claudia just long enough for Max to make an escape. He replayed the little scene with the babysitter over and over in his head.

He had reached the south end of the Avenue, just blocks from his destination, when he got a text from Nate: FOUND HIM.

A tightness in Josh's chest released.

At the next stoplight he called Emma to tell her that Max was found. He parked in the loading zone in front of Daddy Rock and left the Rover open. Inside the store, he strode through the aisles and straight for the back. Taking the stairs up, he reached the mezzanine level and spotted Emma in the third office, in an apparent dispute with a guy with bushy gray hair behind a desk. Josh realized the guy was her boss, Leo Grant.

He stuck his head through the open office door. "Hey, Emma."

She spun toward him. "Max?"

"Hey, you. Out! Customers downstairs," Grant yelled. "We're talking here."

Not surprised that the guy didn't remember him from their conversations about setting up the Grindstone concert, Josh ignored him and reached for Emma. "He's okay."

"Where is he?"

"At the beach."

She sagged a little in his hold, but he kept them moving.

"Emma, he's okay. He's with my lifeguard friend Nate. They found him playing in the sand. He did not go in the water. I'll take you right to him."

"Emma, we're not done here," Grant called after them. "You can't just walk off the job."

Emma twisted to call back. "It's my son, Leo. I've got to go to him."

"Fine. You're done, Emma. Don't come back."

Josh and Emma did not talk in the car. Emma sat staring straight ahead, her arms folded over her middle, her hands clasping her elbows. Josh finally made her call Claudia. She would be less frantic if she had something to do.

When she had the other woman on the phone, Emma came back to herself, looking out the window at the beach beyond. Josh pointed out Nate's lifeguard tower as they pulled up in the parking lot behind the Power Plant brewery, and before he turned the engine off, she slipped out of the car and scrambled over the low Strand wall onto the sand, headed for the pale blue wooden tower.

Josh kicked off his loafers, tossed them in the Rover, and closed up the car. As he followed Emma, the sun sent eyeball-stabbing shafts of glare off her hardware. A strong cool afternoon breeze off the ocean blew against her as she struggled across the sand, whipping her hair back from her face, and he caught up when she stopped to kick off her heavy boots halfway across the beach.

Max sat at the base of Nate's tower with another guard in red trunks and a windbreaker. The boy was asking the guy questions. He stopped when he saw Emma and jumped up.

"Mom, I'm okay."

She sank to her knees and pulled him into a fierce embrace.

"Don't be mad, Mom. I really, really like the beach." He patted his mother's shoulder.

"You can't ever go alone, Maxie."

"But you never take me."

"You promised to wait till summer."

"I was mad. You were never going to let me."

"I…" She hugged him again. This time, he stiffened in her arms.

Ah. Josh understood. Emma was one tough mom, but Max had a kid's instinct for applying pressure to any flaw in a parental argument. He was rooting for the boy.

"Can I go in the water now that you're here?"

Emma leaned back and looked at him. "You broke the rules. We have to go home."

Max twisted away. "But you break the rules. You don't want me to see Josh, but you see Josh. You went to his house. I saw you."

Emma looked equally stricken and stubborn, trapped by her own rules. Josh sank to his knees between them and said, "No fair, buddy. Grownups get to do things that kids can't."

"Kids go to the beach." Max gestured with a sweep of one arm. "Why can't I?"

It was an undeniable truth. In front of them, a boy no bigger than Max flopped on a boogie board to catch the shore break. Two small girls chased each other, splashing through ankle-deep water with scarcely a glance from their sun-worshipping mothers. A mom with a squealing toddler in her lap sat where the ends of the waves could wash over their legs. Josh could see the boy's logic perfectly.

"I didn't go in the water, Mom. But I want to. I want to be like regular kids."

Emma's anguished gaze met Josh's. Whatever fear held her back, she obviously didn't know how to let it go.

"Emma, can I help?" he asked. "You don't have to go near the water, but would you let me take Max down to get his feet wet? I won't let go. We'll stay right here in front of the lifeguard tower."

"Say yes, Mom, please."

They stood facing each other between the glare of the sun and the burning sand and the indifferent gazes of Nate and his lifeguard buddy. Without the audience, Emma would likely let him have it for interfering.

He faced her down. The chill breeze whipped her clothes and hair against her and brought happy squeals of children splashing in the surf. "Come with us, Emma."

Josh stood and took one of Max's hands in his while he reached out the other for her. He didn't know if she could reach across that space and take the hand he offered, but he said again, "Come on. Get your feet wet. I won't let you go."

"We don't have towels," she pointed out.

"We'll dry."

"We'll get sand all over your car."

"I know someone who does great car detailing."

"You're dressed for a date...or...something."

"Actually, you're the overdressed one. Let's get some of this hardware off of you." Josh tugged her toward him and reached up to undo the fake piercings, first one ear and then the other while Emma stood with her leather-gloved fists clenched at her sides. Not wanting to lose the moment, he turned to Max and said, "Ask Nate if he has a bag or a bucket in his tower that we could use to keep some stuff in."

Max let out a whoop and scrambled to the foot of Nate's tower to shout the request up to him. Josh heard the exchange and a plop as something dropped into the sand.

"Here's a bucket," Max announced.

"Good work," Josh told the boy, but he concentrated on Emma. He took her hands and pulled off the rings and the black gloves and reached for her wide leather belt with its threatening metal studs. Undressing a woman on a public beach under the professional gaze of two lifeguards was a new experience, but he wasn't going to stop. If Emma was letting him touch her, he was going to do this.

"Max," he called, "what's the water temperature today? Check on Nate's chalkboard."

Max dashed to read the answer and returned to report, "60 degrees."

Cool enough to take care of Josh's reaction to her once they got into the surf. By giving up her armor, Emma was having her usual effect on him.

"Thanks, Max. Emma, put your hand on my shoulder and let's get rid of those fishnet stockings."

She glanced back across the sand. "I left my boots behind."

"You don't need them. You got fired. The stockings have to go, too."

For a brief moment their eyes met, hers full of doubt and appeal. His, he was pretty sure, were just full of naked desire.

She finally did as he requested, putting a hand on his shoulder while he steadied her at the waist. When Emma reached up under her black Band-Aid of a spandex skirt and tugged on the ragged fishnet pantyhose until they sagged around her knees, he knelt and helped her out of them.

He emptied his own pockets into the white plastic bucket Nate had offered them while Max rolled in the sand at his side. He had Max stuff his shirt into the bucket and put it under the lifeguard tower.

"Ready?" he asked.

Emma shook her head, but she took the hand he offered. Max gave a little leap and grabbed Josh's other hand.

Josh took a firm hold and pulled the pair toward the dark ragged line of debris the ocean chewed up and spat out with each wave: shiny brown kelp pods and leaves, colored bits of plastic litter, empty crab shells. That line marked the farthest reach of the water where the waves spent themselves before the ocean sucked them back again.

They crossed over onto wet sand that was blissfully cool underfoot. Josh made them run forward to where the foaming heads of the waves hissed around their ankles and paused there to let

Emma enjoy the contrast of cool water and hot sun. Max understood
the game instantly: Run forward to catch a wave, run back when it
comes at you. It was a game of brinksmanship with the ocean like
the game Josh and Emma were playing with their attraction, chasing
each receding wave of longing down the slope and then scrambling
back when it turned and rushed at them.

Max tugged them further out. "Can we jump the waves?"

"Sure." Josh was all for it. He was not above using Max to
get Emma wet again. Whatever worked.

It didn't take long. The inevitable stronger wave in the set got
a second momentum and foamed up at them, faster and harder than
expected. As they scrambled back, awkwardly linked, Emma
stumbled and landed on her bottom in the sand. Josh let himself go
and pulled Max down beside him without breaking his grip on either
the boy or his mother.

The wave came on and swirled up around their waists, lifting
them briefly and tossing them up the beach before stranding them to
hiss and foam its way back toward the shore break. Beside Josh,
Emma tried and failed to struggle to her feet, her clothes soaked and
clinging.

"Again! Again!" Max cried.

Emma turned and buried her face in Josh's shoulder. She
began to cry, great heaving sobs.

Josh let go of Max to hold Emma. "Max, go sit at the bottom
of Nate's tower for a minute, will you?"

"Is Mom alright?"

"She's alright. She didn't lose you." He glanced once to see
that Max had obeyed him then asked in Emma's ear under the roar
of the waves and wind, "Are you going to tell me why the ocean
terrifies you?"

"No."

Her answer came out as a long wail interrupted by gasps and
sobs. Josh tightened his hold on her, telling her with his arms and
body that she could let it all out, and when the sobbing subsided he
made her sit on the wet sand at the farthest reach of the water and
took Max out into the surf where the waves surged and sucked back
around them to let the boy get the feel of it. He let Max get knocked
down a couple of times and come sputtering and laughing back up

until he had the hang of it. Only when Max's teeth began to chatter did Josh finally say enough.

Emma sat hugging her knees, shivering, her fake tattoos sliding down her pale arms in swirls of color like oil slicks on wet pavement, her bare feet buried in sand. With Max's help, Josh collected their stuff from Nate's bucket, helped them up and across the beach to the outdoor showers and then into his car. Emma's boots had disappeared.

On the way home, Max asked a million questions. *Why is the ocean salty? How does the ocean make waves? Why does sand stick to you?* Josh tried to answer every one while Emma stayed silent.

It was near eight when they reached the duplex. Emma insisted on hosing her son off one more time in the driveway before they climbed the stairs. Josh believed it was a sign that her maternal toughness had returned. After she unlocked her door and Max dashed inside, she turned to Josh, grabbed a fistful of his damp sandy shirt, and pulled him to her.

"Thank you."

She kissed him, quick and hard on the mouth, then disappeared into her apartment.

Chapter Eighteen

"You must think I'm a crazy person."

Huntington had to, because Emma thought so herself. She had knocked on his door in spite of herself. He was still a Canyon boy of the worst sort, a careless, gorgeous, idle prince of privilege. She couldn't be certain that he hadn't slept with his date last night. He still wanted sex and self-indulgence, not a dog and a house and a kid. Nothing had changed for him, she was sure, and neither had her goals changed, whatever obstacles stood in her way, like Leo firing her. But she believed in facing facts, and she'd been thinking of this since she'd kissed him earlier. The fact was she wanted him. She hardly knew all the reasons why. She had some vague idea that inside he was not the man he appeared to be on the outside.

It was nearly ten and he was playing a cheesy Lifehouse track, "Hanging by a Moment." Despite his questionable taste in music, he was beautiful. He stood framed in his dark doorway, shirtless and barefoot, in worn khakis that sagged below the tops of his plaid boxers and the reversed parentheses of his pelvic bones. Emma's art history major training kicked in. In some other century he could easily have made a career of standing naked and idle around Rome or Florence for anyone with a block of Carrara and chisel. Except for the sappy music he would fit in some wing of the Getty.

"I tried to keep Max away from you," she murmured, "but you sucked us both in."

He did not look glad to see her. "Did you come to blame me for Max's adventure today?"

She shook her head. He didn't have a clue what she was feeling. "You found him for me."

"You're grateful." He sounded grim.

"Profoundly."

She'd admitted it, so now it was up to him. He would pull her into his apartment, into the big chair.

"There's a reason you're afraid of the ocean," he said instead.

She dropped her gaze to his beautiful feet. For a man who wanted her body, he was strangely distracted. "Mother fangs don't work on the ocean. It's cold and deep and huge, and full of sharks and currents and rogue waves."

Her answer wasn't enough for him, apparently. He reached out and lifted her chin. "Emma, what did you lose to the ocean?"

He was touching her, which was progress. But what she didn't need was for him to get all smart and probing on her. "You do understand how grateful I feel *right now*?"

"So, you are knocking on my door to offer a favor in return for finding Max."

Apparently there were things he did not understand at all. He didn't even recognize that he'd done a good thing. She was grateful. He could not know what it meant to have your heart drop like a wounded bird from ordinary blue-sky happiness to the deepest blackest pit of fear in an instant. Yet what she wanted from him had nothing to do with trading favors. She could admit that to herself now.

"You said you wanted to take me to bed."

He straightened. "You know what I want. I don't have a lot of resistance here."

She nodded. "I don't know why you're resisting at all. You said you always eat the marshmallow."

* * *

Josh stared at Emma. He had not recovered from undressing her on the beach, let alone from the kiss she'd planted on him at her door. Now she was here, scrubbed and fresh, all traces of the death metal maiden washed away, wearing one of her oversized, lost-and-found state college T-shirts and a pair of khaki shorts, her feet bare like his. She was putting the marshmallow on the table in front of him, daring him to eat it.

Lifehouse was telling him to let go of all he'd held on to, to let Emma take all of him now. The song suddenly struck him as appallingly lame. He needed to change the music. But even as he had the thought, a strange new realization took shape in his brain. *Maybe now I don't want to eat the marshmallow. Maybe now I know that there is something more to be had if I wait. If I earn it.*

That couldn't be right. He couldn't be disappointed that she wanted sex. Something must be wrong with him. His wires were crossed since he'd lost his trust fund. Since he'd moved into his half of this below-market dump of a duplex, he'd found himself attracted to women who felt grateful to him as if he were some kind of hero. He missed the old Josh, the guy who was attracted to all the Bethanys of L.A., cheerfully lust-crazed women who couldn't find their way with a moral compass even if the needle on the thing pointed due north.

Emma looked a little lust-crazed, and he knew he could drive her over the edge. Now was not the time to grow a conscience. Now was the time to listen to Lifehouse and let go of all he'd held on to. Emma would probably stop him if he gave her any chance to call it off.

Still, he hesitated, letting the moment stretch out until he hit on a compromise. "Let's start in the chair where we left off."

Josh stepped aside, and she walked in. There was nothing deliberately seductive about her movements, yet the action was a straightforward declaration of intent that was as erotic as anything he'd ever experienced.

He turned down the music, settled in the chair, and pulled her into his lap. It felt right to have her there, her bottom nestled in his crotch, her back against his chest, their feet on the ottoman. Leaning down, he kissed the side of her neck, inhaled the scent of her, and brought his hands up to cup her breasts through the soft T-shirt.

No bra.

His brain froze. Luckily, his hands knew what to do. "You think you're ready for this?"

"Ye-s-s." The word wobbled out on a ragged exhalation of pleasure.

"Emma, do you have some form of protection?" He had to ask before they went any farther. His brain probably had only a few minutes of blood flow left.

It took a while for the question to register. Finally she said, "No."

Okay then. They would have to stop, or he would have to get her to his bedroom.

He did neither. He went on teasing her breasts with one hand, while his other hand sought the waistband of her shorts, found and undid the closure, and slid downward to cup her sex. He had wanted this from the day she'd caught him lying on her kitchen floor, a skyscraper of an erection lifting his shorts from her nearness, and on his belly a wet glob of grease and decaying matter from his botched attempt at fixing her sink.

"Why," she asked on a gasp, "did you study piano?"

Her question was distracting, but he answered. "My father hated it."

He hadn't thought of the fact in a while, how satisfying it had been to fill the house with music; the more complex the better, the longer it took to master a piece the better. In his father's view, making music was both unmanly and unworthy, an activity for street performers with their hats out on the pavement.

"Do you still play?" she asked.

"No." He'd gone on annoying his father with his piano playing until he found other misbehavior more effective.

Conversation was difficult. His fingers had found the neat tight folds of Emma's sex, slick with desire. She wanted to talk, but that was only her way of fighting to stay in control. He wanted only to stroke and coax and open and fill.

"But…you…still…sing?"

He had to get her to stop talking. He shifted his thumb, and Emma jerked in his lap. Her hand clutched his arm.

"Let go, Emma," he whispered. He went on coaxing and teasing until he thought she might rise up out of the chair, then stopped and kissed her neck and let her catch her breath.   "You have a lot of power here. You can say when and how much."

"And if I say *now* and *everything*?"

"Then we check on Max and retire to the bedroom."

* * *

Emma was not surprised by his thoughtfulness. Huntington was as good as his word, steadying her on her feet as he took her hand and led her across the entry to her unit to check on Max, who slept soundly, one arm flung out. She had rarely seen her son so dead to the world.

Back in Huntington's unit, Emma discovered that his bedroom was the mirror image of hers in size and layout, but like his bathroom, worlds apart in comfort. Where her bedroom had only a sleeping bag and quilt and some baskets on the sad old carpet, his had a large bed with a dark wood headboard and fresh new carpet soft underfoot.

The long narrow window above the bed framed the faint city glow of L.A. Without letting go of her hand, he turned on a bedside light, pulled back the covers, and sank down on the side of the mattress. He reached for the drawer in his bedside table to pull out a string of condoms she recognized from the day she'd washed his car.

He pulled her to stand between his legs. She studied his face, looking for signs of enthusiasm. Her own body could hardly contain the energy coursing through it, a wholly new experience. Being turned on like this was being hyper-alive, having every sensation amplified, especially touch. Touch, which seemed so quiet, so subtle a sense, without any of the pop or pizzazz of vision and none of the drama of hearing, had suddenly consumed her other senses.

Huntington was watching her as if he understood that she was about ready to come out of her skin. He said, "You're a mystery, you know. Are you going to tell me how all this seems so new to you?"

"I'm not a virgin," she said. "I have Max."

"So you went for a results-only approach to sex and got lucky? One time, you hit the jackpot, got a baby, and never went back?"

Emma shook her head. She was not going to be led into any revelations. "No more talk. Promises were made. You said you could make me forget past experiences."

And he did. He knew how to kiss and touch and hold and press and rub and look until her clothes were shed and her skin was on fire. His hands circled her waist and cupped her bottom. His hot mouth took each of her breasts to taste and tease. She clung to his shoulders to keep from coming apart as her legs trembled and the tension rose in her...and then it came to her that he was doing all the giving. She had accused him of being the selfish one, but he wasn't.

The idea of a generous Huntington was a new thought, startling, really, but Emma didn't waste time lingering over it. She might not know much about sex, but she knew a lot about giving, and that's what her body ached to do. Leaning down, she kissed the top of his golden head and pushed against his shoulders, freeing herself from his hold. He looked puzzled and definitely mindless.

She smiled at him, put her hands to his chest and shoved, tumbling him back onto his luxurious sheets.

He stared up at her. Emma reached for the fastenings of his khakis, unbuttoning and unzipping, letting his fully adult male penis spring up through the slit in his boxers. She took hold of his khakis and tugged, and he lifted his hips and let her pull the pants away. For a moment then, she didn't know what her next move should be. He sprawled there, golden in the light of the bedside lamp, and, well, clearly enthusiastic about their lovemaking. Just looking at him made her body clench and ache in a tight spasm of her inner muscles.

She climbed onto the bed and crawled up over him, kissing him hard, trusting him once again to know what to do. His hands found her hips and pulled her down to straddle him. Their bodies met, and Emma let herself sink down, his hands coaxing her to slide back and forth across his erection, an exquisite friction as smooth as a needle in a groove, its tiny vibrations rocking her whole body.

He sucked in a breath, caught her by the hips and rolled her under him. Without breaking the connection he rocked against her, hot and slick and hard, until she gasped and shook from the pleasure of it and the need for still more. He broke the kiss, holding himself above her on taut arms.

"We're...not...stopping this time."

He sounded like a runner at the end of a race. She reached up and cupped his face and nodded so there could be no misunderstanding.

Huntington kissed her and rolled away to reach for the string of condoms on his nightstand. When he came back, he settled himself between her legs and slowly pushed into her, watching her face, his mouth set in a tight grimace. Her body stretched and clenched around him, wet, aching, swollen, and so relieved to take him in that she shook with the rightness of it, at the perfect startling fit, the bells-and-flashing-lights-win-a-million-dollars answer to her body's urgent question,

"Move with me," he invited, his voice cracking as he rocked up into her.

Emma slid her hands down his back to cup his hips and catch his rhythm, slow at first until she caught on and matched him. She realized that she had underestimated the hard muscular strength of him. She thought of him sprawled bonelessly in his chair, indolent, coolly at ease, apparently disinclined to sweat or strain or even hurry, but now in his restraint as he watched her face she knew the taut power of him. When she put her hands to his hips, she discovered that his usual cool manner hid quite a different person, one she could only catch in glimpses through deep urgent kisses and the possessive claim of his body on hers. For a moment in their bodies' meeting she felt they had come self to self…and then surges of happy energy shook and lifted her away from all thought, and he shuddered and groaned and spent himself inside her.

She must have dozed. Emma came to, curled warm and damp against him, clasped in his solid arms. He smelled of himself and sex and faintly of the ocean. She had not anticipated the brain-melting effect of so much skin-to-skin contact. She had held naked newborn Max to her chest, the feel and scent of him healing the lonely fears of her pregnancy, but now she was the one being held skin to skin.

Oh. She should move. She should find her clothes and thank Huntington for a good…time before he woke fully. "Time" was a chicken way to say it, though. She had guessed all along that he would be good at…it. She'd been wrong about something else, though. Maybe sex was all it was hyped up to be after all.

She should write him a thank-you note:

Dear Mr. Huntington, Thank you for taking the time to show me the pleasures of sexual intimacy. Your patience and thoroughness and willingness to attend to my desires made our encounter a memorable and satisfying experience. Thank you again, your neighbor, Emma.

But it wasn't just the sex she was grateful for. He had done so much more than light up her body and set off its internal fireworks. The thought that had come to her earlier returned. Huntington was truly generous—and insightful. He had understood instantly her need to find Max, and he had also somehow managed to release her from the tight grip of fear that had held her back from letting Max explore the world. She owed Huntington a whole lot more than sandwiches and carwashes.

When her brain switched back on, she would figure it all out.

* * *

Josh suspected Emma operated pretty much by the laws of physics: *For every action there would be an equal and opposite reaction.*

It was too bad, really, but she had broken too many rules and crossed too many lines not to react against the great sex they'd had. She had climaxed more than once in body-wracking spasms. Her conscience would come down hard on her for that. Nor would Emma feel good about the emotional release she'd had on the beach. She had not been willing or able to tell him what made her so afraid of the ocean, and he still wanted to know, but what he wanted more than anything, before she left his bed, was a strategy for getting her back into it.

He waited until he felt her start to squirm in his hold then let his left hand drift down from her ribs to cup her belly, his palm flat, his fingers spread wide. "Don't blame yourself for ending up here, Emma."

"Excuse me." She sounded instantly offended. "I knocked on your door. I walked right in. I said 'yes' several times when you asked." She squirmed again.

"You couldn't help it. You resisted as long as you could."

"Are you saying I had no choice?"

He smiled to himself at the instant return of her resistance to him. It was so like Emma. "Why fight it? And now that you're here, when are you coming again?"

"Is there no limit to your ego?"

She was fully awake, her sexually sated body obviously taking a backseat to her usual independence and sense of responsibility, so he shifted against her backside to make it clear how he was feeling. "There's no limit to my wanting you. That's the key fact here. Take it as the compliment it's meant to be."

Something in what he said or did stopped her movements. She did not reply. He kissed her bare shoulder while he waited for her to decide how she felt.

"Thank you."

Josh didn't move. He just waited for the rest of what she was bound to say.

"I've got to get back to Max now. I'm supposed to be a mom."

She sat up, slipping from his hold, disturbing the sheets so that a sobering wash of cold air hit him. He had a brief glimpse of her slim body in the lamplight before she pulled that white state T-shirt over her head. He was growing fond of that T-shirt, which hung loose to mid-thigh and left some very sweet Emma parts open to him.

Scooping up her shorts and panties, she cast him a look over her shoulder that jolted him out of bed, his brain processing its meaning a beat late. She had her hand on the doorknob when he caught her. He flipped her around and pressed her back against the door with his body and his mouth, and when he let her go, he said, "Emma, you are a good mom."

"A good mom sets the rules, keeps all her promises, takes care, and always pays attention."

"That's you, damn it. You have sterling mom qualities."

"Well, I face facts at least. It's a fact that I've been naked for three hours with my landlord while my kid slept alone next door."

Josh shook his head. "Stay focused here, Emma. You love your kid, and he gets it. You've got a hug that tells him you'd die or kill for him. But you and he are two separate people. He gets to go to the beach sometimes. You get to have sex."

She stared at him. "You have it all figured out, don't you?"

"Yes. He's still safe. He's still loved." Josh pushed back from the door and pulled her into a hug. "You want to come back. I want you to come back. So, don't make it hard on yourself. You may have broken an old rule, but here's one of mine: Don't mess with what's working. This thing between us *works*."

Emma said nothing.

"I won't keep you, but if you knock, I'll answer," he finished, not sure what else to say. "Consider it a perk of living here."

He watched her leave.

Chapter Nineteen

Emma woke in her sleeping bag, a little stiff, a little sensitive, aware of an unfamiliar stretch in her muscles, but she told herself she was still capable, still basically on track. She might have eaten the marshmallow, but she just needed a little time to think. The smart thing to do today would be to get as far from Huntington's distracting presence as she could.

Emma was not one to go back on a choice she'd made. She'd chosen sex with Huntington, a choice she'd made not only because he turned her on, which he did, but also because some feeling she could not contain had taken over as she'd watched him teach Max to play in the surf without fear. She didn't want to use the word *love*. Love was what she felt for Max, for Maria, and even for her grandparents. It made more sense to call the feelings she'd had for Huntington in that moment—helpless, foolish, unreserved feelings for what he had done for her and for Max—gratitude. The tricky thing was that whatever she had felt or might feel didn't change who Huntington was or make him a good candidate for a full-time role in their lives. He had told her he considered great sex between them a "perk" that came with their living arrangement. So she had a big decision to make before she saw him again.

She called Claudia, whom Max owed a big apology. The woman invited them to join her family's usual Sunday BBQ, and Emma snapped up the chance to go back to the old neighborhood. Now that she'd been fired, she had her first free Sunday in months.

They left before there was any sign of life from Huntington's side of the duplex. It took patient waiting at bus stops and two long routes across the South Bay to reach their destination, but Emma's spirits lifted when Max dashed happily across the grass toward a gathering of familiar faces. In the crowded park, radios broadcast the L.A. Dodger game in English and Spanish, competing with the sounds of kids playing pickup baseball and smaller kids having tantrums. Dads grilled meat, and barbecues sent up a haze of flavored smoke. Moms hovered over cloth-covered picnic tables, setting out platters and caddies of condiments and utensils. Emma tuned in and out of dozens of conversations in two languages. Her body sat on a bench at a shaded picnic table, but her brain hovered somewhere in the hazy atmosphere above the park stuck on a replay of the night before.

She accepted a plate from Claudia's husband loaded with a burger and potato chips, shocking Max by breaking a half dozen food rules. She immediately reached for the cherry tomatoes she'd brought to the picnic and tried to regain some clear-headedness about her Huntington problem. First and foremost, she was Max's mom. Her job was to protect Max from heartbreak even if she could not protect herself. Neither she nor Max was in any danger from Huntington's charm while they were here at the picnic, but Emma needed to know how she was going to act when they returned to the apartment.

She had certainly underestimated complete sexual satisfaction. It was a thrill ride and a spa day rolled into one. She had occasionally treated Max to rides at amusement parks, and the thing with those rides was that once was never enough. No sooner would she and Max slide, glide, or splash to a breathless, giddy halt than he would demand to do it again.

She got that now. Her body was certainly crying "again," even while her head was saying, "wait." The emotional ride of making love with her landlord was harder to understand.

Claudia joined her at the table and began to retell the story of losing Max the day before, but when she came to the part about Huntington helping her with the laundry basket on the stairs, Emma's heartbeat picked up. It was crazy, but she realized her real problem with Huntington was much more serious than mere sexual attraction. He was gorgeous, with that golden hair and those blue eyes and that really nice musculature, but more than that Huntington had been instinctively kind to a stranger, an ordinary woman with a laundry basket. He had also done some kindness to that redheaded Annie James which made her believe in him and kiss his cheek with gratitude. So, Huntington was both giving and kind. If she was honest with herself, Emma had to admit that she had been seduced as much by his personality as by his good looks. It was his kindness that made her do dumb things like climbing into his lap and letting him deliver great sex.

Her heart still raced a little. Good sex with Huntington remained a problem not because it emptied her body of all its restless energy and left her with a happy afterglow of satisfaction, good sex with him was dangerous because it dulled the sharp edge of wariness that had guided her for years and allowed her to protect both Max and herself. Good sex made her feel a strange sympathy for Huntington and believe that he needed more than just her body. He actually needed her to care for him.

He had accused her of hiding, but maybe *he* was the one hiding some kind of pain behind that gorgeous, careless façade. She wondered who besides herself had told Huntington that he was not a good man.

She knew what she would do when they got home.

* * *

Josh was operating on coffee fumes. That's what mind-blowing sex could do to you.

Today he was overseeing the arrival at Canyon of the trucks bringing thousands of pieces of equipment needed to construct the concert stage. There was a carefully orchestrated sequence required to get everything into the service yard; there were trucks with the light cans, sound boards, the decking system, the steel columns and birdbath rigging that went overhead, the giant video screens, and monitors for every element of the show. The work had been scheduled for the weekend not to interrupt classes and to keep security tight on the concert location. Each truck had to pass Ryker's people—they were thorough—before being checked off on Josh's list. The instruments themselves and the grindstone and axe would arrive separately during the week.

It struck him about eight hours into the day, as he signed off on the delivery of a pair of giant metallic curtains that suggested chain mail, that he was actually working. A bigger revelation was that he liked the work. Unlike the job he'd landed at Canyon when his father first threatened to take away his trust, the job he was doing for Ryker entailed real responsibility. Ryker, who apparently could not leave that chair without assistance, was counting on Josh to get the Canyon venue ready for the concert.

There were a number of things about the job that were tedious to be sure. His time was not his own. He had to give his attention to details that were not sexy or entertaining, and the conversation was pretty limited. Not a lot of humor from Ryker's security guys. At least the guys driving the trucks and doing the lifting and the carting of heavy objects had more to say.

One good thing about working was that it interrupted the tiny niggling doubt he had that Emma would return to his bed. While his parents would be appalled at his getting his hands dirty for a paycheck, he wondered whether Emma might reconsider her assessment of his character if she saw actual sweat on his brow. Whenever there was a lull in the flow of trucks, he checked his phone. The only person who'd called him was Mae Sloan to learn if he'd found the lost boy. He called her, thanked her, and reassured her. He told her a little bit about Max, and she invited him to bring the boy to her house to play with her dog sometime.

He tried not to read anything into Emma's phone silence. Most women he'd had sex with would leave him a teasing text or other sign of their continued interest the next day. Not Emma. He had no idea where she'd gone today, or how she felt about their lovemaking—probably conflicted. He recognized when a woman felt satisfied, though most of the women he knew wouldn't fight the feeling as Emma did. But she had her rules, and she had hang-ups to get over. That's why he'd told her to consider their lovemaking a perk. Sex with him would only help her, and she wouldn't have to change her plans or make any promises. As for him, sleeping with her was the perfect solution to his dry spell. If she wanted it, they could have lots of sex before he left the duplex and went back to his regular life.

Of course, he didn't know if she'd see it that way. He'd done his best that morning before they'd parted to neutralize the rules she lived by, rules that punished her for enjoying anything. He wanted a string of nights, as many in a row as she was willing to give him. He wouldn't know whether he'd won even one more night until he heard her knock on his door again.

* * *

She did knock. It was almost midnight, and she heard Green Day playing its saddest song. If his musical choice was any clue, he had not expected her to return.

She cut the music, took Huntington's hand, and urged him up out of the chair. "Did you think we were done?" she asked in a whisper.

She led him across the entry into her apartment and down the hall to her bedroom. It was a compromise. She wouldn't be thinking about Max, but she would not be out of earshot if her son needed her.

Standing in the gloom at the door to her bedroom, looking at her sleeping bag and quilt arrangement, she faltered, uncertain how to navigate from the upright fully clothed position to the naked in bed position. She glanced at him and saw understanding in his eyes.

Just like that, he took over.

In the aftermath they lay panting, spooned on their sides, wrapped in her quilt. Emma could feel the hard surface under them where her right hip made contact with inadequate layers of quilt, sleeping bag, and worn carpet, but her body basically sent a message back that she had never expected to hear from her own girl parts: *So what? Focus on the main thing here. You just had great sex—again.*

The sex should have been awkward, clumsy, and uncomfortable, the two of them making love on her sleeping bag, but he had managed it with his usual skill. They had not spoken. He'd used his hands to ask or coax. *This? This? That?* Somehow he'd kept her on top of him through a timeless stretch of kissing, touching, and joining, as if she'd been as light as a leaf or a stick riding a rain-swollen creek toward the sea. She still had her T-shirt on. He'd managed that, too. She realized that it meant he'd had lots of sex in tight places, but she tried not to let that thought intrude further.

"You know," he whispered, "I have a yoga mat in the garage."

Of course you do.

"You should talk to your landlord about this carpet."

"My landlord?" Emma said.

"The guy should replace it for you."

"You apparently don't know my landlord."

"I don't?"

"He's not your ordinary sort of landlord. He would probably replace this very functional shag carpet with tatami mats from the Intercontinental Hotel in Bali and double my rent."

"I think you've got this guy all wrong."

His voice was lazy. For once she was the more alert of the two of them, and she turned in his arms so that they lay face to face. "Do you have a middle name?"

"You're not really worried about the rent, are you?"

She would not be distracted. "In my mind I think of you as 'Huntington,' but...well...now..."

He was her lover, not her boyfriend or significant other or some casual hook-up partner, but her lover. He was like the heroine's competent, suave lover in a French film, the kind Emma had watched one term to fulfill the language requirement for her art major. The heroine had been an awkward deaf girl, and the hero an ex-con. They had had seriously hot sex in a small car, but the scene had been set at night in dim lighting and Emma had not learned much from it except that a woman could take charge of her sex life and her working life and demand that she be satisfied with both.

She glanced over at Huntington. So, both of them wanted the marshmallow. It made no sense, but it was a fact. There was something more, too. They were in tune in some way. Maybe because they had lived side by side for months. On the beach Huntington had understood that finding Max was the only thing that mattered. He had understood her crazy fear of the ocean—not the why of it, but the hold it had on her and how she wanted to be released from it.

He moved slightly, and her breasts flattened against his chest. "You object to the name 'Josh'?"

"On you," she managed. Josh was a name for his careless outer self, not the real man she suspected he kept concealed. "It doesn't fit you exactly."

"Interesting." His glance shifted away so that she could not read his expression. "At Canyon we all had last names and nicknames, no first names. I'm used to 'Huntington,' if that suits you."

"What was your nickname?" she asked, conscious that face to face, warm and snug under her quilt, it might be hard to keep a serious conversation going.

"Oh, I'm not sharing that."

"So, what am I going to call you?"

For answer, he closed a hand over her breast and kissed her.

They did not make love again, and his kisses could not make her forget the thoughts that troubled her. It had not mattered that she deceived him with a false name for months as long as he was merely her landlord, but now he was this other thing in her life, a lover. It felt wrong to lie with him and also lie about who she was. Every twist and turn of her thinking led her to another life rule she was breaking.

"Tired?" he asked.

She nodded, and he left her bed as easily as he'd entered it. In the dim light of her room he was a pale figure like the sculpture she'd once imagined him being. He pulled on his boxers and shorts, and she rose and walked him to her door. Careful and quiet, they kissed once more.

"Mom?" Max's voice came from his bedroom. "I hear talking."

Emma instantly turned from Huntington. "I'm saying goodnight and thank you to Josh. He just got home." He might not want her gratitude, but he'd always have it.

Huntington opened his door, making a small truth out of her statement.

"Goodnight, Josh," Max shouted from his room.

"Goodnight, buddy," Josh called from his side of the entry.

Chapter Twenty

On Monday Josh was back in the Hall of Canyon men as the build-up to the concert continued. The whole week promised to be crazed with last minute details to arrange. Worse, he and Leo Grant were now standing in front of the life-sized black-and-white portrait of Grindstone taken at their 2008 concert, and the two were sharing a moment of mutual hostile recognition.

"You're running this thing?" Grant snapped. He'd come to consult on some of the more technical staging details.

"Ryker is running this thing. I work for him."

"You're the jerkwad who took Emma."

"You fired her. Her kid was missing."

"Her kid? Are you the dad or something?" Grant's eyes narrowed with suspicion.

"Just a neighbor."

"Yeah, well, you cost her. Let's get on with it. I haven't got all day."

The man was clearly an ass, and Josh could see that he would get nowhere trying to get justice for Emma. No halfway decent guy fired a single mom for caring for her kid in an emergency. Josh hadn't figured it out yet, but if Emma got behind on her rent...well, maybe they could work something out. She and Max could move in with him and he could rent their unit. He'd be getting one more check from Ryker, and it was nothing like his trust, but he could manage as long as he had rent from the north unit. He had a funny thought that he hadn't missed the things he usually spent money on as much as he'd thought he would.

He handed Grant his clipboard. "Take a look at this crew list. We're trying to match the original group."

The guy looked it over, glancing up at the picture from the 2008 concert. He handed the clipboard back to Josh without comment.

"So," Josh prompted, indicating the picture, "who are we missing?"

Grant pointed out a tall, long-haired guy in a black sleeveless T-shirt with seriously inked arms. "Pete Williamson, now the front man for Masters of the Heist. He ripped off every lead break Saxon played." His finger moved to a man with long, straight blond hair. "Kurt Cooper did lighting, now works in films."

Josh nodded. Looking at him, then at the list one more time, Grant pointed to a short, wiry man second from the far right with a head of thick blond curls. "Ron Newsted. He was the band's pyro tech. Got the band in deep trouble by selling backstage passes to underage girls. He took off on his motorcycle after the 2008 concert and crashed in the desert." He handed Josh the clipboard back and said, "Got it?"

"Newsted's dead?" Josh asked.

Grant nodded.

Josh looked at the face in the photo again. He'd glanced at this picture several times a day since he'd started working for Ryker, but he'd always focused on the four band members in the center. Newsted's face and hair struck him as familiar, but no direct connection came to mind so he put the thought aside.

Grant was watching him. "You know, Emma's a nutter. I *had* to fire her. Music's a business, man, and she was losing focus. She was super intense about getting into this show. Even believed that stupid old fantasy about the black chair and rose on stage for the dead debutante. You should warn security about her. Never know what she'll do to get to Saxon. Now *that's* a girl bent on laying some famous pipe."

Josh's brain balked at the off-the-wall idea that Emma, his rookie lover who thought a coed shower was a daring sexual act, wanted to get to Steve Saxon. He weighed the satisfaction of his fist smashing Grant's face with certain inevitable consequences of that move. His mouth managed, "Dead debutante?"

"A legend. Saxon groupies hardly came from the upper echelons of society," Grant said with a laugh. Then he walked off.

* * *

Emma met Max at school at the end of the day on Thursday. Since she'd lost her job, she had not needed to send him to the Center. He skipped and bounced and talked nonstop on the way home. Most of his conversation was about the beach and Josh, and when they might go again. His talk made Emma conscious of the double life she was now leading, cautiously keeping her son away from Huntington while secretly counting the hours until their landlord returned. She almost suspected that Huntington had a job. He said he was doing a project for a friend and that later he'd tell her about it, but the work kept him away from early to late each day. His absence actually made it easier for her to protect Max, no matter the risk she might be taking with her own heart.

This afternoon she steered Max toward Daddy Rock. She had hoped Leo would relent and take her back, but so far he'd refused to see her. When she checked, she found he'd left the last of the money he owed her at the front cash register. So, at least she could pay some rent even if she wasn't going to get a ticket to the Grindstone concert out of him.

As far as she knew from talking to the other Daddy Rock employees, *no one* had a pass to the concert. Leo was just being as tight with them as he had been with her, and no one had any real information about the venue. There was a good bit of grumbling about that, in fact, that the concert was a private party for high rollers. So Emma's main problem remained. Her father was making his first trip outside of Sweden in seven years, and she did not yet know where his band would perform or how she would get into his concert.

She would not give up in spite of the feeling that time was running out. She had a Plan B.

She had put on her death metal gear once again, and from the record store she led Max over to the taco shack where she figured she'd find Brandon and Todd. They'd show up there eventually. She just hoped it wouldn't be a long wait.

Tacos Jalisco proved a good distraction for Max. After customers ordered from the window and picked up their baskets of small, soft, meat-filled shells, they could add ingredients from two long tiled bars with wells of salsas, chopped vegetables, and cheese. Her son might not be hungry, but he was curious. Emma told him he could pick three things to put on his chicken tacos. He had questions about every one. The crying tongue chilies led to the longest conversation, as Max tried to imagine his tongue shedding tears and Emma tried to explain the metaphor.

Their tacos were cold, and Emma was feeling pretty desperate when Brandon and Todd finally showed up and sat at the picnic bench opposite her and Max. She smiled idiotically at them, and Max moved closer to her on his side of the table.

"Did you get a pass to the concert?" Brandon asked.

"Not exactly."

"You haven't been at the store this week."

"Listen," Emma said, cutting off any further questions. "Are you guys still planning to go no matter what?"

They exchanged a glance. "Duh. Yeah."

"And you know where it is?"

"Yeah." Again, the two looked at one another. Then Todd said, "And we know how to get in."

Emma felt herself sag with relief. "Do you think you can take me? You said before that you might take me."

Brandon cast a dismissive glance at Max. "You're not going to bring the kid, are you?"

"No," Emma said.

Max tugged her sleeve. "Mom, are you going somewhere without me?"

Emma reached out and pulled him closer to her on the bench. "Only to a concert, and only for a few hours. You'll be with Claudia."

"Can't I be with Josh?"

She shook her head. "Finish your tacos."

He pushed the plastic basket away. "I don't like the green stuff."

There was no point in telling him that he had picked it, so she leaned over, recovered the basket, and scraped most of the salsa off one taco. "Try it like this." She turned back to Brandon and Todd. "Where's the concert?"

Todd laughed. "It's seriously weird. At a prep school."

"A prep school?"

"Yeah, some rich boys school on the West Side up near Sunset."

"You don't mean Canyon, do you?" Emma asked. She thought Huntington's project was at Canyon. He might know whether Brandon and Todd were right about the concert being held there even if he had nothing to do with it. She wondered why he hadn't told her what he was doing.

"Yeah, that's it," Brandon said. "The Canyon School. Big fancy sign out front. Do you know it?"

"Why there?" Emma asked.

"Don't know, but we followed Leo until he went in through the gates. Then we went around through the back entrance. A lot of big trucks with equipment there, like stage-building equipment. And lots of security. Big men with shades and earbuds."

"So, what's the plan?" she asked. "For getting inside on the night of the concert."

She listened to Brandon and Todd explain their scheme while Max picked at his tacos, and as the two young men talked her spirits rose. Their plan to get in might actually work. Without a backstage pass or the help of an insider like Leo Grant, these two seemed to be her best chance.

"Listen," she said. "If I wanted to meet Steve Saxon and didn't have a backstage pass, what's my best strategy?"

"Meet Steve Saxon?" Two incredulous pairs of eyes turned on her as if she'd uttered a sacrilege. "You are seriously not his type."

"I want to meet him, not sleep with him," she said. Was sex all women wanted from her father?

"Oh," said Brandon and Todd, and she could see that the idea did not compute.

"I have something to give him."

Brandon picked up a neglected taco from his basket, and after a minute Todd suggested, "Well, if you could get on stage and get in exactly the right spot without anyone seeing you, you could ride down in one of the lifts at the end of the show and follow Saxon backstage. That might give you enough time to…give him the thing."

"I like it," Brandon said. He put down his taco and licked salsa from his fingers. "It's sort of subversive, sort of like the audience breaking the invisible barrier between them and the band. I mean, musicians do it when they dive into a mosh pit, so you could do it in return. Yeah, you could definitely try to get on stage when they do their fog thing."

"How would I get on stage? Fly?" Emma asked.

The two young men looked at each other then shrugged. Brandon said, "Oh, we can get you onstage, but you'd have to find just the right place to wait. And your timing would have to be perfect."

"Okay, thanks," Emma said, wondering if relying on her anarchist friends was a bad idea after all. "I'll think of something maybe. Ready, Max?"

Her son jumped off the bench.

"No, wait, Emma," Brandon said. "Don't bail out on us. We can do this. You can count on us. We'll be like the Ninja Turtles."

"You can be April," Todd added.

As the two happy would-be anarchists beamed at her, Emma nodded. Their plan *was* crazy, but what other choice did she have? She had worked at Daddy Rock for over a year just to get a chance to see her father, and she would not give up now. After the concert he would return to Sweden, out of reach. So she made plans to meet her own personal teenage mutant ninja turtles on Saturday.

Back at the apartment, Emma challenged a lagging Max to a race up the stairs, and her son dashed ahead, making the metal steps ring with his footfalls. The race ended abruptly when they caught sight of a woman standing in the entry looking down at them.

She was tall and spare, and approaching fifty. Her impeccably tailored gray silk suit established an air of elegant efficiency. She wore her dark hair in a neat bob, concealed her sharp-eyed gaze behind oversized red-rimmed glasses, and carried a designer bag that would fund Emma's rent for a month. She also held a man's black garment bag printed with the logo of an exclusive Beverly Hills tailor in one hand, and over the crook of her other arm hung a basket filled with bags of specialty roasted coffee beans, packages of scones and biscotti, and little pots of jam and cream.

Max stared openly. "Hello," he said. "Are you looking for Josh?"

The woman, whose quick assessing glance took in both Max and Emma, nodded. "I am."

"Are you his mother?" Max wanted to know.

She laughed. "No, but I know his mother. I'm bringing him some things from her." She lifted the items in her hands.

"Oh. Why doesn't his mom come herself?"

"Max," Emma cautioned. "Too many questions." She reached the top step. "Can we help?" she asked the stranger. "We're the tenants here across from Josh."

"I see." If the woman made any judgment based on the contrast between Emma's leather and metal gear and her own designer silk, she did not betray it in her unchanging facial expression. "I'm Margot Miles, Mrs. Huntington's personal assistant. I'm bringing Josh an item he needs for his next…engagement, and a little gift. You wouldn't have a spare key, would you?"

"I don't," Emma said. "He only leaves his key with me when he's away on vacation."

"I see." The woman glanced around the little entryway and at the street beyond, as if deciding whether it would be safe to leave her items at the door.

Emma did not know what conclusions Margot Miles might be drawing about her relationship with Josh, but she wasn't going to explain or apologize. But she decided to stop being offended. Margot Miles was only doing her job.

"We could keep the things for Josh if you'd like," she suggested. "Did he know you were coming? Do you want to leave a note?"

"Thank you," the woman said. "That would help. I'd like to be sure that he receives these items in time for an event this weekend. His mother's expecting him."

Emma fished her keys out of her pocket and handed them to her son. "Open up, Max."

Max took the keys and spun round to their door. He managed the lock and then disappeared inside. Emma stepped into the doorway and faced the stranger.

"What is he, six? Or seven?" Margot asked. Once again, her glance took in her surroundings without reaction.

"Six," Emma confirmed.

"Well, you have your hands full, I see. He must have lots of energy."

Emma reached out to take the gift basket. As her son returned she said, "Here, Max, can you put this on the kitchen sink until Josh gets back?"

Max took the basket, and Emma reached out for the garment bag.

"Thank you, Max," Margot said, smiling at him as he reappeared.

"We kept one of Josh's jackets before, didn't we, Mom?" Max confided.

"We'll get these items to him as soon as we see him," Emma said. She gave her boy a quick hug. Discretion was not a six-year-old concept. She'd have to work on training him not to overshare with kind strangers.

Margot pulled a phone out of her bag. "You are…?"

"Emma."

"Thank you," the woman said. "I'll just text Josh to find his things here with you."

Emma turned her son to face the kitchen. He hadn't really touched his tacos and was probably hungry. "Max, why don't you fix a snack? You can have hummus and carrots."

He headed off, and Margot looked up from her phone. "Thank you again, Emma."

"No trouble."

The woman didn't move. "I beg your pardon for asking this, but…Josh hasn't made you any promises, has he?"

Emma straightened her shoulders, not willing to acknowledge the implication. Her relationship with Josh was no one else's business. "He's our landlord. As landlords go, I've had worse."

Margot slipped her phone back into her bag. "That's good then. Thank you again."

Behind Emma, Max had the refrigerator open. He was humming to himself, and Emma held her breath waiting for Margot to go. Just when she thought that would happen, the woman turned to her one last time. Her expression was sober if not unkind.

"You do know that he lost his trust, don't you?

Emma nodded. She knew because she had heard Annie James mention it. What did that have to do with anything?

"Good. And what he's doing to regain it?"

Her heart suddenly in her throat, Emma managed a small shake of her head.

Margot took a deep breath. "He's dating a series of women his mother designated. It is her hope to see him happily settled soon. She's prepared to make the trust fund payments his father cut off. He's…an expensive young man."

Emma stared blankly at the woman, who shouldered her expensive bag and left. It was true. Josh Huntington was expensive. He could not exist on air. No doubt he needed to do something to pay his bills. Now she knew what that something was. Emma hung the garment bag over the back of a chair and closed the door.

"Mom," Max called. "Can I have peanut butter instead?"

Chapter Twenty-one

It was late, after midnight, when Josh sank deep into his chair in the living room. He didn't turn on any music. For a moment or two he'd just enjoy the silence. Then he'd cross the entry to Emma's place.

He hadn't known he could be this tired, what with his days at Canyon and his nights with her. He seemed to be living two lives, neither of which he recognized. His daytime life required all the energy and decisiveness that his father admired, but it was in the service of a musical performance to launch a video game. Even with the philanthropic intent behind the event, it was a temporary job that would not get his trust back. In fact, it would probably just annoy his father.

He smiled at the thought. He was rather proud of how he'd managed to turn Canyon into a venue for Ryker's concert. When it was over, he could tell Emma about it. And it might be worth it to send his dad a selfie standing beside Steve Saxon, just to raise the old man's blood pressure a notch. Josh guessed that he had been the subject of some familial discussions recently, because his sister had sent him a text of solidarity from New York: *Don't cave. Don't move home. Come here and sleep on my couch if you must. Sibs forever.*

As for sleeping with Emma, that was pure selfishness; that was just for him. It was not part of any plan, exactly, for together they made no plans, not even from one day to the next. Having sex with her for the past five days had been like that cheesy eighties movie where the lovers shape-shifted from man to wolf and lady to hawk and could only meet for a few minutes at dawn or dusk. He and Emma existed at night.

Daily his mother's executive assistant updated him with reminders about the Glen reunion, which conflicted with the Grindstone concert. Today he had glanced at another text from her about a jacket he was supposed to wear that she'd left for him somewhere. He would have to decide what to do about the conflict with the concert. At the moment the women on his mother's list seemed unreal to him. He couldn't remember whether Bethany had had blue or brown eyes. After being with Emma the first time—he hadn't really thought of other women.

Two weeks earlier he'd been complaining about having nothing to do. Now his phone was never quiet. Sloan called him several times a day, and they had gone together on Wednesday night to answer questions for the Canyon Board about ex-Headmaster Chambers. Sloan had even hinted again that Josh could return to Canyon if he wanted. Meanwhile, Louisa at the Center reminded him that she would like him to drop by as soon as he was free, as she was hoping he would think about working there as the youth director. He hadn't said anything about the work at Canyon, but he thought he might tell Emma about Louisa's offer. Emma would probably be appalled to think of him as a youth role model.

Despite their lovemaking, Emma still hadn't opened up to him about her past. He wondered when and if she would be ready to do so. Thinking of that, he should ask her about Leo Grant's weird comment about her interest in Steve Saxon. He should also take a moment to reassure her that he wasn't worried about the rent.

Josh had dozed off in his chair when Emma appeared, coming to him sweetly at that hour when the city quieted its roar and one could hear waves breaking. She moved quietly past his chair until he snagged her wrist and pulled her with him to the bedroom.

He thought of these quiet hours as their time, but from the first kiss he felt something had changed. He didn't want things to change, though, so he concentrated on blowing her mind with good sex and making her forget everything but pleasure. He was good at that.

He held her as they descended weightlessly from the high. They lay pressed together in the near dark, breathing raggedly like runners, and he remembered fireworks displays over the lake at camp in summer, the way the bright bursts of color froze for a moment in their most dazzling brilliance then crumbled silently through the dark sky: He knew he had only a few minutes before her restless energy would return and the change he'd sensed in her would take over again.

Another wave broke outside, a big swell he guessed from the sound of the crack it made.

"So," he said, while he had her half-dozing in his arms. "What did the ocean take away from you?"

It was no fair, he knew, asking the question when Emma felt so blissfully at ease. She tried to stir, but her limbs, limp with satisfaction, didn't get the message. Even better, she answered. "My mother."

Her mother? He uttered a silent curse. Her bad luck was worse than he'd thought, and his heart went out to Emma, though his thumb brushed her belly, distracting her from waking up and realizing what she was saying. "Tell me."

"I was a baby. One night she left me with my grandparents and took one of my grandfather's cars. She was going back to my father. He was somewhere in Santa Barbara, but the car went off the coast highway into the ocean south of Oxnard. She hit her head or something and never got out. She drowned. Someone from the naval station found her the next day."

* * *

Emma stiffened in Huntington's arms. She had said it aloud. Her young mother had drowned in the sea while she was a baby.

Facts were facts, smooth or rough-edged, but always hard as stones. Still, they looked different in different lights when one took them out and held them in one's palm. She had held this fact in her palm many times since she'd learned the truth, studying its contours in the light of her grandparents' harsh grief. She had looked at her mother's death again as a new mother with baby Max in her arms and thought only of the sweetness and joy her mother had lost. Now she picked up the stone of her mother's death and saw it in another light, the light of Huntington's embrace, and she held her breath waiting to see what the new light would reveal.

The room was quiet. Emma had no idea of the time. She should get up and check on Max, she knew. She could feel the roughness of the hair on Huntington's legs which twined with hers and recognized the subtle shift of his limbs that said he was ahead of her, already alert, no longer drifting in a haze of sexual satisfaction. So there was no putting off any longer the conversation she meant to have with him.

She lay on her right side, facing him, his left arm around her shoulders, her hand on his chest. Looking into his eyes she said, "You know, you haven't told me what you're doing now. Do you work? Are you earning a living?"

He tensed slightly. "I'm covering expenses."

"How?"

"Emma, what is this? An interrogation?"

His voice was light, but she could hear an edge to it. He wasn't going to make the conversation easy, and he wasn't giving anything away.

"It's important to me," she said, thinking again of Margot Miles. "I know we don't open up to each other much."

"I told you. I've got a gig going helping a buddy of mine. And your rent has helped."

Her heart missed a beat. "What if I don't get another job and can't pay it?"

He looked at her. "Well, you and Max could move in with me, and I could get a different tenant for your place."

Emma's breath caught, and she waited for him to say something more. But what he'd suggested so casually was a reminder of how he lived from moment to moment. He was her charming, affable neighbor, accommodating and helpful. He was her wonderful lover. But he wasn't a man ready to choose being an all-the-time dad for a kid or a committed partner for a woman, and he wasn't choosing independence as she had done. His trust waited for him like his jacket and his basket of expensive whole bean coffee; he could slip back into his old life any time. She wondered what he'd ever done to be denied it.

"That would be convenient," she found herself muttering. She hadn't meant the sarcasm, exactly; it just came out. Her eyes immediately stung with unwanted tears, and she rolled onto her back.

He slipped his arm from under her so that they lay side by side then rolled to face her and cup her chin in his hand. There was just enough light coming through the high window to impart an evil glitter to the sprayed-on ceiling, the one cheap thing in his bedroom. "Emma, you've lost me here. Why are we talking economics?"

"We're talking facts."

"Facts? You're as stingy with facts as anyone I've ever known. You don't get to grill me on my finances when you haven't answered the least of my questions. Like, how you got to know Tony Orlandi—and why Leo Grant really fired you."

Emma's pulse instantly kicked up, and she jerked away from his hold. She felt her cheek brush his hand, and she knew he caught the moisture there. When he spoke, his voice sounded raw.

"Emma, why are you messing with a good thing?"

"I just want to know where we stand here, and I think I do now."

"Nothing's changed," he said. "I want you, and you want me."

"I know."

Emma rolled away from him and scooted off the bed. Her feet landed on her discarded clothes. She shook a little with the cold as she scooped up her T-shirt and pulled it over her head, conscious of an ache in her chest. Her heart protested that they had begun to evolve a way of being together, that she knew him, that she had learned the things he liked and that drove him over the edge. Her head said to put that knowledge away like something learned to pass a test and not needed again.

She faced him where he lay in the bed. "You're right that there are things I haven't told you, but you also know that I'm a grownup. I pay my way by what I earn. I don't depend on anyone who might ultimately control me or influence the decisions I make for Max and me."

He looked annoyed. "Are you saying I'm not a grownup?"

"I'm saying we're on different paths. They sort of merged for a while, but now they're splitting. Today your mother's assistant came and brought you a jacket to wear this weekend wherever you're going. If I understood her right, and she was quite direct, your mother hopes you'll meet an appropriate woman to marry. I put the jacket over one of your chairs and the gift basket of coffee next to your bean grinder. So, you're good to go."

"Wait a minute, Margot Miles was here?"

He was sitting up, throwing off the covers, but he wasn't denying the facts. Emma backed up a step and said, "Ms. Miles thoughtfully explained to me how you were working to regain your trust."

He swore. It was the first time she'd ever heard him do it. He sat on the edge of his bed, unmoving. She'd shocked him. Apparently he didn't have a lot of experience facing facts. She was sorry to be the one bringing him the opportunity.

He stared at her. "Answer one question, grown-up Emma. All this time, what have you been doing here? Were you just paying a debt, maybe for that day on the beach? Did you think I wanted sexual favors for liking your son and offering my help when you needed it?"

She swallowed a painful lump in her throat. "Consider us even."

She said it as brightly as she could. It was the smart thing to say. He was hurt and angry, and this was the quick and painless Band-Aid removal approach to ending whatever it was they had. They weren't meant for the long run. She had promised her kid a house and a dog, and maybe a real dad, and when that time came she wanted the man to be someone Max could count on. Huntington wanted sex—great sex, great temporary sex. And he wanted the expensive things he'd always had, things he'd never earned, things he couldn't give up. That's who he was. Whatever her heart might say, her head knew it was time for them both to go back to their real lives.

She turned, took hold of the door handle and did just that.

Chapter Twenty-two

The next morning Emma's alarm woke her early. She felt heavy-eyed with lack of sleep, but she knew she'd done the right thing. She had chosen her path months earlier—years earlier—and she was not going back now no matter how much her heart hurt.

She got Max up for a project that had come to her in the night. Skipping breakfast, the two of them left early, while the fog was in and Huntington's Rover still sat in the driveway.

Walking Max toward his school, she asked him to help her find three perfect stones, and she had him cup the palm of his hand to see the size she meant for him to collect. Instead of walking on the sidewalk as they usually did, they walked down the curving path through the planted median where railroad tracks had once run, and Emma let Max wander to either side of the path, scouting under bushes and trees in the sandy soil for round, smooth stones. She carried a canvas grocery bag to hold what he found, and soon it was heavy with candidates. For every stone Max collected he had at least three questions, and Emma realized she was inadequately schooled in fundamental geology.

They had time, so she broke their normal routine further by not continuing on to school, instead taking Max for muffins and juice at a café on the Avenue. They sat outside at a small table and spread out the stones.

"We're now going to pick three from our collection," she announced.

Max's leg kicked the table as he sat. "Why?"

"We're going to give them as a present to someone."

"Josh?" Max asked.

"No, someone else."

"Who?"

"Someone you have not met yet, an important someone. Now, line the stones up, and tell me which ones you like best."

Max moved the stones around on the table, talking about their shapes and sizes and textures until their food came. He and Emma paused to break the warm muffins apart and spread butter and jam on each piece; then Max made a pile of stones that equaled the size of one truly impressive muffin. Once he took a bite, however, he concentrated on eating, and Emma didn't want to rush him. This was too important a task.

Customers came and went as the day brightened, carrying away sacks of muffins and paper cups of coffee. Traffic imperceptibly grew heavier. Surfers returned from the beach with boards under their arms and the top halves of their black wetsuits dangling around their knees. A school crossing guard showed up to help kids across the Avenue.

Max looked up as he finished his muffin. "Mom, we're breaking so many rules, can we go to the beach?"

She almost laughed. "Nope. We have to choose our three stones, and then I'll take you to school."

"How do we decide?" Max asked. The waitress came and took away their crumb-covered plates and empty glasses.

"Well, think of one stone as you and one as me. Which stone seems like your stone?"

Max did not hesitate. He picked up a smooth gray specimen with a band of whiter rock running through the middle. "That's me, because I'm Max Gray and I have light hair."

He picked up a smooth shiny black stone next and declared it to be Emma because it was pretty. She thanked him and put the two stones in her pocket then studied the remaining pile one more time, although she had already spotted the one she would keep. She picked it up and added it to her pocket.

"What will happen to the others?" Max asked. He was standing, ready to leave.

"I'll put them back along the path on my way home. Help me fill the bag again," she told him.

Minutes later Emma left him at school. She took the path back to the duplex, lingering to scatter the extra stones along the way and taking a detour up to the Coast Highway to a shop that had other supplies she needed for the project.

When she returned to the apartment, Huntington's Rover was gone. She spread pages of a paper flyer that came in the mail on her worktable and gave the rocks a coat of sealant. She puttered around until that dried, and then she painted a name on each rock: Max's, her real name, and Huntington's. Then she sat down and reread the letter she'd written at seventeen and never delivered to her father.

It was no longer right. She tore it up and began again to write the most fearless and loving letter she could, because being a mom had taught her to be fearless and loving even when you were scared witless. She told her father of the questions about him that had consumed her as a child.

Who is my father? Where is he? Why don't I live with him?

Emma told him her true name and birth date, and of the DNA-testing she had done to confirm her parentage. She told him of how she had come to know him only as the cause of her grandparents' terrible loss and grief. She told him of how at seventeen she wanted to rewrite her mother's story so it was more Elizabeth Bennet and Mr. Darcy and less Juliet and Romeo.

She told him of her first foolish attempt to meet him and its consequences. She told him how challenging and satisfying it was to be a mother, and how being a mother meant growing up and becoming independent in ways she had not imagined as a girl. She told him of the people who had helped her, of Maria, and Tony, and even Huntington. She told him of her months in the vinyl store and all she had learned about his music and his band's story. She told him that she hoped he would tell her his story himself some day in his own words.

She told him she was going to give her kid a house and a dog.

She offered him two of the stones she'd prepared. She told him that she and Max were facts, as real and solid as stones. She invited him to carry them in a pocket or take them out and hold them in his palm and look at them in different lights, and she told him where he would be able to find his daughter and grandson if he so wished. Then she wrote, *We are here to know if you care to know us.*

Emma folded her letter and placed it with the two stones in a small box, wrapped the box in brown paper and string, cleaned up the mess from her project then began to pack up the apartment for one last move.

* * *

As soon as the students left the Canyon campus for the weekend, Josh's job got much harder—which was good for his anger. He had never claimed to be a hero, but he'd been a pretty decent guy with Emma, and for her to accuse him of holding back when she was the queen of keeping secrets was too much. He shouldn't have to be the one to explain about his parents and his trust when she hadn't shared her history with him. And if she had been honest, she'd have admitted that she'd been enjoying the sex between them as much as he was. Nor did he appreciate her telling him that he was not a grownup.

He tried to remind himself that he didn't do anger. Why was he getting steamed about Emma's crazy worldview? She was the one who had issues. But the angry thoughts came and went as he worked down the punch list of concert preparations. Saturday's concert schedule required crews to do a substantial amount of construction on Friday before ten p.m. Most of his job was watching and keeping communication going between the different teams of technicians assembling the stage, with its jutting front and long wings, giant backdrop for video screens, and tall columns to support the lighting and sound systems. The food truck people had sent samples to keep the crews happy as they worked, but Josh wasn't hungry. He just wanted the whole thing to be over.

His phone buzzed repeatedly with texts from his mother's ever-helpful executive assistant, his mother, and his sister. Margot Miles wanted to know if he'd received the things she'd left with Emma. His mother wanted to advise him on how to behave with decency if he could not accommodate a date, clearly having heard from Bethany, and his sister reminded him that her couch was available. Each time he turned away from his phone, he was glad to get back to the work.

It was one in the morning before he left Canyon. He made it to his bed by two and crashed. He didn't even glance at Emma's place.

By noon on Saturday, when he stepped outside the hall to check on how the stage plot was coming, the set looked nearly complete. A wide black backdrop rose seventy-five feet above a performance space that jutted out into the quad fifteen feet above where the guests would stand. It wasn't U2's Claw or Genesis's steel crown, but it was impressive nonetheless, dwarfing the Spanish Colonial architecture of Canyon's main buildings. Behind the band was a huge screen where the video game trailer would play. Speaker stacks towered on either side of the stage, and overhead, techs hung huge black light cans from an open grid of steel pipe. To either side of the main stage, a long narrow runway allowed room for the musicians to prowl freely. And the black chair that cynical Leo Grant had mocked sat stage right, as specified in the band's current rider, a sentimental tribute from the 2008 reunion tour to Saxon's dead lover of long ago.

A special platform had been erected for Ryker to view the show surrounded by security men and guests, placed discreetly in front of a stand of palm trees on the upper slope of the quad lawn. A hydraulic lift like the ones Grindstone used would raise him in his chair up to the viewing stand. He wouldn't have his dog with him, but he'd have one of his trusted security men. Clear, bulletproof plastic panels surrounded the platform like he was the Pope or a president. Whatever Ryker had done as an arms consultant, he clearly believed his enemies had a long and dangerous reach.

Below Ryker's platform was a set of wide risers for a group of brain-injured veterans who were his special guests. The early part of the program before the band played would feature speeches and introductions and recognition of this group, Marines wounded in action, all from a unit that had seen the worst of it in a small town in Afghanistan during Operation Bulldog Bite in 2010. The pieces of the puzzle that was Ryker were all assembled now: wounded Marines, arms deals, Ryker's injury, his tattoos, and the enemy he expected to come after him. Josh figured he would be able to assemble that jumble of pieces to form a clear picture of his old classmate's story—if only he were less distracted.

The work continued until, by five, there was only a last-minute security check and they'd be good to go. The taciturn Ryker actually thanked him, which Josh realized should give him enormous satisfaction—a job well done, blood, sweat and tears and all that—but he felt hollow inside. His zeal for the project was gone. The whole thing reminded him of the Canyon gala. He'd thrown himself into a project, earned himself a piddling paycheck and zero satisfaction. His efforts had backfired in some way, and he'd ended up with zilch for trying to do a good deed. He really needed his trust back.

He took off his laminated ID badge on its lanyard and tossed it on the front seat of his Rover. His job for Ryker was essentially done. He could return to Canyon when the concert was underway, but he doubted that anyone would need him then. His plan was to get a quick shower at home and then head for the Glen event. It was time to get back to his real life. There was a good chance he could leave with Mackenzie. His mother and Margot Miles could hug each other over that, if either of them did hugs, and that would be good for his bank account.

He turned up the music to blast away all thought of Emma, but it didn't work. She didn't really know him, and she'd misjudged him just because she had taken the hard road in life while he had always taken the easy one. She thought independence meant everything had to be earned and paid for by one's own efforts. She thought there was some kind of virtue in cleaning your own floors, in keeping an old heap of a car going, in making do with third-rate towels because you paid for them with your own money. She didn't know how to accept a favor or a gift. He doubted she knew how to have fun. No wonder she didn't appreciate him.

Well, it was her loss. He was done with her wrong-headed judgments on his lifestyle. No matter what he had to do, tonight he would set about regaining his trust and his real life. He had no idea why he'd ever considered anything else.

Chapter Twenty-three

Emma wore all black. She skipped studs and piercings that would catch the light and only applied tattoos low on her arms and collarbone. Without a ticket or a backstage pass she was going with Plan B. Brandon and Todd would get her in, then they would help her disappear onstage in the fog of the finale. All she had to do was to remain invisible in that chair until the moment came for her father to see her.

It was a crazy plan.

Brandon complimented her on her look. He had borrowed his father's black luxury sedan to get them to the concert. The vehicle hardly suited his anarchist leanings, but he insisted that breaking into the concert would balance the score and keep him true to his principles.

He parked in the posh residential neighborhood above the arroyo that separated the Canyon school from its neighbors. The car looked right at home there, if he and Emma did not. At the end of the residential block they turned onto the broad boulevard that ran past the school, but before they reached the gated main entrance they left the sidewalk and scrambled down through the scrub oak, Manzanita, and grasses of the arroyo. Walking along its dry stony bottom, they disturbed nothing more dangerous than rabbits and then headed up a narrow animal track to a vine-concealed gap in the school fence.

The gap had been Brandon's idea. He had not watched a lot of thrillers for nothing. He figured that if they made a concealed gap a feature of the fence before the concert, surveillance would not detect it later as an anomaly. Todd was the inside man. He had used the gap the night before and camped in the wooded boundary along the fence. He had been onsite as the concert began, scouting the scene for security details, reporting the color of the required wristbands and the design of the hand stamp.

Brandon signaled for silence, and Emma turned off her phone. She reminded herself that Max would be okay while she was gone. Nothing would happen for the next three hours that Claudia couldn't handle, and she had told her son that he absolutely had to stay with his sitter this time.

She and Brandon slipped through the hole in the fence. No one came. No beeps or buzzers sounded. Then Todd was there, and

from his big pockets Brandon fished out neon orange wristbands that
would pass all but really close scrutiny. Todd drew a red Grindstone
axe in a circle on the inside of each of their wrists.

"Okay, one thing," Todd said. "Turns out there aren't too
many chicks here, Emma, so keep your hood up."

Todd explained that he'd been watching the show from high
up on the hill. Nothing had happened yet but speeches and
introductions and stuff. They had arrived a little late to avoid the
heaviest initial security. The descending sun created long helpful
shadows as they skirted the edge of a gravel service yard crowded
with vehicles for band equipment; then Todd led them up a path
behind a storage shed to a hillside that led to the athletic fields.

Emma took a steadying breath and reminded herself how far
she'd come and what mattered. Seven years ago she had survived her
first failed attempt to reach her father and even turned her misfortune
into something wholly good, her son. This time, she would succeed.

The plan was to merge with the crowds returning from the
stands of Porta-Potties at the edge of one of the fields. It worked.
Emma, Brandon and Todd strolled around the farthest Porta-Potty,
and no one paid them any attention. As they emerged from the end
of a building into the shallow sloping valley that contained the
school and caught the first blast of Grindstone in action, Brandon
and Todd flashed each other the sign of the horns.

Emma tried not to think about getting tossed out or arrested.

* * *

Max crawled from the back seat to the front of the Rover and found
the button that undid all the door locks. He pressed it, heard the
doors release, and waited. Then he poked his head above the window
to check his surroundings.

From the front seat he could see a long brick garage with five
white doors for cars. Lights above each made the cars in the
driveway shiny. The Rover was the last car in the row. Max guessed
the garage and house belonged to Josh because of the way he had
talked to a man at the gate as they turned in right before the ride
ended. In the car Max had thought about popping up and surprising
Josh, but he'd waited to be sure they were too far away for Josh to
turn around and take him back. They were far from the beach

apartment now. He knew because it had taken a long time to get here. He had counted the songs Josh played until there were too many.

He had figured out that his mom was keeping him from Josh on purpose. She didn't have her job anymore, either, and today she'd packed up their things, which meant they would move soon. So, he really had no choice. He had to talk to Josh about being his dad before it was too late.

He watched three men in red jackets talk to each other and take turns moving cars around a big cement circle out in front of the house. They were not policemen or firemen, but they moved fast and acted in charge. They would not see him if he stayed sitting in the car, but it might be a long time before Josh came back, and his mom might hear from Claudia that he was gone again and worry. Once Max and Josh talked, Josh could call her and everything would be okay. Just like when he'd gone to the beach. His mom had stopped being angry as soon as she hugged him.

He looked at the house. It was bigger than any house he'd ever seen. Tall white poles held up a roof over a big front door like a giant's. From the Rover he could not see a doorbell button.

Max climbed into the driver's seat, away from the men in jackets, pulled the door handle and slowly pushed the door open. No one seemed to notice. He slid down out of the car and let the door almost close behind him, crept around it and behind other cars until he came to some bushes. He scooted fast into these before anyone could see and then pushed his way out onto a lighted brick path.

He looked both ways. From the front of the house came the sounds of men talking and cars moving. From the back of the house he could hear people talking and laughing. It sounded like a whole lot of moms talking at once.

Max started down the path toward the voices. Another time it would be fun to crawl under the bushes, but right now he wanted Josh.

* * *

Josh had to admit that the women here were beautiful, sparkling and shining under the lanterns in the fragrant garden. Groups of friends found each other and exchanged enthusiastic hugs. Cocktails sloshed in glasses, driving the merriment to a high pitch. Mackenzie Burke had looked out for him from the beginning of the party, reminding him of the names of women he'd managed to forget.

It was a hot night in L.A., but his mother's garden remained cool and fresh with its whispers of splashing water. A repeating slideshow flickered on a pair of screens, playing shots of Glen girls ten years earlier in their plaid skirts, white shirts, and blazers. Recognition of past moments drew peals of laughter from the guests, and it didn't take long for Josh to catch the rhythm of the gathering and fall into easy conversation with a small group of Mackenzie's friends. They knew the people he knew, and the restaurants and hotels. He was reminded of happier days, days of plenty. Things with Mackenzie looked promising.

He had his arm around her waist. She was explaining with charming self-deprecation how she had utterly bombed a job opportunity as a paralegal at a swank law firm.

"I was all wrong for them apparently. They didn't like my Miu Miu shoes or my perfect Agnes B skirts. No one had the least interest in my ideas, and they wouldn't allow me to schedule my vacation—it was *my* vacation, I mean I earned it, a day for every six weeks—whenever I wanted. I just wanted to go to Fashion Week. I never miss New York Fashion Week. I mean, I didn't even ask for Paris."

Josh gave her waist a squeeze and tipped his glass against hers in a light salute. He got it. She'd made a visit to the real world and discovered it wasn't for her. Effort and hard work were overrated, and besides they interfered with life. Emma had it wrong, and he'd been misled briefly by her attitudes because he'd lost his trust, but now that he and Emma were over he would get his old life back. He preferred the lazy drift of it to Emma's version of a forced march through responsibilities.

Mackenzie smiled at him. "The way the manager explained it, and she was twenty-five—*twenty-five,* with seriously bad taste—'If you take their money, you have to play by their rules.'" She shrugged. "Well, I don't need their money. I have my own money."

Everyone laughed, and the conversation turned to travel adventures. Josh was recommending a great place for street food in Kuala Lumpur when he saw women at the other end of the patio guarding their drinks against spilling and stumbling back in heels to make way for something lurching through the crowd. Female voices oohed with the sort of universal sympathetic sound the gender made in the presence of puppies. Josh expected a loose pet. Instead he saw Max Gray emerge, looking warily up into adult faces and ducking to avoid hands that reached out to ruffle his hair.

"Hey, buddy," Josh called, surprised and baffled at the boy's appearance in his mother's garden. It was as if his two lives had got mixed up. He slipped his arm from around Mackenzie's waist and took a step forward, while Max turned a look of profound relief his way.

"I found you."

A space cleared around them. Josh stuck out his hand, unexpectedly glad to see the boy, and the two exchanged the Canyon handshake. Max gave a sigh and moved to stand close beside him.

In spite of himself, Josh's first thought was of Emma. "Does your mom know where you are, Max?"

The boy shook his head. "I came in your car."

Josh tensed. That meant the boy had been gone more than an hour, and if Emma was looking for him, she would be out of her mind again.

Mackenzie spoke up from behind him. "Who's your little friend, Josh?"

Something in her tone caught his attention. He'd momentarily forgotten his audience, but as he looked around and into the faces staring at him and Max, he saw the possibility dawn in their eyes that Max was his. It would be easy to deny, to say that the boy was his tenant's son and dispel the suspicion he read in those eyes that he had knocked up someone from outside their elite world and produced this embarrassing result. Instead, he put his hand on Max's shoulder.

The boy looked around with his natural curiosity, taking in the women in their finery, the catering staff in black and white, the music, and the big screens with their steady flow of images. Josh knew Max's questions would start soon.

Josh's mother stepped out of the crowd into the space near Josh and Max. She wore a champagne-colored sheath and those pearls of hers that came from oysters on steroids.

"Darling, do you need a moment to sort out this lost boy's situation?" She gestured with one hand away from the patio. "I'm sure one of the staff can take him in hand and see that he gets back to where he belongs."

"Thanks, Mom. He and I will sort it out just fine."

Max looked up at Josh's mother. "Josh is my friend," he announced.

Josh's half-smile turned grim. Emma would not be pleased to learn where her son was. He dropped down to Max's level and said, "Max, why did you come here?"

"To see you."

"I live next door. You could knock on my door."

Max shook his head. "Mom packed up all our stuff."

Josh felt his gut clench, but he kept his cool. "When?"

"Today."

"Where is your stuff?"

"It's in Claudia's car. I wanted to talk to you before we went away."

"Okay. But your mom doesn't know where you are, does she? We should tell her before we do anything else." He might be angry with Emma, but he didn't want her frantic, so he pulled out his phone and texted her.

Nothing happened. There was no notice that his message had been delivered. Her phone must be off.

Beside him, Max's gaze shifted to the big screens again. He tugged Josh's arm and pointed urgently at one of the images. "My mom has a skirt like that."

Josh followed the line of Max's pointing finger to an image of three Glen girls striding across a green lawn in the Elizabeth Hutton Cobb Academy uniform of perfect preppy girlhood: pleated plaid skirts, white collared blouses, and navy blazers.

The image faded, but another appeared. This time the girls wearing the plaid skirt had parodied the uniform. One had hiked the skirt up to hooker-length and wore it with red stiletto heels. Another had cut the pleats so that they hung in thin strips like a grass skirt and paired it with flip-flops. A third had tie-dyed the thing and draped herself in beads.

An inescapable truth smacked Josh where he knelt: Emma Gray had been a Glen girl. The first time he'd seen her she was wearing that skirt and he'd thought her a teenager. After that he'd only seen the skirt out of context, mixed with her death metal gear, and he'd never made the connection, but the pieces suddenly fit—her knowledge of Canyon, her car that came from a mechanic who worked for vintage car collectors, her clever art history paper based on a private collection. For months she had scoffed at his privileged self-indulgence and looked down her short, self-reliant nose at his idle ways, and yet all this time she'd been hiding a pampered upbringing of her own. He wanted to make her own up to every bit of deception she'd practiced on him, pin her down on his luxurious sheets and...love her senseless.

He stood up and looked down at her son. "Right you are, Max. Come on, we're going to find your mother's picture in a book."

"In a book?"

"Yep."

Josh led the way past whispers and a few louder, more pointed comments meant to be heard to a set of elegant woven outdoor chairs and sofas around a huge low glass table where women leafed through old Glen yearbooks and laughed over memories. He borrowed a yearbook from a class two years behind his own, his twin cousins' class. Emma would be a sophomore, he figured. Of course, she wouldn't be Emma Gray, so he had to hope that her sixteen-year-old self looked familiar.

He sat Max next to him on a large sofa, the boy's feet sticking straight out.

"Mom has her picture in this book?"

"In one of them, and we're going to find her."

He figured she was four grades behind him in the class of '09. He picked a likely yearbook from the pile and started in on the sophomore class, arranged in rows of smiling faces, all wearing the Glen collared shirt and blazer. He skipped the blondes and forced himself to go slowly over all the brunettes. He thought he might have to look at other classes when Max suddenly said, "There's Mom."

He pointed to a girl in the next-to-last row. Josh looked at the print column on the right for her name.

Morgan Ashley Winterbourne.

M. A.

Emma.

She hadn't gone far to find an alias.

The inside of Josh's head rang with silent curses. He ripped the page out of the book and stood.

Conversation stopped. Women looked up, startled.

"How rude! You can't tear up people's yearbooks!"

He waved the torn page at the suddenly silent group. "Anyone know a girl four years behind you—Morgan Winterbourne?"

There was a murmur of indignant voices. Josh waved the yearbook page again, and finally a petite redhead spoke up.

"She's the one who disappeared, isn't she?"

"Disappeared?"

The redhead looked around. "Didn't the school hold a vigil or something at graduation?"

"Disappeared?" Josh repeated.

"She went somewhere—a concert, a party, somewhere—and didn't come home. Her grandparents went nuts about it."

Josh's mother appeared at his side, pearls gleaming. "Darling, you are parading unnecessary baggage here. It's time to turn the boy over to someone else." She linked arms with him and offered a smile to her guests.

Josh didn't move, just stared at her. "Do *you* know what the story is about this Morgan Winterbourne?"

"Like mother, like daughter."

Josh thought the acid in his mother's voice might dissolve the pearls. Max tugged at his arm, and he let go of his mother to keep the boy close, resting his hands on the kid's shoulders.

His mother arched one of her perfect brows in a way that didn't even wrinkle her forehead. "Must you give people something to talk about?"

"Mom, the story," Josh prompted.

She indicated that they should walk away from the crowd.

"I know more about the girl's mother, Helen Winterbourne," she said after they had taken a few steps and the guests returned to their conversations. "After her debut, she ran off with some appalling rock musician in leather who couldn't even keep his pants closed on stage. The family did their best to hush it all up, to get the girl back. Then she died—drowned, I think, in a car accident. Satisfied?"

For a moment Josh's ears felt stopped up. The party noise faded away, and he could hear Emma telling him her story. *My mother drowned.*

He knelt beside Max, another piece of the puzzle striking him. Steve Saxon was Emma's father, and Emma at seventeen had run away to find him. *Like mother, like daughter.* He didn't know what Emma had found when she tried to reach Steve Saxon, but he knew when she'd made the attempt, at the time of the band's last reunion tour. That's when Emma would have been a senior in high school. As a schoolgirl she would have come up against the hardened crew of rockers in the picture he'd been staring at for days. Suddenly he guessed where Max got his hair.

"Where is your mom tonight?" he asked. He had to ask, but he had a stomach-dropping feeling that he already knew.

"She went to a concert with those guys," Max said.

"'Those guys'?"

"The music store guys."

Josh stood. He knew who Max meant, and he hadn't heard anything about her metalhead friends getting tickets, so that meant Emma was going to sneak in. She didn't have a clue what she was up against with Ryker's security team on the job. "We'd better go find her."

Max gave a little leap. "Just like before!"

Josh grimaced. "Not quite. Before, you were the lost one."

His mother watched this exchange, allowing the faintest frown to crease her brow. "Josh, darling…" She put out a hand and touched his jacket sleeve. "Find someone else to take the boy to his mother. You don't have any responsibility for him."

He stared at her. "Oh, but I do."

Her hand fell. "You can't be serious. What about…what about Mackenzie?"

"She'll survive," Josh said.

"We had an arrangement. You agreed."

"But I didn't really. Now I know what I want, and I won't find it on your list. Thanks for trying to help, Mom."

"Oh please. Come to your senses. You can't live without your trust."

Josh shook his head. His mom had meant him no harm in offering her deal. She just didn't understand that he'd changed. He made himself speak gently. "Turns out I want to do things a different way. I'll pay you back, Mom, but I think I can make it on my own, thanks."

She stared at him, uncomprehending. "This isn't a joke, Josh. You can't toy with me. Walk away, and you say goodbye to your trust. I wash my hands of you. You won't be welcome here."

"Ouch." His mom clearly meant her words to hurt, and they might have, if she and he had ever been close. But when he glanced down at his blazer, slacks, and loafers in search of gaping wounds, he found none. He felt rather free. "No blood, vomiting, unconsciousness, or visible bones. I'm good to go. Come on, Max, let's find your mother."

Chapter Twenty-four

Emma was grateful to Brandon and Todd for getting her into the concert, but now she needed them for the most important part, giving her a boost up onto the stage. They had worked their way to the front of the swaying crowd of Grindstone's mostly male, slightly older, and mostly shirtless demographic, to an inner corner of the giant, jutting stage. She kept her hood up and her head down, grateful for the deepening dusk.

Despite their years of retirement, Grindstone delivered what fans expected—rebellious songs at industrial-strength volume. Lights pulsed and flashed and changed color. Guitars screeched and wailed and shredded single notes into cascading, stuttering beats of sound, or thrashed with total precision. The beat invaded the listeners, taking over minds, bodies, and the movement of swaying hands held aloft in the horns salute.

Immediately before the set ended, the band would reportedly play the never before heard track that would appear in a soon-to-be-released video game. Otherwise, they were doing their classic song order, a sequence designed for dramatic effect leading up to a moment when all seemed lost and the lights would go completely dark before the finale with the grindstone and the axe.

Emma's father dominated the stage from his lead-guitar position. He sang and moved in ways familiar to her from watching the band's videos. As she had at seventeen, she felt an almost visceral response to him. There were things about his face, his mannerisms, his stage strut, that broadcast Emma's own biology. That was DNA, though, not love or the connection of being a family together. Still, she would start with the fact of it. He was her father. His stage personality was only one aspect of who he was. There was another Steve Saxon backstage whom she intended to meet.

Anticipation had Emma edgy and tense. This time around she was being much smarter. She was not accepting favors or drinks from anyone. Her letter to her father and the stones were in their box, hidden inside her black hoodie. She was going to meet him, and she was going to hear the truth about Steve Saxon's feelings for her mother. That's why she'd come, and there was no way she was going home without success.

209

Her father's feelings for her mother made a stone that Emma had not yet held in her palm. Saxon had done outrageous, excessive things for years, and then he'd stopped, disappearing somewhere in Sweden. Those seven quiet years did not mean he was changed man. Her grandparents might be right about his excesses. But he had not done any terrible things to Emma. The thing he had done to her was simply to remain ignorant of her existence. He might want nothing to do with her or with Max when he learned of them, but she would at least give him the chance to decide which her grandparents had denied him for years.

It would be terrifying, climbing up onto that stage and opening herself up to him, but nothing was possible until Steve Saxon knew that she and Max were facts. The shock of meeting her and knowing she existed might not make for the smoothest of conversations, but that's why she'd written the letter. It would give him a chance to think about the facts on his own terms. It was a baby step Emma could take to end the hatred and anger her family had sent his way.

So, talking to her father would be difficult, but the thing that worried her at the moment was security. As she had guessed, there was no question of getting backstage without a pass; seriously large and scary men barred access to the stage from various angles. So, the empty black chair looked like her only chance to get close to her father.

It was good that they were following their 2008 reunion show order. The moment to act would be obvious. She'd coordinated with Todd and Brandon, and the song she waited for told the story of a guitarist trapped in the machinery of modern society desperate for some primitive energy to wreck the trap so that he could break free. It would end with Steve Saxon on his knees in a shower of chains unable to play, the guitar's last chord dying away in a wail of pain. Then the stage would go black as if the concert had ended in failure.

Moments later the finale would begin. Fog would pour from the stage, and the sound of the axe placed against the whirling grindstone. Sparks would fly as steel met stone. Lights would come up again on a giant figure sharpening the axe. He would give it to the kneeling guitarist, who would rise up, shackles clanking, shake off the chains and wield the axe to break their last hold on him with a mighty swing. Then the band would play its final song, and in the hush after the last note Steve Saxon would place a single red rose on the empty black chair. The chair for her mother.

Emma inched forward, wedging her way through the tight-packed swaying crowd to the lip of the stage.

* * *

With Emma and her two anarchist buddies about to test Ryker's serious security team, Josh wanted to set land speed records; however, he would settle for getting to Canyon without getting stopped by a cop. He distracted himself from worry by prompting Max to give him the full story. He made the boy call Claudia on the speakerphone so he could briefly reassure her the kid was okay.

"How did you get to my mom's house, buddy?"

"I rode in your car. I was very quiet, and you always play your music. I counted the songs."

"You said you wanted to talk to me? What about?"

"Well...Mom said I had to wait until summer."

"For what?"

"A dad."

Josh felt gut-punched. Emma was headed to that concert to find Max's dad—who happened to be dead.

"She says she'll look for one later," Max added.

Josh could breathe again, but he was missing something in the story. "So, she doesn't already have a dad picked out for you?"

Max kept talking as if he hadn't heard. "But I want a dad now when I'm a kid, and I want to pick my own dad."

"Have you and your mom talked about this?"

Max nodded solemnly. "I told her you would be a good dad."

Josh almost laughed. He wondered when that little conversation had occurred. It explained a lot. "What did she say?"

"What she always says. Wait until summer."

Josh paused, thinking. "Max...you do know your mom gets to decide this matter, right? Because moms and dads have to be really close friends and live together."

"You live close," Max said. "You live right across from us. You like mom. So you could be my dad."

Josh could now see what Emma had been up against, especially since he knew Emma's opinion of him as dad material.

"Max," he said, "I want you to find me something in the car here. It's a plastic badge on a ribbon."

Max held up the lanyard. "This thing with your picture on it?"

"Guard it, buddy. That's the way we get to your mom."

It wasn't as bad as he feared. At the Canyon gate, Josh got lucky when he recognized the security man on duty, and the man let him through with Max as his guest. He parked the Rover and headed for the Hall of Canyon Men, which was basically where he figured Emma would go to reach her father. He hoped she wouldn't do anything dumb; he didn't want to think about her tangling with Ryker's security people. Of course, he didn't even know whether she and her conspirators had made it inside. The whole situation made him a little crazy.

He lifted Max and tucked him under one arm as he trotted up the drive past the food trucks. Walking between buildings that led to the quad, he could hear the music blasting at full volume. Grindstone was finishing the piece just before their video game track.

Security was even tighter at the hall. Josh showed his pass, but the hulk looking at it still wanted to know why he should be admitted during the show. Josh's navy blue blazer garden-party attire wasn't helping, but finally he got the reluctant security man to call Ryker's second-in-command.

They didn't want to admit Max.

Josh started to argue that Max was a kid, not any kind of threat to Ryker's security, when the boy himself spoke up. "My mom's in there. Her name is Emma Gray. We have to find her."

Emma's name caught the guy's attention. He reached for a clipboard.

Josh put his hand over the man's list. "She's with Daddy Rock, and we're meeting them all backstage."

It was as close as he would come to pulling off a Jedi mind trick. The guy hesitated long enough for Josh to whip Max past him and enter the maze under the stage that led to the Hall of Canyon Men. If the security man figured out that Emma shouldn't be here and decided to alert his team...well, that might help Josh find her. As long as they didn't haul her off in chains.

The hall was quiet inside and nearly empty. A few techs wearing headsets monitored screens and control boards and did not look up. Ryker's black dog lay next to Ryker's usual chair, and Max squirmed from Josh's hold and squatted down beside him, reaching out to pet him. Josh felt his heart skip a beat, but the dog accepted the boy's touch.

Josh pulled Max upright, turned him around, and told him not to go anywhere. "Your mom and I will be coming for you here. Nowhere else. And don't go with anyone. Got it?"

Max nodded.

Josh took his lanyard and draped it around the kid's neck. "This is a special guard dog, so let him guard you. *Don't go anywhere.*"

Max sank down beside the dog. "I promise."

Josh exited the hall and made his way back through the maze. He reached the crowd in front of the stage just as the drums lowered to a low ominous murmur, and Saxon was on his knees, his head bowed, his hands on his guitar, both the instrument and its notes sliding away from him. Loops of heavy chain rattled down from above, clattered to the stage floor and twisted to pin his arms to his sides.

Josh turned away from the spectacle, scanning the upturned faces of the crowd, looking for Emma. At her height her face would be about armpit level in the mass of raised and swaying arms, and he had no idea what she'd be wearing.

Brandon. He suddenly saw the face of her tall friend, with his long hair and black coat standing right at the edge of the stage, his hand on one of the underpinning trusses. Josh shoved forward through the crowd.

A single wailing note hovered high in the air. Then the lights went out.

* * *

Everything went dark. Brandon's hands found Emma's waist, and she put her own on his shoulder, her foot in Todd's, which were cupped. Brandon tossed her upward. Todd pushed her feet, and with a final surge she flung her arms and chest across the lip of the stage. She felt one more boost from the hands holding her feet and flopped down and lay flat.

Success. She'd scraped the underside of her arms on the stage lip and banged her chin on the floor; she tasted blood, but she was on the stage and didn't think she'd been seen. To her right she could hear the crew moving the grindstone into place.

Machines started pumping fog. Emma snaked on her belly along the edge of the stage, skirting light cans and amp boxes until she reached the place where the wing turned out. She turned in, wriggling across cables and cords, angling left until she felt the base of the platform that held the black chair.

The chilled white fog was at least three feet thick now, and the crew's movements had stopped. Emma pulled herself up into the chair, turned, and sat with her hood pulled low, her head down, and her hands tucked into the folds of her black sweatshirt. Her heart pounded, her knees and elbows ached, and she felt dizzy from breathing the theatrical fog, but she held herself perfectly still. She also prayed that she was right about her father's onetime love for her mother.

* * *

Josh kept his focus on the spot where he'd seen Emma's friend Brandon and waited. Within a minute a cool white fog began to foam across the stage and spill over onto the spectators at the base of the stage.

The grindstone began to turn with a whirring sound. Then came the first touch of the axe to the spinning wheel. Sparks flew from the contact of steel and stone. The lights began to come up, and a giant figure in mail appeared, holding the axe to the wheel. Lighting from the edge of the stage cast the giant's huge shadow across the backdrop.

Josh looked for his man and couldn't see him anymore, but he saw security guys in brisk, purposeful motion headed away from the stage. He followed their movement toward Ryker's platform, and when he looked up over the heads of Marines he saw the platform was empty.

But that was impossible. The guy had to be there. Security men were converging on the scene, but Josh turned back. Emma first.

On stage, the giant took the axe from the wheel and held it over his head. It gleamed cold and sharp in a carefully directed spotlight, and he swung it in wild, vigorous arcs. Then he placed it in front of the trapped Steve Saxon.

A vibrating, heavily detuned blast from a bass guitar sounded. Saxon clasped the axe handle and rose. His chains loosened, and the guitarist turned in a circle, unwinding their hold on him until only one chain from a heavy iron collar around his neck remained, shackling him to a great log. He lifted the axe with great ceremony, paused a moment then brought it down to smash the chain. Freed from the log, Saxon picked up the guitar and the band went into their signature finale.

He had to admit, Grindstone were as good as ever. Josh felt the pulsing beat vibrate inside him as his eyes swept the crowd for Emma, and as the song blasted to its crashing conclusion, roses fell from the grid overhead in a scene that lived up to the band's artistic mantra: Anything worth doing is worth overdoing.

The crowd loved it.

Josh's eyes went back to the stage. Saxon had knelt again, and he picked up a single red rose. He kissed it and turned toward the empty black chair…and Josh found Emma.

Chapter Twenty-five

Emma lifted her head and looked straight into the startled gaze of her father. She didn't flinch. She simply held out her hands to receive the rose. He placed it there with the same bow she had watched him make countless times on Internet video clips of the band.

The crowd, oblivious of their interaction, roared and whistled then shouted for the encore. Her father did not miss a beat. He turned back to his raving fans, and the band struck up the video game track.

One more time, Grindstone brought the crowd to screaming, deafening applause. Emma shook with suppressed emotion. She'd done it. She'd reached him. It was thrilling and terrifying. The music stopped. Showers of sparks descended from the pyro cans, and the stage went dark. The house lights came up over the crowd, and a voice came over the loudspeakers telling audience members to leave in a safe, orderly fashion—and also that there was plenty of Grindstone merchandise available at the concession stands near the exits.

The moment her vision adjusted, Emma met her father's dark flashing eyes. He was still onstage, and he was pumped and angry. He had been known to take the axe to parts of the set after a show.

"How the hell did you get here? No one sits in this freaking chair!"

He might be fifty, but his bare inked chest and arms were muscled and taut. Heavy bands of iron circled his wrists. The huge chain from the iron cuff around his neck hung down his torso. His shoulder-length black curls glittered where stray light from the arena caught beads of sweat.

He removed his guitar in short jerks of motion. He'd spoken quietly, but the sharpness of his tone had made the others on stage turn and pause. Emma kept her eyes fixed on him.

"I have something for you."

"Oh, you have something for me! I've got something for you—charges for trespassing. You could have seriously screwed up the show."

"A letter."

"You're frothing mad. Whatever happened to the post office?" He looked out over the crowd streaming toward the exit. "Where are the freaking security guys?"

"I'm your daughter."

Emma dug her fingers into the black velvet arms of the chair in which she sat. Steve Saxon swung around to rake her with a long, sneering scrutiny. There was a moment of silence. Then: "Not a chance. I bang birds your age. I don't have a kid your age."

The stage lights came up, and across the stage Emma could see the bass guitarist Jed Rezford unplug his instrument. Rezford swung a curious glance their way, and she could tell he was listening.

"Nevertheless, I'm your daughter," she repeated. "Helen's daughter."

Her father's mouth opened and closed. For the moment at least she had rendered him speechless.

Rezford came over. Standing beside Saxon, he looked Emma up and down. "Sweetheart, I haven't heard that one before, but you're pressing your luck. Security will show in a minute, and you don't want to tangle with them. They can be seriously rude."

Emma looked at her father again. She was not going to budge. Facts had a power of their own. She had to believe that was the case. "My name is Morgan Ashley Winterbourne. My mother was Helen Winterbourne."

Her father flipped open the iron ring on his neck then tossed off the cuff and chain, which clanked to a heap at his feet. "I don't care what kind of fan fantasy you're having, Morgan whatever. I don't have a daughter."

"You might, man. You and Helen were quite a pair." Rezford's voice was quiet. His gaze was thoughtful. "Listen to her, Steve. You're really Helen's kid?"

Emma nodded.

Rezford rested a hand on her father's shoulder. "Sweetheart, if you are who you say you are, and you look a bit like her now that I can really see you...you didn't get a prize dad, but he was crazy about your mother."

Emma smiled. "I wasn't expecting Atticus Finch."

"He never knew he had a kid. She didn't tell him," Rezford said. "He thought she left him. Part of the reason the band broke up."

"She had me and died trying to get back to him."

Her father shook Rezford's hand off his shoulder. "Cut the rubbishy, touching exchange." He pointed at Emma. "You look nothing like Helen. She was gorgeous. You belong in a dog show."

He stalked to the front of the stage and yelled out into the emptying courtyard, "Hey, where are the fracking security swine when you need 'em?" He glared back at Emma and added, "You better hope they show, girl, and you better move, because I'm gonna smash that bleeping chair to bits."

He turned, his gaze shifting to the floor nearby. There was nothing but a tangled pile of chains lay.

"Looking for this?"

Emma glanced toward the new voice, a voice she knew well. *Huntington*. He stepped out of the shadow of the giant grindstone. He looked like the quintessential Canyon boy, wearing a navy blue jacket, khaki slacks, and his imperturbable charm, but in his hands he held the double-bladed axe—easily, lightly, as if it weighed nothing. Emma couldn't think what he was doing there, how he had stepped from his other life into the middle of hers.

Her father spun Huntington's way, halting abruptly at the sight of the axe. Then he started swearing, calling everyone idiots, demanding that security arrest everyone who wasn't part of the band.

"Security have their hands full at the moment."

Huntington spoke in his usual unruffled manner. As he did, Emma could see a knot of large men gathered around someone on the ground of the quad. An ambulance appeared and started beeping as it backed toward the group around the downed person on the grass.

"Who are you?" Saxon asked.

"Doesn't matter. Emma's with me. Don't insult her."

"Hey, I'll insult whoever. It's my axe. It's my freaking chair, and I want this crazy chick out of it. I don't care what you do with her, but take her away. We're done."

"I don't think so."

Emma had no idea how Huntington had come to be here to find her face to face with her father, but it didn't look like he was going anywhere, and it also looked like he was keeping the axe. She had to admit it gave him a certain authority. Of course, she was the only one on stage who knew he had the strength to use it.

Josh looked at her. "Still want to give him your letter?"

"I do." She drew it out of her hoodie. "I have to give him a chance to be my dad. My grandparents never did."

Those words apparently penetrated her father's ego shield. "Effing give it to me."

* * *

Josh watched Saxon snatch the simply wrapped box from Emma. It rattled, and the guitarist shook it hard, swore some more and planted himself on the edge of the drum deck. He tore off the wrapping, opened the box, and pulled out a pair of stones then held them in his hand as he removed the letter. Then he began to read.

Around them, techs and roadies had gathered at the edge of the set. They watched the scene, but Josh watched Emma, full of pride and love. Saxon had thrown one of his worst bad-boy rocker tantrums at her, hoping to scare her away, but she hadn't budged. Josh couldn't tell what she hoped for from the encounter, but he knew she was stubborn enough not to quit until she got it.

He also realized he'd got this whole thing wrong. He'd thought she came to find Max's dad, but she'd come to find her own. He didn't know all the details, but he could guess most of her story. She'd left behind the privileged life her grandparents provided to find her birth father, living on her own as a single mother in order to have the freedom to search for him. Nothing had been easy for her. No wonder she had scoffed at his first pathetic attempts at self-reliance.

Saxon looked up from the letter. His gaze grew speculative as he looked first at Emma, and then at Josh. Then he started shaking his head.

"I am too freaking old for this stuff. She's got a kid. That makes me a..." He shuddered. "Who are you, the kid's freaking father?"

Josh saw Emma tense, her eyes full of sudden wariness.

He called out her name, drawing her gaze to him. "Emma. Max's father is dead." He said it gently. He had no idea what it would mean to her. But she needed to know. Especially if she'd come here not only to find her father, but also to find a father for Max.

* * *

Huntington looked straight at her as he said it, and Emma knew he had figured it all out. Everything. Saxon, Max, her years on the run...

She released her grip on the arms of the black chair. She had no idea how Huntington had figured it out, but she had never doubted his intelligence or his kindness. With his revelation of Max's dad's death, he had freed her from yet another fear. She had been willing to face Max's father here if that was the price for finding her own father. She had not wished him any ill except for a few bruises from her boots. If she had not wanted to share Max with him, she had never wished him dead. And now she would always be guilty of the selfishness of keeping Max all to herself, of being more like her grandparents than she'd realized.

Huntington watched her face as if he read some of her thoughts. He didn't say anything. That was the trouble with Huntington. He was very perceptive. It was how he fooled people who only saw the smooth surface of his unruffled manner.

Rezford spoke up from the side of the stage. "Time to get a move on, folks. The limo's waiting." He nodded to the roadies at the edge of the stage then walked over and gave Emma a friendly pat. "Nothing goes right for you, does it, sweetheart?"

"It does now." It was Josh who'd spoken. He turned back to Saxon and said, "Take the axe if you want it. Make kindling out of your past if you think it will help. Do your worst. It won't change Emma. She's not a fantasy you toss a rose at. If you're lucky she'll let you in her life, but she'll expect you to act like a grownup. If you do, she might even let you meet her kid...*Grandpa.*"

Frowning, Saxon offered him a one-fingered salute, but his other hand still held Emma's stones. Emma offered a silent prayer that he was thinking as hard as it appeared.

* * *

Looking at Emma's father, Josh was betting on her power to get her man. Maybe not today, maybe not tomorrow, but soon.

He turned and handed the axe to Rezford. "Give us a few minutes?"

The bassist nodded.

"Emma?"

She came up out of the chair and gave him her hand, his death-metal maiden. He led her across the stage and down a flight of stairs until they reached a place with grass under their feet and stars over their heads. He led her beyond the quad to where he could yell at her for a few minutes or kiss her senseless, whichever impulse won when he got her there.

When they were truly alone, he pulled her into his arms and kissed her as he hadn't been able to for two days. "Just so you know what I want."

She pressed her face to his chest and rested there in his hold.

"You mocked me for eight months for my towels and my boxers."

"For your garage full of toys and your music."

"For my dark glasses and my condoms—which we used up, by the way."

"For drifting through your life on a cloud of privilege."

"As if they don't know you on Rodeo Drive, Morgan Ashley Winterbourne! You knew how to keep your wreck going because your grandfather is a notable collector of vintage cars. You wrote your impressive art history paper on your grandmother's art collection, am I right? You looked down your self-reliant nose at my trust when you're the only child or grandchild in a family with a substantial net worth."

"So…" She pulled back in his arms.

"So?" He could only push Emma so far.

"So, what do you want to do about all my lies and deception?"

Josh allowed himself an unseen grin in the darkness. "You know, I've given some thought to that. I finally decided upon pinning you to my 400-thread count sheets and loving you till your hard-headed, self-reliant, list-making brain melts."

Even in the dark, he knew she smiled back.

She laughed, and before she could say another word, he kissed her again. Inevitably, after a mindless time her responsible self took charge.

"I have to get back to Max. I left him with Claudia."

"Brace yourself. Max is here. He's backstage."

"Here?" She pulled back in his arms. "How did he get here?"

"Long story. Very determined kid. It might be genetic."

"Claudia will be frantic!"

"I called her. Come on, I'll take you to him. And then, Emma Gray Morgan Ashley Winterbourne, we have more talking to do."

They found Max curled up asleep on the floor of the Hall of Canyon Men. He was leaning against Ryker's dog. Ryker was again sitting in his chair, his hand on the dog's nape.

"Lose something?" he asked.

"What happened out there?" Josh said. "I saw the security guys but not you."

"We had a little episode. It's all taken care of now. Is this one yours?"

"He is." Josh scooped up the sleeping boy in one arm, and Emma slipped her arm through his other. "You okay?" he asked Ryker. The guy looked exhausted.

Ryker nodded. His dog stirred, and Ryker took hold of the beast's black nape, and the two of them visibly relaxed. "Later, Huntington."

Josh shifted, accepting the dismissal for what it was. He hoisted Max up onto his shoulder and took Emma's hand, and they left the hall and passed through the abandoned quad where the cleanup crew was tossing bulging orange trash bags into an electric cart. At the car, Emma opened the door so he could settle Max in the back and buckle him in. The boy didn't wake.

"Where am I taking you?" he asked her.

She paused a moment then said, "To my grandparents' house. It's not far from yours, you know."

Josh looked at her. "Let's call them to let them know you're coming. It's been a long time, hasn't it? Maybe it'd be good if I spoke first."

She nodded and murmured, "Thank you."

He gave her his phone and let her put in the number; then he stepped aside to make the call. It was late, and he imagined the slight alarm of a phone ringing at such an hour.

A deep older male voice answered with the slight perplexity of the newly awakened. When the man on the other end of the line identified himself as Arthur Winterbourne, Josh introduced himself and explained that he had good if unexpected news about Morgan Ashley Winterbourne.

After her grandfather acknowledged a desire to speak to her, Josh handed the phone to Emma.

"Hello, Grandpa, it's Morgan. How are you? Is Grandma okay? I've missed you."

Josh did not hear the reply, but he held the girl leaning against him while tears ran down her face.

"We'll be there in an hour," she said.

In the front seat, Josh took her in his lap as he had once before and just held her. She let him, and after a moment she moved her mouth close to his ear and whispered, "Do you remember when I asked you for your middle name?"

He moved his head so that she could feel him nod. His throat was too raw for speech.

"I asked because...well, we were both being false. I knew you weren't the player, the careless Canyon boy you pretended to be, but if you were pretending, so was I. I realized how deep in I was. My lies hadn't mattered when you were my landlord, but suddenly they did. I thought if you were honest with me, it would be a signal."

"But I wasn't."

Her embrace tightened briefly. "It was one of the moments when I realized we weren't on the same path."

"So you pushed me away."

"I didn't understand you well enough."

"Do you now?"

"You *are* a fraud in a way though," she said. "You don't let people know you. You pretend to be so cool and indifferent..."

"I believe the phrase was 'irresponsible, idle, self-serving, and manipulative,'" he reminded her.

"I should never have said that. I was wrong about your character. Max was right."

"Are you sure about that?" Josh mocked himself with the question. He wanted her to be right about him. He wanted to be the man Max Gray picked for a dad. "I will hold you to that statement."

"I'm sure," she said. "You pretend to care about things that don't matter to you and pretend not to care about people. You pretend to be heartless, but you are kind and generous and heroic."

He reached out to embrace her before she got too carried away, but she started punching him with wild, ineffectual punches that turned to clinging. She continued by saying, "You fooled me for months, but you can't fool me any longer. I know who you really are."

He didn't need any more compliments. He'd done plenty of dumb empty things in his life, and he was humbled and ashamed when he considered the hardships she'd gone through in order to find her father. He tried to shake his head, but she caught his face between her palms and kissed him, hard.

"I love you," she said.

They kissed again.

When they paused to breathe, she looked at him and asked, "How did you know about Max's father?"

"I'd been looking at the picture of the band in the Hall for weeks now, and then Leo pointed out one man as crew who would not be present for the reunion. He told me the man died in a motorcycle crash right after the 2008 concert. I didn't realize until tonight why the guy always looked so familiar. Max has his face and his hair. I thought you were coming here to find him…to give Max the dad he wants."

Emma gave him a solemn look. "No. Max's dad and I were never together. I met him when I went to find my father. He…took advantage."

She stopped speaking, and tears choked her again. Josh silently cursed the man and held her through what she couldn't or wouldn't say.

"Were you hiding from him?" he finally asked.

"I hid because I wanted to make my own decisions. I didn't want anyone—not him, not my grandparents, not *anyone*—making decisions for me. My grandparents made all the decisions for my mother, and she rebelled and lost everything. I almost followed in her footsteps, but I got lucky. I had Max…and I paid attention to what I learned from him. "

Josh held his breath. They had reached a moment of truth. She might love him, but he was unworthy, and she had more than proved that she was capable of taking care of herself and Max all on her own. She might visit her grandparents to reconcile with them, but Emma would not give up her independence.

"Will I see you again? Max said you packed up your stuff."

"I can't pay the rent," she joked. "And I owe my grandparents some time and some explanations and a chance to know Max. But yes." She touched her fingertips to his mouth. "You will see me again. Sometimes you have to wait for the marshmallow. Believe it or not, sometimes that makes it better."

"I love you, too," he said. "Just so you know."

"I know."

Josh lifted her off his lap, and she gave him a small smile from the passenger seat as he started the Rover. The food trucks were gone. The campus was silent again except for the click and spray of the automatic sprinklers, and as they passed through the Canyon gate Josh saw that the sign out front was still standing.

He took that as a good omen.

Chapter Twenty-six

Three weeks later

A knock on his door at noon woke Josh from a dream of floating in a lazy circle on an air mattress pushed by the intake flow of his mother's pool. Whoever it was knocked again, more sharply, and it reminded him of Emma's knock, but she was gone so he groaned and turned over and pressed his face deep into his pillow.

The sun was shining beyond his bedroom, penetrating even the drawn shades. The knocking became banging, this time as if two people were going at it, the second person adding a rapid, irregular counterpoint to the first.

Josh rolled onto his back and opened both eyes. The sprayed-on ceiling of his apartment glinted wickedly in the half-light of the dim room. Nothing had changed in his sleep. He was still in his half of the beach duplex he'd taken over when his father took away his trust, living in a hell of his own making without Emma. After dropping her at her grandparents he'd found a note in his mailbox that said *Thank you* and held the last of her rent. That was the only message he'd received, and she'd clearly written it before the concert. Her stuff had vanished, and he couldn't help thinking she had no reason to return. She'd said she loved him, and he tried in the face of her empty unit to hold on to that fact.

He had kept himself busy putting his new post-trust-fund life in order. He had his father to thank for cutting off his trust to begin with, but it was Emma who had truly freed him to stand on his own two feet in the world. He had kept only what he could afford of his old toys and he'd dug into his new work at the Center. In his spare time he'd tackled Emma's rundown unit.

He had not yet put a FOR RENT sign in the north unit, so whoever was knocking really had no business doing so. He jerked upright and swung his feet onto the floor, ran a hand through his hair and over his unshaven face. One of these days he'd go back to shaving, probably before Sloan's wedding.

He headed for the door in his boxers. Whoever was knocking would regret having a conversation with him before he'd had his coffee.

He yanked the door open. There stood Emma and Max. The boy had a blue striped towel over his shoulder and a yellow boogie board under his arm.

"Emma," Josh said.

Max barreled through the door and hurtled into him. He caught the boy and staggered back, barely keeping his balance.

"We're going to the beach," Max yelled. "Together!"

Emma smiled at him, and Josh thought he saw the love he'd seen in her eyes on the night of the Grindstone concert. Maybe even more. She looked like she really believed he was good, great, all-the-time dad material after all, and that she was going to give him a chance to prove it. He prayed that was the case.

"Coffee?" she asked, offering him a tall, lidded paper cup.

Max released Josh from the hug and began to tug him by the hand toward the door. "Get ready. Let's go. She might change her mind."

Josh glanced at Emma, or Morgan, or whatever name she was using now. Still a little stunned he asked, "Where are we going?"

Max flung his arms wide. "The beach!"

Emma smiled serenely at him. "I won't change my mind, Maxie. It's made up about whole lot of things."

She slipped a canvas bag off her shoulder and set it down on Josh's kitchen table. When she leaned forward to kiss him lightly, his head buzzed and he had a feeling that he'd fallen into another dream entirely. Then she put her arms around him and laid her head on his shoulder, and his heart beat erratically. With his free hand he pulled her up against him and tried to get his bearings. The rush of happiness was overpowering.

"Did you think I wasn't coming back?" she asked him.

"Once or twice an hour."

Max bounced impatiently in front of them. "Mom, can I see our old apartment? Josh, can our old apartment have dogs?"

"You have been busy," Josh said to Emma. "Max, take the key from that table, and go take a look."

The boy spun, picked out the key, and dashed off. Josh heard him manage the lock across the landing.

He studied her. She had a new look; not that her hair or eyes had changed, just that happiness now lit her features in some indefinable way.

"I heard from my father. He sent me the lyrics to the song he wrote when he thought my mother left him."

Josh shook his head. "Poor Steve Saxon. He's no match for you. You'll make a decent grandpa out of him yet." He let himself kiss her because he could, because she was there and real and not an elusive dream any longer. He almost missed her next question.

"What have you been doing?"

"I'll show you," he said as Max came charging back.

"It's all different, Mom," the boy announced. "Come and see."

Emma looked at Josh.

"You'll especially like the bathroom," Josh said in response.

He took her hand and led her across the landing. Her eyes widened at the changes she saw, the new paint and new carpet.

"How did you manage it?"

He shrugged, not wanting to give away all his secrets. "Sold a few assets." *Just a garageful.*

Josh followed Emma through the rooms with Max chattering the whole way. He watched the realization dawn on her face of how much money he'd spent in the remodel, and she turned so abruptly in the narrow hall outside the bath that they collided. He took the opportunity to slip his arms around her.

She pushed back, her palms against his chest. "Not… You didn't sell the Rover?"

He grinned. "I didn't go that far, but you'll find the garage quite roomy now. And I took a job. At the Center."

"I see. So, you gave up on your trust entirely?" She was smiling at him in a particularly promising way. "Why?"

"You and Max. You are the reason for everything I've done since that night. Maybe since even slightly before that. So, don't even think about living in your old unit. We need the rent from it."

"Where will we live then?" Max asked, sounding worried.

Josh looked at Emma. "I thought you'd live with me. Forever."

"Can we, Mom?" Max asked, jumping up and down.

"Wait, Maxie," Emma warned, and Josh's heart gave a stuttering beat. Then she told the boy, "I need you to go back to Josh's place and get our present for him out of the canvas bag. Then wait there. Can you do that?"

"Okay." The exuberant six-year-old skipped off.

Josh and Emma were alone, briefly, in her transformed unit.

"You know," she said, "I like the forever part of the plan, but isn't there one more thing you need to say to me?"

"I love you?" Josh said with a laugh. "I thought I already told you."

"Worth repeating—often," she replied. "And, I love you back."

She took his hand and led him across the landing to his apartment. Max stood just inside the door, bouncing on his feet.

"We brought you a present! Mom said you'd really like it even if breaks all the rules." From behind his back the boy produced a clear plastic package with unmistakable contents. "Marshmallows! For your hot chocolate!"

Over the boy's head, Josh looked into the laughing eyes of the woman he was going to marry just as soon as he could.

ABOUT THE AUTHOR

Kate Moore's first romances were "True Romance" comics read at a cabin in the woods by Lake Tahoe. She rediscovered her love of Romance while teaching at a boys prep school in L.A. and quickly moved from reading Austen and Heyer to penning her own stories set in Regency England and contemporary California. Her heroes are honorable loners, and her heroines are warm-hearted practical princesses with long to-do lists. Now a multi-published author, three-time RITA finalist, and Golden Crown winner, Kate lives north of San Francisco with her surfing husband and her children's dogs. She loves to hear from readers.

Did you enjoy this book? Drop us a line and say so! We love to hear from readers, and so do our authors. To connect, visit www.boroughspublishinggroup.com online, send comments directly to info@boroughspublishinggroup.com, or friend us on Facebook and Twitter. And be sure to check back regularly for contests and new releases in your favorite subgenres of romance!

Are you an aspiring writer? Check out www.boroughspublishinggroup.com/submit and see if we can help you make your dreams come true.

Made in the USA
Charleston, SC
20 March 2016